I0714785

HEARTLESS HETTE

M. L. FARB

Heartless Hette. Copyright © 2021 by M. L. Farb.

Morgan Horse Publishing

All rights reserved. This book or any portion thereof may not be reproduced or used in any manner whatsoever without the express written permission of the author except for the use of brief quotations in a book review.

This is a work of fiction. Names, characters, places, and incidents are a product of the author's imagination. Any resemblance to actual persons, events, or locales is entirely coincidental.

Editing by Annie Douglass Lima

Cover design by Wynter Designs

Contact the author at mlfarb.author@gmail.com

❀ Created with Vellum

CONTENTS

PRONUNCIATION GUIDE

Long vowel sounds are represented by "ae", "ee", "ie", "oe", and "oo" for a, e, i, o, u respectively.

- Hette: He-tae
- Konrad: Kon-raud
- Friedrich: Freed-rich (soft "ch" almost a "sh")
- Johannes: Yo-hon-es
- Bestian: Best-i-an
- Demuth: Dae-moot
- Erasmus: Er-ras-moos
- Peter: Pae-ter
- Georg: Gae-org
- Nyx: Nix
- Rätsel: Rae-tsel
- Blitz: Blitz
- Tollkirsche: Toel-kir-sha

For James,
A deep well of wit and wisdom.

THE BARD

*T*HE SCENT *of mildewing straw filled the barn while John's lantern light, mixed with the winter sun, struggled through dust-thick air. The floorboards bowed beneath him.*

This was not what he'd anticipated when he signed the contract as the new steward of the Zachary estate. The other two barns were in good condition. But this third one—John shook his head—it would take the rest of winter to prepare it for spring. He should have checked the full situation beforehand. Now he was paying for his haste. Though the holdings contained rich farmland, the retired steward had been lax. How the land was managed would have to change.

"So you're the new steward?" a voice crackled. "You be a young one. Thirty at most."

John spun around, his boots scraping the grimy floor. "I'm Master Bailey."

A wizened man hunched over his walking stick and tilted his head sideways to look at John with bright eyes. "Ah no, not to me. I'm long past me years work'n the estate. I was just stopp'n by to get my grandson, Ned. Ned Gibson. I know I'm a bit early, but I walk slow and—"

"I'm afraid not. No worker is leaving until this barn is cleared of the old straw."

"*Now, young'n,*" *the grandfather said, twisting his bent body to look more fully at John.* "*Ya can't do that. Ned's a good lad. He works hard, does his part. And if the last steward let this barn get a little ragged, well it wasn't really needed, was it?*"

"*It will be in use, and as steward, I must make sure it is ready. Ned will not go yet.*"

"*Please, sir.*" *His voice edged upward.* "*Ned will work extra hard after his rest-day, but you must let him go now.*"

"*Why must I?*"

"*We're gonna listen to the Bard.*"

John sighed. He'd heard that title slip in conversations between workers as he toured the estate. Even Sir Zachary had hurried off to get changed for the evening, leaving John to see the last barn on his own. No wonder the estate needed a new steward if this was how the master prioritized.

"*Old man,*" *John said slowly.* "*Your grandson may leave when he's completed his work, not before.*"

The man thumped his walking stick in the mildewing straw. "*You heartless—*"

Heat rose along John's neck. "*I am the steward. My job isn't to care for the workers, but to make sure the estate is cared for. Be off with you.*"

With the clump of the walking stick, the elder shuffled away.

John calmed himself by walking through the barn, noting where floorboards needed to be replaced, where ice speared through holes in the roof, and so on. He nodded with satisfaction as he patted a beam. The barn still had good bones.

"*John?*" *Sir Zachary stepped into the barn.* "*What is it I've heard? You've forbidden my workers to leave?*"

John bowed to the gentleman. His master was an imposing sight in his velvets and furs, his middle-aged face creased into sternness.

"*Sir,*" *John said, straightening.* "*My duty is to care for your estates. Your workers are soft and unused to authority. I must show them a firm hand from the beginning, or they will never listen to me.*"

"John, I promised my workers an early day off. I will not renege on my promise. The barn will keep, as it has for the last fifteen years."

"But sir—"

"This is my order."

"Yes." John clenched his jaw. He'd heard much good about his master but hadn't expected this—meddling in his duties. How was he supposed to accomplish his responsibilities when so hindered?

"John."

"Yes, sir."

"I would like you to come this evening. You may sit with my family."

"Is that an order, sir?"

Sir Zachary lifted his brows. "It would please me if you came."

John's shoulders rounded as he suppressed a grimace and followed Sir Zachary.

Later, as they approached the mayor's house, voices swelled out the open door. John's grumbling was lost in the jostle of elbows and chatter as hundreds bustled about, finding seats. He settled on a bench, and one of his master's wiggly children was placed in his lap. The ocean of voices pushed against him on every side.

Time inched by.

Why had he signed the contract? If this was how his master ran his estate, then no steward would have much success.

The silence hit him harder than the waves of voices.

A woman now stood on the hearth at the front of the room. Her olive skin and tight black curls contrasted with the room of fair faces. She couldn't have been older than sixteen. A slightly built child in a woman's fur trimmed dress.

John scoffed silently. He had no time to listen to some foreign young woman tell tales in broken English. If only he could just slip out. Instead, he let his mind wander back to the numbers and plans of earlier. At least the time wouldn't be completely wasted.

A clock bonged seven times in the corner of the great hall.

"Some order their lives by the ticking of a watch." The young

woman's voice carried like a tenor recorder; clear, sweet, penetrating, richer than it should have been for a near child.

John focused on her with surprise. She spoke perfect English, but for a slight rolling of her "r"s.

She dangled a pocket watch from her slender fingers. The gold watch twisted on its chain and flashed in the firelight. "Life is lived by another clock, one that starts before the first breath and continues till the last gasp. But what would happen if the watch and the heart were combined?" She raised her thick eyebrows and quirked a corner of her mouth.

"Come to Germania, to where a clockwork heart rules and a fool advises. Journey to a place of powerful magic and precise engineering— where a laugh can bring both to their knees.

"Come, see."

PART I

PROPOSAL

"*THE SAFETY of the people is in the heart of the ruler. And a ruler who does not love is a danger to the people.*"

The words of my father's chamberlain, Herzog Heinrich, itched in the back of my mind. He'd never quit pestering me to marry. But why should I? Was I not as capable to rule as my father, even if I was a woman? He'd ruled without a spouse since my birth, and his wife's death, twenty-eight years before. And now that he lay dying, his life shortened by extravagance in food and women, it was time for me to rule. I'd be wiser than he. I'd never let my heart lead my decisions. And I'd never marry.

The memory of another of Heinrich's constant arguments jabbed me. *But what of an heir?* I strode across the rose-paneled receiving room to the mirror and tugged at the stiff lace collar that stuck out around my neck like the ridged gear of a clock. My dark hair, about as lovely as mud, or so my father said, was pulled back in a tight bun, making my narrow face sharper and my coffee-brown eyes more serious. I had the face to make people pause before speaking. I pulled on the curled blond wig, adding an imposing height to my shortness—an element that made it worth the itch. The thick layers of my dress fitted around my body like embroidered armor.

I lifted my chin and practiced the bored annoyance that had ended the last suitor's visit.

What of an heir? Did I not have cousins? I'd train one up as an heir. But until my father's death, I had to respect Herzog Heinrich's wishes and meet with all the suitable, and even more of the unsuitable courtiers. When I was queen, I'd stop this nonsense.

The grandfather clock in the corner struck three, each metallic *bong* a reminder of the coming wasted hour—an hour listening to eloquent wooing, full of empty praise, self-importance, and little else. Tiresome fellows. They didn't appreciate time or brevity. Nor did they appreciate direct responses. Wars could start over such honesty.

A gentle knock warned me to settle onto my straight-backed chair. The chair had once been padded, but Heinrich had traded it out for an ornate wooden chair that made even the cold chamber pot seem comfortable—no doubt to get me to sit on the tiny couch with the visiting courtier.

I composed my face into gracious indifference as the door swung open. Three guards marched in, followed by two servants laden with platters of coffee and crisp pastries, the rich scents wafting both bitter and sweet.

Lastly, the courtier entered, and my composure slipped.

The man's grey eyes were rimmed with black. Not black lashes —those were as pale as his flaxen hair that curled at his neck—but black rimmed piercing grey irises. They were royal eyes, distinct to my family's line. Was this a distant relation? He stood a little taller than most men and had broad shoulders over a lithe body—all characteristics of the royal family. Though I'd inherited neither height nor eyes.

He bowed. "Your Highness, your time is valuable, and I will not waste it. I seek to wed you and rule beside you."

I laughed. A cold, disbelieving laugh.

"Does my offer surprise you?" He inclined his head. "Is it not what all other suitors seek, but will not say?"

Intriguing. I motioned for a servant to pour coffee while I sorted his words.

He was unlike the others. Compelling and blunt. If he was also obedient, I could use his services. Maybe make him a baron, and councilor to the crown. What was his current rank and position? Who was he? I'd have to make sure Heinrich told me more. I'd stopped caring years ago who he sent to meet with me, but this time it might have been beneficial.

"True." I offered him a delicate Dresden cup, brim-full of coffee. "And why?"

He sipped and hissed. The coffee sloshed over the edges of the bird-painted cup, leaving trails of black against pastoral peace. He glared at the spreading stain on his forest-green breaches.

He was a dandy after all, and not the first one to be irritated by the coffee I offered. But if a man couldn't handle coffee hot enough to sear meat, then he had no place seeking to rule my people.

He set the cup on the table and spread a silk handkerchief over the stain. "Well played, Your Highness. How many have you frightened off with that trick? But you asked why I would want to marry you?"

"Yes." I blew across the surface of my coffee and sipped, carefully funneling the liquid so it left no permanent damage.

He raised his brows.

I found that brevity pulled more information than lengthy questioning. I waited.

He laughed. "Do you wonder why I don't court one of the other princesses of the scattered kingdoms of Germania? A more willing one? Your kingdom isn't the largest or the richest. Why would I waste my time on a woman who is cold as winter frost?"

His words rubbed against old scars. He said nothing that

others had not said before. I offered him a pastry and waited. He'd answer my question—eventually. Even if he posed many of his own first.

He bit the pastry, and flakes tumbled onto the handkerchief in his lap. When it was gone, he dabbed his lips and nodded. "You have something the others do not—a fire."

"A fire?" That was a new compliment. I brushed a pastry flake from my stiff lace collar. "But am I not as cold as winter frost?"

"That is what others say. They don't see the real you." He studied me with his black-rimmed eyes, as if my thoughts lay naked before him.

I shivered. "And what do you see?"

"I see a woman who sits in an uncomfortable wooden chair, facing dreary marriage proposals from those who don't care a whit about her, because her father wants her to marry rather than pass the ruling power to her. I see a woman who is stronger than the king, and is ready to do whatever she needs to, to retain her power."

My cup clanked as I set it down. How could he see all that?

"Do you know what else I see?" He leaned forward.

I gave a stiff shake of my head.

"I see a stuffy room. Our conversation would be better out in the gardens. Come walk with me, Your Highness. Let us talk of politics and power, and how to keep from losing it to others."

"And of marriage?"

"That too." He stood and offered his arm. "If you will allow."

A smile tugged at my mouth. *No, I won't smile.* But his bluntness was refreshing. Perhaps I would find a place for him in my court.

I took his proffered arm, and we stepped through the balcony doors and into the garden. Knee-high hedges lined the paths that curved in geometric perfection. From the palace roof the paths appeared as lilies, vines, and fountains. Exactness and care kept the gardens. Just as I would keep my kingdom.

My guards trailed after us at a respectful distance.

At this proximity, my suitor's perfume became apparent. It wasn't the strong, head-aching perfumes of my other suitors. Not rose, lavender, or violet. Not even a blossom. Sandalwood—with an almost sweet overtone.

"Pray tell me, who are you?"

He raised an eyebrow. "Did your councilor not tell you?"

"I stopped asking for names months ago."

He made a sweeping bow. "Friedrich. Your humble suitor, at your service."

"Humble?"

He half-smiled and offered his arm again. "Your suitor, at your service."

"And what have you to offer, my most proud suitor?"

"Power."

"Power?" I rested my hand again on his arm. "Most suitors offer love."

He turned down a side path. "Do you want love?"

I stumbled at his question.

With quick grace he lowered my arm and steadied me with a light touch on my back. Part of me wanted to pull away, and part of me wanted his hand to remain. Why? I didn't want love. It was empty.

I lifted my chin. "I have power. I will rule when my father dies."

Friedrich dropped his hand from my back and continued walking. "Do you think you'll keep your throne on your own? Your neighbors will be happy to gobble up this kingdom."

"They haven't yet. Though my father hardly rules." I quickened my pace.

He lengthened his easy stride. "He's a man. He has a court who supports him. He throws parties and money at his nobility to retain their favor." He stepped slightly in front of me, forcing me to either dodge around him or stop and face him. "What have you done? Who will support you?"

"I'll rule by law and reason. Justice will support me."

"And does justice have armies and gold?"

"Why are you here?" I stared into his dark eyes and then dropped my gaze.

"Hette."

I shivered at my name in his calm voice. It struck with more emotion than if he'd added all the swooning praise of my last suitor.

"Hette, I offer you power. You care not for love. You would retain the throne alone, grasping the book of law in fingers that grow old and wrinkled, surrounded by your subjects. Always above. Never to have an equal. With me beside you, no one will take your power away. I will protect you and your kingdom."

What if he could? Would I give up part of my freedom to marry him? Would I give up all my freedom? *No.* I stepped away from him and firmed my face into an impassive mask. "Sir Friedrich, you said that with you beside me, I'd never lose my power to another. But how will I keep from losing my power to you?"

"Because I promise."

Of all the words he could have used. *Promise.* Like my father promised me family. Like my tutor promised me respect. Like the young man who'd traded kisses for empty promises. *Promise.* A word to be broken at the slightest inconvenience. I lifted my chin. "A promise is but the stomach's wind after dinner, all stink and no substance."

Instead of scowling, his eyes brightened. "Ah, I like you. Maybe one day, I'll even love you."

Ugh. Love and promises. He was no different from the other pompous fools who'd courted me. "Sir Friedrich, go court another princess. Fill her ears with your lies and empty promises." I lifted a hand to call over the guards to escort him away.

He caught my hand, pulling me under a rose-twined arbor. "What if I give you more than a promise?"

I raised an eyebrow. "How?"

He reached into his breast pocket and pulled out a silk-wrapped object. It vibrated in his hand, expanding and contracting like the ticking of a clock. "This is my heart. I will give it to you as we stand before the priest on our wedding day. If you injure it, you injure me. If you destroy it, I will die."

My eyes widened. "You are a sorcerer."

He nodded. "But even a sorcerer grows lonely. I have no place for silly women. But you, with your logic and reason—you, I could see spending a lifetime with. I'd use my magic to support you in your rule."

I touched the silk cloth. It pulsed beneath my fingers. "You'd give me your heart to seal your promise? You'd give me control over your life?"

He handed the bundle to me.

It fluttered in my hands like a rapid breath.

Could I? It didn't have to be love. Could I marry him, bear his children, and let him rule beside me, knowing that if he ever betrayed me, I could crush his heart?

I looked up into his dark-grey eyes. "Why would you trust your life to me?"

He cupped his hands over mine. "You are not the only one who wants to make a difference in the world. I see a new age with you as queen and me as king. We'll build universities, improve medicines, and foster inventions. Our small kingdom will influence all of Germania and then the whole world. Generations will look back to our day and speak of us."

I pinched my lips against the pull of his words. "We could do all that and not marry."

He traced his fingers over mine as his heart thumped between our hands. "Are you so afraid?"

He hadn't answered my question. Just as he hadn't answered most of my other questions. "I'm afraid you'll play me for the fool." I handed the beating silk back to him, making sure he had a firm grip before stepping back. "I'll install you as master of the university. I'll fund your inventions. But I will not marry you."

His eyes hardened. "Oh. In that case, I lied. This is not my heart, but it will be yours." The pulsing silk glowed.

A burning pain spread under my ribs. *Guards!* I tried to scream, but only a tiny gasp emerged as the world narrowed, tightening into an airless tunnel. My legs gave way and strong arms caught me.

As dark closed over me, a voice whispered, "I hold your heart. In time it will melt at my touch and believe my every whisper. One day you will beg to marry me."

My chest flamed as if I'd swallowed a coal and it would burn a hole from the inside out. "Never." The word stuck on my lips—a breathless silence, as the thumping of boots encircled me.

"Your Highness!" It was one of my guards.

Friedrich's voice pitched with concern. "She fainted. Please, help her."

And sound slipped away along with pain.

A dull pain radiated with each breath. I lay in softness, but something hard lay within me, a stone weighing in my chest. What had happened? I rolled to my side, fighting to move against weariness.

"My lady." It was my maid's voice. "Oh, my lady, you're awake. We thought you'd never wake. I must tell the physician." The soft slap of slippers on the stone floor faded into the distance.

Never wake? Had I been injured?

My mouth was sticky-dry. My eyes seemed glued shut. A stale scent of sickness filled my nose.

Had I taken ill? What had happened?

Memories slipped through the fog.

A grey-eyed courtier. The gardens. An offer and then a threat. Pain.

"Curse that sorcerer!" It came out a raspy croak.

What had he done to my heart? He hadn't taken it, for it still thumped inside of me, each beat a dull aching reminder of the coal-hot pain. But he'd done something to it.

"Curse him to the slave mines!" My tongue stuck to the roof of my dry mouth with each word. *Water.* Where was my maid?

I rubbed my eyelids, abrading them with sleep sand, then forced them open. I lay in my bedchamber. The forest-embroidered curtains were drawn back, allowing in a slanting western sunlight. It was evening. It had been early afternoon when I'd met with the sorcerer. Had I slept half a day? More likely a day and a half.

First order of business—after water—sentence the sorcerer for his crimes against the crown. Death? No, I needed him to remove whatever curse he'd placed on my heart. Sentence him to the slave mines? If he wouldn't remove the curse immediately, then that would bend his will. And when he removed the curse? Life imprisonment.

I nodded. I couldn't have a powerful sorcerer running around my kingdom laying curses on my people, or worse, marrying into a neighboring kingdom and taking up arms against my own.

Now where were my maid and that physician? Why hadn't he been in the room, watching over me as she had been? The tall clock in the corner of my room clicked at the passing minutes. A closer clicking pattered slightly off-sync from the clock. Had the physician left a pocket watch at my bedside? How annoying.

I covered my ears, muffling the discordant ticking of clock gears. But the closer clicking continued—*click, thump, click, thump*—preceding and matching the beating of my heart.

It was a clock, and it was attached to my heart!

The *click, thump* quickened, then a sliding sound of a larger gear, and a heavier beat.

Or was it? Did I still have my heart, or was this the pulsing silk bundle he'd let me hold? Had he replaced my heart with a mechanical pump? If so, where was *my* heart?

His words came back: *I hold your heart. And in time it will melt at my touch and believe my every whisper. One day you will beg to marry me.*

"Never!" I sat up, throwing the down cover from me, and wavered, light-headed, clinging to my bed curtain. "He'll never control me."

Bestian, the grey-mustached physician, entered, followed by my maid. He was a large man who looked more like a butcher than a doctor, and he took no nonsense from his patients. He was brutally honest and honorable. Unique attributes in the court. He'd help.

He set his bag on the table. "Your Highness, lie down. You've been very ill."

I clung tighter to the curtain and swung my legs over the edge of the bed, my bare feet brushing against the sheepskin rug. "Bring me the sorcerer!"

My maid rushed to my side. "My lady, please. You've been asleep for three days. You must be thirsty. We've only been able to moisten your mouth with a sponge." Her gentle pressure on my shoulders was more than I could resist, and I fell back onto the pillows. She poured a glass of wine and held it to my lips.

I leaned forward as she supported my back. The wine was thinned to a sweet and bitter water. It slid over my chalky mouth and down my parched throat. I gulped, coughed, and gulped more. Some spilled and spread over my white nightgown.

"Now," I said, pushing the cup away. "Bring me the sorcerer!"

"What sorcerer?" asked my maid, her freckled face broad with confusion and worry.

"The one who did this to me? The fowl-brained, sow-scented —oh, I would the Fool were here to make a proper insult—my words are too weak for his crime! The one who—"

"Be still." Bestian held out a second cup. An acrid scent wafted from it.

I scowled at him. "You will not drug me."

"I would rather not give you an anti-hysteric. But if you do not calm yourself, I feel it is my duty."

I closed my eyes and hissed a breath through my teeth. If he gave me that drought, I'd not be able to think clearly.

"That is better." He set down the cup and turned to my maid. "Let a fresh breeze in."

My maid bobbed a curtsy and scurried about opening windows. The breeze pushed at the stale air.

Bestian laid two fingers on my wrist and whispered, "Your Highness, it would be better if the maid didn't know of the clock-work heart."

"You know?"

"Hush. I would be a poor physician if I couldn't tell a heartbeat from shifting gears. But if your father or anyone else in the court learned of it, your power would slip away."

I shuddered. If they knew of my cursed heart, I'd become a monstrosity in the court—something to be laughed at and ignored. I'd never become queen in anything more than name.

"Bestian," I asked, keeping my voice low, "where is the sorcerer?"

"He helped carry you in and acted with all courtesy and

honorable worry. But by the time I checked your heart and realized what had happened, he was gone."

"Then he's not imprisoned."

"No. It was too late. I told the court that he gave you poison. Soldiers are looking for him as we speak."

I nodded, cold reason already smoothing over the earlier errant emotions. "Good. When they find him, we'll force him to restore—"

My maid returned to my bedside.

I stiffened. Had she heard our words?

"Good doctor," she said with a curtsy. "What can I do now to help my lady?"

"She needs sustenance. Bring a gentle broth and soft rolls, fresh from the oven."

She bowed again and left, giving us the opportunity to speak freely.

"Bestian, you have kept that secret, and I will ask you to keep more. The sorcerer threatened me as he took my heart. He said because he held my heart, he'd make me believe his every word, and I'd beg to marry him."

Bastian's brow furrowed. "Do you feel any love toward the man?"

"Love for him?" I rubbed my breastbone. A dull, heavy ache lay under it, along with a mechanical ticking. "Only love to lay him across the rack or under the whip. Both of which I will do when I find him, and leave him under their various pleasures until he's restored my heart."

"Then perhaps his spell didn't work on you."

"Even if it didn't, I want my heart back. But how to find him? I'm sure whatever he told Herzog Heinrich was as much a lie as what he told me. He's probably not even called Friedrich." As the last word left my lips, my chest burned as if the sorcerer was taking my heart again. I gasped, and the world narrowed. An aching as though I were standing outside on a winter night with desperate need for a fire coursed through my limbs. But it wasn't fire that my body longed for. *Cool fingers traced over mine, grey eyes peered into my soul, a mouth curled into a satirical smile. Lips parted, inviting.* I closed my eyes, waiting for their touch—

—that didn't come.

The ache grew into pain as cutting as my father's slaps and my tutor's cane.

"Your Highness." Bestian's voice came through a muffled fog. "Princess Hette."

A sharp scent burned my nose. I coughed as my eyes watered.

Bestian pulled away a vial of smelling salts. "Your Highness?"

I swallowed against the longing that still coursed through me and took a shaky breath. "I think saying his name triggered the love-spell."

He waited, his expression neutral.

Did he think I'd turn against him? That the sorcerer would control my every action? No. I wouldn't let him control me. I couldn't. "My heart may not be mine, but my mind is." I closed my eyes and breathed deep to bury the cursed longing under calm.

Black-rimmed eyes seemed to smirk in the grey beyond my eyelids. Mocking, beautiful, perfect eyes.

I lifted my chin. "Friedrich," I carefully said his name in icy tones, "If you want to control my emotions, then I just won't feel."

FOOL

I SAT on an ornate chair next to the empty throne.

A dust-covered captain knelt before me. He'd led the soldiers sent two weeks ago to search for the noble who'd "poisoned" me. His face was wan with exhaustion, just as mine must have been. The sorcerer's spell on my heart was worse at night and kept me in vivid dreams instead of restful sleep.

I extended a hand and motioned for him to rise. "You may report."

"Your Highness, there is no Baron Friedrich in the Grand Duchy of Mecklenburg."

So, he did lie. Of course he did. Anger rose within me and slanted sideways, toppling into desire. Friedrich stood before me, a ghostly apparition in the throne room. He smirked and beckoned with a tilt of his head, a simple motion that dug like nails into my chest, creating a painful need that only he could satiate.

I shuddered and pushed aside the anger and desire. How many times would it take before I remembered that the curse turned any strong emotion into yearning for him?

My vision cleared, and the captain stood waiting with concern slipping through his weary face. I rang a bell, and the treasurer strode forward. "Give him and his regiment an extra month's pay for their services."

The captain bowed his thanks and exited with the treasurer.

Now what? What clues did we have to his location? He said I'd beg to marry him, but even if his spell left me in that state, how did he expect me to find him? Did he plan to wait until I was a shell of myself, then ask for my hand again? He was an accused poisoner. He'd never be allowed to marry me. Unless he was waiting for my father to die, which could not be many more months. When I became queen, would he approach, expect me to pardon and marry him?

No. I breathed to calm the rising anxiety. I wouldn't wait until then. The sorcerer would wear me down, eventually, if the royal court didn't notice first.

Bells jangled at the other end of the throne room. The court Fool strode through the arched doorway, the bells jingling at the ends of his two-pointed cap. His motley garb was a clash of stripes and diamonds in shades of reds, whites, and greens, made all the more ridiculous by his overly tall, lean body—part giant, part scarecrow. Curly reddish-blond hair sprang from under his cap. Even his mouth was too wide for his narrow face, stretching in grimaces or grins like a puppet. Probably the first reason my father brought him in as a fool. His very appearance caused laughter.

But laughter was not what I needed.

Halfway across the room, he stumbled forward, caught himself on his hands, and sprang from a handstand into a flip. He somersaulted thrice, launching off the marble floor with his hands each time, and landed on his feet for a moment, before dropping to a knee and sweeping off his belled cap. "My lady."

"I did not call you."

He lifted his head and winked one amber-colored eye. "Nor have you ever, my lady. You have no need for fools when the court surrounds you with them. And none of them have ever made you laugh. So, what hope have I?"

I let bored annoyance fall over my face. It was not a strong emotion, and thus one I could still experience without the curse activating. "Why have you come?"

"At first, I thought to invite you to an entertainment in the gardens, but remembered that last time you walked thus with a man, you almost lost your heart, and so I—"

I stood and stepped toward him. "What did you say?"

He grinned and tilted his head, his hat-mussed curly locks falling across his eyes. "Would you care to stroll through the painting gallery? The physician suggested it would be good for your further healing."

Bestian sent him? That didn't mean that the Fool knew anything. His comment about my heart could have referred to an error I'd made in my youth.

I stepped from the dais. "Is there a particular painting we should see?"

"The one that tugs most at your heartstrings." He set his cap back on his head and strolled away from me.

Heartstrings? No, he can't know. I hastened to catch the Fool.

My guards didn't move from their posts. The Fool was the Fool. He was as loyal to the royal family as any sworn guard. There were even rumors that he'd saved my father's life from an assassin ten or so years earlier. He'd been around since my early memories, a gangly boy who grew into a mocked man, bearing the court's cruelties with a droll smile and mocking them back with sharper wit.

I'd avoided him. But now Bestian sent him to me. Why?

"Fool? How do you know the royal physician?"

"I've known him longer than I've served your family."

That was not what I meant. Why must he always twist words?

He chuckled. "And I've known your family since your fifth

birthday. I was hired to entertain you but had little luck. You were a solemn-eyed child."

"You weren't more than a child yourself."

His rolling gait slowed. "I was eleven and orphaned. I was no child."

I shrugged aside pity. It was too strong an emotion, even before the curse. It helped nothing and only made sleep more difficult. "And you know Bestian how?"

"So you do know his name? That is a high honor. Most of us are titles and roles to fill. Fool, king, maid, courtier…"

We entered the long gallery. Paintings of my family stretched down both walls, starting from my ancestor who first drove the barbarians from this land, all the way to me. He motioned to the painting of a solemn-faced girl. "Even, princess. Each of us to be categorized like butterflies pinned to a board."

My jaw tightened. My butterfly collection. The one where he'd swapped all the labels. My father let him go with a pat on the shoulder for a good joke. Even after sixteen years, the injustice stung.

Angry memories tilted and slid into a whispering caress. *Hette.* Friedrich's voice brushed like gentle fingers. My knees weakened.

Large hands caught my shoulders. "Steady there."

I took a shuddering breath, pulling myself back into a shell, blocking out all but thought—though the cursed caresses continued.

"Apologies, my lady." The Fool released my shoulders and studied the painting of me as a child. "You've always had a good control of your emotions, but I had to know how quickly the curse takes hold. It is important if we are to find the sorcerer and bring him to justice."

Bestian did tell him of my curse! Why? I pushed down the flickering anger before it could activate the curse with worse torture than Friedrich's caresses. I needed to focus on more practical matters, such as how the Fool planned on getting my heart back. "How do you suggest finding the sorcerer?" I said, coldly. "The soldiers couldn't. We have no clue where he is."

"I know how to find him." His smile turned grim.

"You know where to find him? Why did you wait till now to tell me? I could have had my heart back instead of this clockwork one —" the world tilted again as sandalwood perfume twined around me. I gritted my teeth. "You will guide a platoon of soldiers and capture the sorcerer."

"I'm afraid the soldiers won't help."

"Why not?"

"He's a sorcerer. He'll just disappear. But..." He inclined his head. "If *you* go, he will wait for you. That is when we'll capture him."

"I will not be bait in a fool's madcap plans."

"Even if it's the only chance to retrieve your heart?"

"You'll have to convince me that it is a chance at all. Who will corroborate your story?"

"Bestian."

"My physician?"

He nodded. "If Bestian vouches for me, will you come with me to catch this sorcerer and restore your heart?"

I raised a brow. "Come. We will speak with Bestian. We'll see if your story holds anything more than fireside boasting."

Bestian sat on one of the padded chairs in my sitting room, his grey physician robes properly solemn. The Fool lounged against the wall beside him, his garish red-and-green clothes clashing with the peach-toned wallpaper. I stood with hands clasped behind my back and my chin stern. Betrayed anger simmered below, along with the whispering lies of Friedrich.

"Bestian," I said with an icy edge. "Did you tell the Fool of my curse?"

He squared his broad shoulders. "Yes, Your Highness, I did."

My anger pushed upward and slid sideways. A translucent Friedrich appeared in front of Bestian and bowed to me, then held out his hand. Delight sat in his fingers. All I had to do was take it.

I clenched my hands behind my back and glared at the wall near the ceiling. "I trusted you to keep this secret."

"I apologize, Your Highness." He spoke calmly. "You see, Konrad has—"

The Fool stood from his lounging position, his height bringing his bell-capped head into sight. "Don't burn Bestian in your anger. He didn't tell me until after I guessed it."

"And how would *you* guess that?"

He pulled out a parchment from a belt pouch and unrolled it. It was an accurate sketch of the sorcerer—one of the notices being hung in every village square throughout the kingdom. He pulled out a second parchment, this one brittle with age. As it unrolled, a face appeared: a lean, handsome face with black-rimmed irises and pale, wavy hair. The two pictures were of the same man, the one who continued to pull at me in cursed and ghostly form.

I pressed a hand to my chest as the mechanical heart jittered.

He held out the older picture. Cracks ran along the faded page. "This man cursed one of my ancestors. My family found the sorcerer's abode, and the path was passed down to me. When I saw the notice in the market square saying this man had poisoned you, I guessed it wasn't poison but rather a curse that afflicted you. Then I watched you for a week and saw how you reacted to emotion; the glazing over of your eyes, the sweat that pricked along your forehead, the wavering on your feet, and *especially* the pressing of your hand to your chest. He's impacted your heart in some way."

I dropped my hand.

He set the pictures on a small desk. "Don't worry. Others are concerned but attribute it to poisoning. Your secret is still safe." His mouth quirked. "Most don't see the world as clearly as a fool does."

I raised my brows, waiting for him to continue.

He nodded in return. "When I approached my honorable friend Bestian with this knowledge and the offer to serve my future queen, he admitted that your heart had been impacted by a sorcerer, but he didn't tell me how. *You* are the one who told me you have a clockwork heart."

Surprise and chagrin drove out the other strong emotions, except for the cursed ones. The ghostly Friedrich smirked. I shook my head to clear it. The Fool had guessed all that just by observing me? It was necessary I get my heart back before others also realized what had happened.

I folded my arms. "Bestian, even if you didn't tell him my curse, you still sent the Fool to me, which means you believe he can help me. Is this true?"

"I don't just believe. I know." Bestian motioned to the Fool. "Konrad is trustworthy and capable."

That was not the answer I expected or wanted. "Fool," I said, "how do you propose to find the sorcerer and to get my heart back? The specifics, please."

He grinned. "I'll be as specific as possible without turning this into a year-long lesson in my family history."

"No history," I said. "Just your plan from this point forward."

His grin widened. "The practical matters. As I told you, I know where to find the sorcerer. He cursed one of my ancestors. It is quite the tale."

"The plan."

"Ah, yes. In short, my plan is to lead you to the tower of the sorcerer, and while he's distracted by you, capture him and force him to restore your heart. After all–" He chuckled. "Our nation cannot have a heartless queen."

I stiffened my spine and looked over his shoulder at the wall. "What makes you think you can capture him or force him to do anything?"

"First, I successfully disarmed five of your guards in a practice brawl."

It was true. I'd watched the humiliating event. Despite the Fool's gangly build, he was quick and had used the guards' strength against them. "However," I said, "the sorcerer is not a magicless guard."

"And thus my second point: I know the sorcerer's true name, the one that will give me power over him."

Startled, I looked back at his face. He had a way to overpower the sorcerer? This, in addition to his knowing how to find the sorcerer, could work. "What is his name?"

He raised a brow. "I'm afraid there are criteria to revealing a true name, and the easiest to fulfill is being in the presence of the name's owner."

"Then use his name without me."

The Fool shook his head. "I have to get close enough to touch him when I say it. I doubt I, or anyone else, will get close enough without you there. Why would he run from the one he seeks to wed? Especially if she has little to no protection." His mouth quirked. "At least not visible protection."

My head ached as he addressed my arguments. It seemed, if I wanted my heart back, I'd have to go to the sorcerer. I couldn't just leave it to an army or even a single assassin. The Fool's plan had merit, if what he said was true. "Bestian, do you trust all he is saying?"

Bestian clasped my hands in his. "My lady, I've known Konrad longer than I've known you. I'd trust him with my life, and the lives of my wife and children. If you knew his history, you'd see the reason for my trust."

The Fool chuckled and his cap bells jangled. "I shouldn't waste Her Highness's time with the annals of my family."

"True," I said. "We've had enough irrelevant topics."

Bestian snorted softly. "Then you'll just have to trust me, as you often have before. Konrad knows the way. He will safely guide you. The path is difficult. But in the end, he will get you to the sorcerer. Konrad may act the fool, but if anyone can guide you safely and retrieve your heart, it will be him."

My stomach turned. Bestian was both honorable and a good judge of character. He wouldn't vouch for the Fool if he didn't truly trust him. But going with the Fool meant leaving the palace and venturing into the unknown.

"Fool," I said, "where is the abode of the sorcerer?"

He raised his brows. "A place hidden to all but those who know how to see the path."

Fear and frustration combined. Why couldn't he be clearer?

Lovely Hette. Friedrich's sultry voice whispered behind my ear, and a cool breath tickled my neck. A lifetime of this if we didn't find the sorcerer.

"If I go with you, what will you do if I fall to the curse?" A tremor marred my contempt.

The Fool knelt before me, his face, for once, serious. "I've been pulling at your emotions from the moment I entered the throne room. If you can coldly withstand the mockery of a fool, you'll withstand the sorcerer."

Why did it have to be the Fool to guide me? I pinched the bridge of my nose. "Very well. But we need a convincing cover story. I'll not have the kingdom gossiping about my running away on holiday with you."

SKEIN

I sat sidesaddle on my white mare, sweat collecting across my shoulders from the early afternoon sun. I wore a brown brocade, suitable for traveling by horse, but not for sitting in direct sunlight with no breeze. At least I didn't have to swelter under a wig. My hair was pulled into a simple bun.

Servants scurried around the courtyard checking the straps on saddlebags bulging with food and clothing, slipping a few final items into side pouches, making last-minute adjustments for my travel to the baths. It was to aid my recovery from the poisoning. Only two would travel with me. The baths were but a few days' journey, and a maid and one guard were enough. The baths' staff would care for and protect me once I arrived.

Or that was what we'd told them.

To my right, a peasant woman sat astride a dappled grey horse: a niece to the physician and apprenticed in the healing arts. She looked to be in her mid-twenties and was solidly built like her uncle Bestian, with a placid face. She'd serve as my maid.

To my left, the Fool slouched on a horse that looked like a pony under his lanky frame, though the chestnut was as tall as mine. A sword hung from his saddle. He juggled three knives, their blades winking in the sun. He'd be my guard.

A stable boy ran up to the Fool with a cluster of grapes. The Fool caught each knife and placed it in his belt, then bent over. "And what be this mournful face and sweet offering?"

The boy shuffled in the dust. "It's from all of us. To make a dull journey sweeter."

The Fool plucked one of the grapes and tossed it into the air, leaning his head back. It bounced off his nose, then his eye, and landed on his shoulder. He jerked his shoulder, the grape flew into the air, and he caught it between his teeth.

I turned my back on the Fool as the courtyard filled with laughter. He was why it was taking so long to leave.

The boy's complaints carried over the laughter. "She shouldn't take you. She should take one of her guards."

"Should she?" bellowed the cook. "The Fool could whip any of those soldiers, or five of them together. You remember when the royal guard challenged him, thought they'd make a fool of him, but oh-ho." She chuckled.

The two guards at the courtyard gates scowled at the cook as the boy continued his complaints. "She's never liked your jokes anyway."

"Your concern is heartening," said the Fool. "But who knows if the sphinx will learn to smile? It is worth a fool's life to try."

"Even a sphinx has more heart than she," the boy retorted.

The Fool laughed. "Then all the more delightful the challenge."

I tamped down the rising emotions. Their idle prattle wasn't worth a retort. I flicked my reins, and my mare clipped forward. "It is time we left."

When the castle stood as a grey monument in the distance, the bustle of town was a muffled echo, and hedgerow-edged farms surrounded us, I turned to the Fool. "Will you be trying my patience every day?"

He plopped the last grape into his mouth. "Patience?"

"The *time*, Fool. You wasted half the day."

He shrugged. "We couldn't leave before the clock tower rang the second hour."

"Why?"

"Because time is as much part of the path as the direction."

"You will tell me the path, both time and direction."

"Nay, my lady." He tossed the cluster of grape stems into the hedgerow. "Only one person can know the path at a time. If I were to tell you, then it would vanish."

Rising anger merged into confusion. My brows crinkled. "That's not logical."

"Magic isn't logical, my lady. Nor is it kind. I know the path because the one who told me died the same day."

Was it true? Or was he just trying to annoy? Either way, he'd not get a rise out of me. I clamped down on the emotions as a whisper of desire for the sorcerer brushed by. "Then magic is like you," I said.

He bowed in his saddle. "Why, thank you, my lady. Though occasionally I am logical."

"And he is often kind." The soft words came from my new maid, Bestian's niece.

I turned. She sat astride her dapple-grey, looking into the distance. Her dark braid swung across her broad shoulders as if she'd quickly turned her head. What was the Fool to her? Bestian had assured me of her honor and discretion.

Oh, it didn't matter how she knew him. She was a maid, and he was a fool. And we needed to find the sorcerer.

"Where to now?" I asked. The road stretched southward ahead

of us, dipping in and out of green hills. A dark forest lay beyond, shrouded in mist.

The Fool grinned. "An inn."

"No." I tapped my horse with my heels. "We've only started. We will travel much longer before we stop for the night."

"We will, but we must stop by the inn first."

"And I suppose it is part of the path?"

He nodded and urged his horse into a trot, passing me, his two-pronged cap jingling in discordance with the horse tack, his bright clothes garish against the green countryside.

Shops and homes towered on either side of the road, nesting together with barely space between for a dog to fit. Red flowers bloomed in every window box, brightening dark timber frames and mustard walls. Songs bellowed from the open tavern. As the buildings thinned at the far end of town, a thatched-roof inn stood with a stable to the side.

In front of the inn, an elderly couple sat on a bench with their heads leaned back, eyes closed, and their lined faces soaking up the afternoon sun. The rich scent of baking wafted by as we stopped in the yard.

The man opened his eyes as we drew nearer, then leaped from the bench and grasped the Fool's hand. "Konrad, what a delight. Please say you are staying the night. You always bring in good customers."

The Fool swung from the saddle and motioned to us. "Leo, may I introduce my sisters, Helga and Irma."

I winced. *Helga and Irma?*

The innkeeper studied us. "Sisters?"

He had a right to be skeptical. I wore a brown brocade, lined with lace, while my hair was pulled into a pearl-netted bun. I could have passed myself off as a merchant's daughter. The maid wore a coarse green-wool dress, belted at the waist with a commoner's pouch hanging from it. Her braid only added to her rustic look. Not even a fool would mistake us for sisters. But a Fool would introduce us as such.

"Yes, my beloved sisters. We sadly must continue on today, but I'd be remiss as a brother if I didn't treat them to your wife's pastries."

The innkeeper nodded as if that explained everything. "Of course. Come and rest yourselves. I'll see to your horses."

We followed the goodwife into the cool of the inn and settled at a round table.

She bustled into a back room, calling over her shoulder, "Konrad, you came exactly on time, as always. It will be but a moment."

"Fool," I said. "Could it be that pastries are the reason we had to arrive exactly now?"

He leaned back in his chair with hands clasped behind his head. "You won't question my timing when you've tasted them."

"I doubt that."

He laughed. "Is there anything that you do not doubt?"

I lifted my chin. "I doubt not immutable truths. Geometry, physics, the planets in the sky."

"Ah. So the shortest distance between two points is a straight line?" He motioned to the fire burning in the hearth. "That water boils over a flame and doesn't freeze?"

"Yes. Of course."

My maid leaned on the table, her arms causally crossed over the dark wood. "I doubt not family nor honor."

I stiffened. *Speaking without being spoken to. She must have learned it from Bestian. It's better in a physician than a servant. At least Bestian's observations are logical.* I looked at the door that led back to the kitchen. Where was that woman and the promised pastries? If we were going to pointlessly stop... The tightness in my chest turned into a ghostly whisper: *Hette. Beautiful, cold Hette. How quickly you come to my call.*

I gripped the edges of my chair. Why did I let frustration turn my emotions? *Stop feeling. Only think.*

Logical thought would have been easier if I wasn't traveling with a fool and a forward maid.

The Fool stood. "Coffee. I doubt not coffee. And that sleeping late is pleasant. I'll go see if the goodwife needs any help and brew us a pot." He strode into the kitchen.

The maid reached over and patted my arm. "Princess Hette, it will be easier if you relax."

I pulled my arm away from her touch and folded my hands elegantly in my lap. "I would remind you that you are here to serve, not speak."

She coughed, though it sounded suspiciously like a laugh. "My uncle said you were bound by protocol. But protocol won't work well on this journey."

My toes curled within my leather boots. *Impudence.* "Are you suggesting I forget my place as princess and your place as maid?"

"Or you can continue to hold to your protocols and make the journey harder on yourself. That curse isn't going anywhere until we get to the sorcerer, and the high emotions just give him more control."

I bowed my head against the dizzy tilting of anger at this maid and longing for the sorcerer. As the emotions stilled, the truth of her words emerged. Clinging to protocol would only increase the times I felt powerless and emotional. I needed to accept that things would differ from the way they were in the palace. But still — "You are my maid. I expect a certain level of respect."

She leaned her folded arms again on the table, watching me with a placid face.

"Do you understand?" I asked coldly.

"I made no oath of obedience. I will do as I see best."

"Then why did you come?"

"Because you can use my help, and my uncle asked."

"And you doubt not family." A mocking tone tinged my words.

She smiled with a little shake of her head. "You didn't doubt him when he said to bring Konrad and me. We're here to help you. Let us be friends."

"I don't have friends." I stood. "I'll see what is keeping the Fool."

As I came to the open door of the kitchen, I stopped.

The Fool stood with his head, shoulders, and arms in the brick oven. The goodwife stood next to him holding a woven bag. Trays of golden pastries sat on a table behind him. Why was he so far into the oven? Did a pastry fall off the tray at the back? Then why the bag?

He emerged, his bright colors coated in white ash, and dropped a large grey ball into the bag.

The goodwife squeezed his hand. "It's finally time."

"If not, it will still end with me."

"Go with God's speed and our prayers."

I ducked back from the door as they turned. What was the ball? And what was it finally time for? If I asked the Fool, he'd never give me a straight answer. Would my maid know? If she had the impudence to speak her mind, then maybe she'd be as direct in her answers.

The squeak of a pump handle, followed by splattering of water, echoed from the kitchen as I returned to the table. "Tell me. Have you stayed in this inn before?"

My maid shrugged. "I've stayed in many. One is like another. They are more pleasant than sleeping on the ground, though we'll have plenty of that ahead."

"Do you know the path the Fool takes, the one that only a single person can know?"

"How could I, if only one person can know?"

I gave an exasperated puff. "You are as slippery in your words as an ambassador."

She shrugged again. "I don't know the path. But I do know the journey won't be easy."

"Ja. It won't be easy." The Fool strode to us, jingling bells with each long stride, and set down a platter of golden pastries. "That is why we will shore up our courage with heaven-sent food." Ash still dusted his clothes, but his face and hands shone damply.

The goodwife followed with a steaming clay jug and three mugs. "None of your flattery, Konrad. They are but apple tarts, and nothing magical or heavenly about them."

"Just take a bite," the Fool whispered out the side of his mouth, "and you'll know the truth of my words."

I'd eat one just so we could leave. Once we were on the road, I'd ask him about the ball he pulled from the oven. And I wouldn't let him slide out sideways from telling me.

The tart crackled as I lifted it from the tray, bits of golden pastry flaking off under my fingers. Heat and rich spicy scents escaped in steam from the open center where green apples bubbled in a glossy sauce. It was like many of the pastries I'd had in the palace. I blew to cool it and took a bite.

Thin layers of crisp pastry melted on my tongue, studded with crunchy granules of sugar. Tart apple chunks, in a buttery sauce, followed. Cinnamon, a hint of hot spice—pepper?—a touch of creamy cheese. Sweet, tart, rich and spicy, melded in my mouth.

I closed my eyes and took another bite.

As I licked my fingers after the last bite, the Fool held out a steaming mug. "Shall we go, or would you like another?"

I reached for a second tart. "Only if the path allows the time."

❧

As we rode away from the inn, a damp and ragged boy ran down the street toward us. Three other urchins raced after him. One drew back his arm and threw. The frontmost child jerked. Another scooped something from the ground and flung his arm. The road puffed with dust where something—probably pebbles—peppered the dirt. The frontmost child ducked his head and ran faster.

I reined in my horse. If the child didn't stop, he'd run in the midst of us and frighten our horses. Nor would I be pleased if the other children hit me instead of their target. "Fool—"

He was already off his horse and striding toward the children. He skipped, then somersaulted, eating up half the distance between the urchins and us.

Three of them stumbled to a stop. But the front most one ran onward with his head still ducked and his hands covering his neck.

The Fool somersaulted again and landed next to the ragged child.

"Bwuh!" The child tumbled to his seat, sending up a large puff of dust.

The danger of being hit by pebbles had passed. I urged my horse forward. My maid and the Fool's horse followed.

The Fool knelt next to the child and spoke softly. Then he pulled a coin from behind the child's ear.

The boy's eyes brightened as his mouth opened in surprise.

Children, delighted by the simplest tricks. I stopped beside the Fool. "Come. It is time we left."

The Fool glanced up. "A moment, my lady." He motioned the other children to him. "Come here, you ruffians."

The other three shambled up, their heads hanging.

The Fool stood and motioned to the boy beside him. "My good friend, Hans, has a large copper that he would like to use to treat you to the best apple turnovers you've ever tasted."

One of the children looked up. "You mean Mistress Krüger's?"

"Exactly. And once you are done, he's promised to help rebuild the dam he broke. You'll have a good waterhole by tomorrow. I hope you'll allow him to swim there with you."

"Ja," said the oldest child. "We won't mind him swimming. Come on, Hans."

The four boys raced each other to the inn we'd just left.

The Fool chuckled as he swung back into his saddle. "Bless those ruffians."

"Must you give away coppers to street urchins?"

He glanced over at me. "A full belly and a forged friendship are worth a little metal."

We left the town and the street urchins behind us. My maid rode to my side while the Fool rode ahead, whistling a tune he often sang at court. Something about life's time being too short for love. It would be a reasonable song if it didn't tend to be melancholy. The sun lay closer to the horizon than the center.

I pulled out my watch and opened it. It sat in my hand like two halves of an egg. The silver hands showed seven minutes before five. We still had about three and a half hours of light.

"Fool," I said, "tell me about the ball that you pulled from the oven."

"So that was you at the kitchen door?" He looked over his shoulder. "Don't worry about the time. Your watch is of little use where we go."

I clipped my watch shut so it sat fully egg-shaped and tucked it into my watch pouch, then urged my horse to canter up beside him. "The ball."

"There once was a shepherd." The Fool's voice fell into the deep richness of storytelling. "He was famous through the whole land for his—"

"What does this have to do with the ball?"

"Questions and answers, my lady."

My maid trotted her horse up next to ours. "Let Konrad tell his story. He won't give an answer any other way."

The road stretched southward ahead of us, and the forest stood two hours away. Or so the map said. Then the road would split and go east and west. The next inn was southeast, about three hours away. We'd reach it just before dark.

If the only answer I'd get was from a story, then we had time. "Proceed, Fool."

There once was a shepherd, famous throughout the whole land for his wise answers to questions. The king did not believe it and sent for the boy. When the boy entered—a lanky youth in tattered clothes—the king believed it even less.

"Tell me," said the king, "how many drops of water there are in the ocean."

The boy gazed at the ceiling, as if he'd not heard the king.

"Boy, answer me."

"I will answer when I've been asked a question."

"Do you understand who I am?" bellowed the king.

The shepherd turned to look at the king. "You are a prisoner, caught in a cell of stone walls, trapped between the demands of courtier and commoner, ever under the sword of rebellion."

"Me, a prisoner!" sputtered the king. "Take him out and behead him."

"Wait," called a youthful voice. The king's oldest son rose from his chair on the dais. He was but a child of twelve years, fair of face and dark of features; beloved by the king. "Father, may I ask him a question first?"

The king's face had turned purple, but he nodded. He'd deny his son nothing.

"Wise shepherd," said the prince, "how many drops of water are there in the ocean?"

"Kind prince," said the shepherd, "if you will dam all the rivers of the earth, so not a single drop runs from them into the sea until I have counted, I will tell you how many drops are in the ocean."

"Father," said the prince, "may I ask him a second question?"

The king nodded again, though his jaw clenched along his high collar.

"Wise shepherd, how many stars are there in the sky?"

"Kind prince, if you will gather all the sands of the earth's beaches, I will count them and that will be the number of the stars."

"Father," said the prince, "may I ask a third question, and if he answers well, will you give me his life?"

The king, who could deny his son nothing, lifted his scepter. "Shepherd, if you answer his question well, I will give your life to him. You will serve him until his death and die upon his dying."

The shepherd held his head high. "My life is not even a drop in eternity. What matters a few years more or less? Do as you will."

"Wise shepherd," said the prince, "how many seconds are there in eternity?"

"Kind prince, in the center of the Black Forest is a diamond mountain, which is two and a half miles high, two and a half miles wide, and two and a half miles in depth. Every hundred years a sparrow comes and sharpens its beak on it, and when the whole mountain is worn away, then the first second of eternity will be over."

The prince clapped his hands and ran to the shepherd's side. "And our friendship will last as long. What is your name?"

The shepherd knelt before the prince. "I've forgotten the name my mother once called me before she died. And I've never taken another. You may call me Shepherd."

"No." The prince pulled the shepherd to his feet. "You are a shepherd no longer. You are my brother. And you shall be called Erasmus."

The two clasped hands, the shepherd towering over the prince, and the penniless youth and the royal child became brothers.

Though the king held a dark heart toward Erasmus.

The Fool drew into silence with the ending of the story. The clop of hooves replaced words.

If the shepherd had spoken thus to my father, my pleading would not have extended his life. But then my words had no influence on the king's actions, not when I warned him of Duke Gerhard's skimping his taxes nor when I exposed his favorite courtier in speaking against the crown.

The shepherd was lucky. A figure in a fairy tale to live a charmed life.

"Fool," I said, "what has the tale to do with the ball?"

"It brought us to the point where I will use it." He withdrew the grey ball from the sack on his saddle and dropped it to the ground. The ball rolled sideways from the road, and a thin metallic thread stretched from it back to the Fool's hand. He tugged on his reins. The horse turned to follow the ball and broke into a trot.

I clicked my tongue, and my horse followed.

The ball rolled, tunneling between the roadside grasses, gathering speed, bouncing above the stalks, then disappearing again into the green. Soon, only the metallic glint of the strand stretching from the Fool's hand showed the direction of the ball.

The Fool leaned over his horse's neck, his right arm extended and his torso turning sideways as if the string was pulling both him and steed forward. He kicked, and the horse broke into a gallop.

We crossed a meadow. I kept a length behind and a little to the left. Bits of soil and plant matter from his steed's hooves peppered the air and my face. A bit of dirt got in my eye. I blinked, then swiped the back of my hand across my eyes. The dirt dislodged, and my vision cleared.

A hedge stood across our path.

The Fool's horse reared up and sailed over.

My horse balked. I clamped my legs tightly around the side-saddle pommels as my body lifted, and I flew over my horse's neck, landing face down on the hedgerow.

"Princess Hette!" My maid's concern came a minute too late.

I sucked in air. My corset had protected my torso somewhat, but also made needed breaths harder. My face fared less well. It stung with a hundred little scratches.

Hands pulled at my shoulders, and the hedge crackled, while bits of my dress snagged. A loud rip accompanied the lace tearing free from my bodice. I sagged as my feet settled on the ground on the same side I'd started on.

My maid caught me and lowered me to sitting. "There now. You'll be all right in a moment. Just breathe."

I caught a few more breaths. "Find the Fool and get him back here."

She glanced over the hedge. "He's too far to call, but he's stopped."

"Never mind. It will be faster if we just go to him." I rubbed my forehead, and winced, as the scratches stung with the touch. How did I end up needing the Fool to lead me to my heart? He did know unusual things. The ball was proof of that. What kind of mechanism powered it? And would it take us to the sorcerer?

"But your face," said my maid. "Let me tend to it."

"No." I stood and mounted, brushing aside her offer of help. If I was to do without a proper maid and protocol, then so be it. I wouldn't let her give pitying help.

In the distance, the Fool knelt by another hedge. He seemed to be lifting something from beneath it.

It took time to find a gap in the hedge, and by the time we

reached him, whatever he had found was hidden, and only the freshly dug earth remained.

"Fool." I looked down my nose at him. "You will tell me, without stories or riddles, what that ball is, and what you've unburied."

He glanced past me, and my maid spoke. "She landed in a hedge when her horse balked. She's uninjured, save a scratched face."

The Fool stood and came to my side. Even standing on the ground, his head was not much shorter than mine when I sat upon my horse. "My lady, we should tend to your hurts."

I didn't want his pity either. I lifted my chin so that I looked over the top of his head. "There is no need."

He stiffened. "Then we shall proceed." He knelt again and pulled a sack from under the hedge.

I leaned over and grabbed his horse's reins. "We will not proceed until you've answered my questions."

"I cannot tell you the path ahead."

"But you can explain the path behind."

He nodded. "Very well. The path behind. Would you like to sit here or ride while I explain?"

"Will it matter to the time of the path?"

He glanced at the sack in his hands, then at the evening sun dipping behind dark clouds. "It's too late to go further today. We just need to find a good place to settle for the night. Preferably under a rowan tree. It will storm tonight."

"Why not an inn? We are close enough to the next town."

"We can't now. Not with what we carry."

Enigmatic man. I glanced around. We were in the open farmlands that bordered the Black Forest. The trees had been cleared years ago and the only plant shelter nearby were the waist-high hedges and narrow lines of trees that defined the fields' edges. There was a scattering of farm houses and barns, but if we couldn't stay in an inn, would the Fool allow even that human shelter?

The wind brushed by with the wet scent of a coming storm. Did I trust the Fool's path? What choice did I have? I couldn't find the sorcerer without him. I released the reins of his horse. "You will explain as we travel."

He didn't.

The wind whipped up, blustering over the open lands and casting up dirt from the road. It prevented conversation until we reached the Black Forest. The sun had long since disappeared into the grey clouds, and by my watch it would soon set. The open grey sky disappeared into a blue-grey shadow of trees as we ducked beneath the spreading branches of beech, elm, and oak.

The wind died within a minute of entering the forest, as if a wall surrounded the trees. But that was impossible. It was just a forest, like many others through Germania. The trees just dissipated the wind. That was all.

A yellow glow came from behind me. My maid held a lamp.

The Fool pulled out another and lit it with a few strikes of his flint and steel, then lit a third. "Look for a rowan. It is the kindest of the trees in this forest."

"Kindest?" Trees didn't have emotion or mind.

He urged his horse backward till he was next to me and handed me a lamp. "Yes. Now keep close. It isn't safe to stray."

Silence settled, even the horses' hooves muffled in the mossy ground. The lamplight reflected off dark trunks and boulders, shadows shifting and scurrying behind them. Ferns and other leafy plants brushed against my skirts, some breaking off and sticking, others snagging and pulling at me. Mist crept between the trees. The ticking in my chest pattered in my ears. *Thump— tick, thump—tick.* An owl cried. It was nothing. *Thump-tick-thump- tick.* The trees were trees. The forest was a forest. *Thump-tick- thump-tick-thump-tick.* It was nothing.

Whispers wound around me. *Hette, do you miss your heart? I will keep it safe for you. And I will keep you safe, too.* His words pulled, drawing me, stretching me out between where I was and where he hid.

"Friedrich."

"Princess Hette?" my maid asked. "Konrad!"

The world blurred together, then darkened.

Pounding. Warmth. Bacon.

My head pulsed as it had the one time I'd drunk my father's liquor. I was wrapped tightly in a blanket, my head on a pillow, but my mattress was knobby. A fire crackled. And bacon scented the air.

Voices whispered above me. "Do you think she'll make the journey?"

"She's strong and stern. She'll make it."

"Does she often faint?"

The man's voice laughed. It was the Fool. "Never before the curse. But she's spent years hardening herself against emotion. She'll not fall to it often, and we'll help her when she does."

"Can't we help in other ways?" That must have been my maid; her voice was a gentle one, and not as annoying as at first.

"If she'd learn to laugh at the emotions—at fear, anger, and even desire, they wouldn't be so difficult to control. But she's never laughed in any way beyond derision. Her closing herself off to all emotion is probably the best she can do." There was a pause, and the sizzle, the bacon scent, intensified. "Though I didn't realize she'd be so frightened by the forest."

"The forest is dangerous," said my maid.

"Yes, but if we keep together and to the path, we'll be safe."

"Will you tell her the path?"

I lay still, listening past the pounding in my head. Would he talk about the path to my maid?

"My dear Demuth, I don't even know the path myself until the tools show it. How can I tell it to her?" He laughed, his bells jingling with his voice.

"You always laugh," she chided.

I would chide him too, if it would make a difference. But I'd learn more if I stayed still. He didn't know the path? What were these tools? What was the grey ball and the things he dug from under the hedge?

His voice quieted. "I laugh because I am afraid. I couldn't face each day without laughter." Leaves crackled with movement. "We should try to wake Her Highness. She needs food as much as anything, and the pork will burn if we leave it much longer."

Someone pulled the blanket back and briskly rubbed the backs of my hands.

I lay still. If they thought I was asleep, maybe they'd talk more.

The chafing increased in pressure, and then someone patted my cheek. "Do you have the smelling salts?"

They wouldn't give up. I groaned and opened my eyes. Dark lines of branches cut across a moonlit sky. I groaned again. We were still in the forest. At least the mist had dissipated.

The Fool knelt over me, one side of his face flickering with firelight and the other hidden in shadow. A bemused grin stretched across it. "I thought you were breathing too shallow to be asleep. How much did you hear?"

I pushed against the constraint of the blanket still wrapped around my legs. "That you don't know the path. That you are afraid. And that you think I should laugh about it."

"A fair bit then." He helped me sit, then handed me a plate with bacon crackling on it.

The pounding in my head intensified, and my stomach turned

at the sight of food. I pushed it away. "Just a little water. I can't eat anything till my head clears."

My maid handed me a cup. "She's right, Konrad. Even though you caught her before she hit the ground, fainting often leads to vomiting. Lie back down, my lady, until you are ready. We have all night."

"Then," I said, "we have long enough for the Fool to explain." I sipped the water, then settled back onto the lumpy ground where my head didn't pound as much.

The Fool doffed his cap and scratched his wild hair. "I'll explain what I can—the path we've already traveled, as you so astutely said. You first asked about the grey ball." He pulled it from a pouch at his side and juggled it between his hands before handing it to me.

It was a metal ball, dull grey and crusted with dirt and plant matter. A bit of looped metallic string stuck out from a hole on one side.

"What is it?"

"The skein of yarn."

"This is not yarn nor a skein."

He took the ball again and slipped the looped metal string over a finger, then dropped the ball. It fell to his lap and rolled until it settled next to a saddle bag. The metallic string stretched between the Fool and the ball. "It is called *The Skein of Yarn*. It's a title."

"Why give it such a name when it obviously fits into a different classification? It is metal, and it is a ball. And it has some sort of mechanism in it. It is a foolish title."

"Yes, many things are foolish to those who only see things in categories. But life doesn't sort so neatly." He gave the string a brief tug, and the ball rolled back to him, pulling the string back into itself. "This is like the yarn a king used to find his children when he hid them from his second wife. This finds the next tools for the path."

So it was magic, or it used some sort of science that was not yet general knowledge. "Why was it in the oven?"

"Powerful tools need prudent protection. The innkeeper's wife kept it safe, just as her mother kept it safe before her."

Pieces of the day clicked together. The timing of our arrival at the inn. The pastries. "Could the ball only be removed from the oven when it was hot?"

He tucked the ball back into his belt pouch. "You are clever."

"Then yes?"

"The stones in the back of the oven will only move at a certain temperature. And the ball could only be removed then. Once a day, and only once."

"What about the other tools?"

He shook his head, the firelight and shadow confusing the shapes of his face and concealing his expression. "That is part of the future path. I cannot tell it yet."

"It is not logical."

He laughed. "It never was."

SEXTANT

After an uncomfortable night's sleep, fraught with nightmares of the forest and Friedrich, and after a peasant's breakfast of cheese and bread, I turned to the Fool. "I am ready to proceed. We will not delay, like yesterday."

He chuckled as he pulled three items from his saddle pack. The first was a book, the second a watch, and the third a sextant. He settled cross-legged on the ground and studied the first page of the book, then clicked open the spherical watch.

I pulled my watch out, too. It would have gotten slightly off with all the riding, but still would be within a few minutes of the time. "You'll have to set it. You may use mine as a reference."

"No need." He turned a knob on the watch, glancing at the open book.

I walked over to see the page.

He snapped it shut. "This is only for a fool's eyes."

"As long as we are not on a fool's errand."

"The seeking of a heart is always a fool's errand."

I spun around and scrubbed my face in the bucket of water my maid had waiting. The cold sting on my scratches settled my emotions. The Fool would use the tools and lead me to the sorcerer. I could live with his company. And I would not let him rile me.

"Princess Hette." My maid stood next to me. "I have a balm for those scratches."

I settled onto a fallen pine and let her apply it. Now that it was day, the forest was the standard place of trees, noisy birds, and chattering squirrels, many of them eating the orange-red berries of the rowan tree. The Fool had found us a *kind tree* to camp beside. As if clusters of fruit and serrated leaves provided any protection. I'd not let the forest rile my emotions again, either.

"It is time." The Fool stood and held the sextant up to his eye. It was a beautifully-made instrument, its triangular frame a dark wood with gold marking the degrees along its curved bottom. Mounted on the side of the frame were three round lenses, almost nested against each other, but each set at a slightly different angle. A fourth lens sat at the top of the triangle, mounted on the adjustable arm.

I stepped closer. Gold scrollwork inlaid the wood—figures of fairies and dryads dancing. The sextant on display in the royal library was less noble.

He looked through the side lens, adjusted the arm, and looked again. But what could he be looking at? The sun hid behind the trees. Whatever it was, the Fool spent a considerable time looking first one way and then another, until he'd spun halfway around and gazed through the sextant at the space behind me. He laughed. "Swan or eagle. But I hadn't guessed crab."

I stepped sideways. Though he was obviously looking over my shoulder into the forest, his words should not have been addressed in my direction.

He strung a length of twine through the open frame of the sextant and dangled the tool from his neck so the triangle of wood and gold sat over the diamond clash of reds and whites of his tunic. He opened the book again and flipped through the pages until about a third of the way in, then traced his finger down as if reading a narrow column of text.

What did it contain? Was this the logbook for the sextant? But how? Everything was mixed up from what it should be. I harkened back to my physician's words. *The Fool knows the way. He will safely guide you. The way is difficult. But in the end he will get you to the sorcerer.*

Bestian would not have said thus unless he knew it. I shook my skirts, dislodging pine needles, and waited.

My maid drew near me, her head tilted as she also watched the Fool. "Princess Hette, you look as though you understand those tools. How do they work?"

"You don't know?" I stepped sideways, widening the space between us. "I thought the Fool confided in you."

"Konrad confides what he can. But he's being honest when he says he cannot confide the path."

"An honest fool?"

"Brutally so."

A smile twitched at my mouth. A motion that cracked against scratches and muscle. "I know how the scientific sextant works."

"Sextant?"

"The tool he has hanging from his neck. But he's not using it correctly. The sextant shows the angle between two objects, the various lenses reflecting the sun in line with the horizon. Then, based on the angle and the time, a person can look up their position in a book of tables."

"Oh," my maid said. "I see why you are concerned. He has neither sun nor horizon to measure against."

I turned and looked at her. She was no dimwit, despite her placid face. "Correct."

The Fool glanced up from the book. "Correct and wrong. But then, many things are. A king's right to rule. A duke's control over his serfs. A princess's—"

"Konrad—" My maid's voice turned sharp.

He grinned, "Ah, yes. We should go."

I turned my back on him. He would not raise my emotions that day.

We mounted our horses and set off through the trees, the Fool leading, me close behind, and my maid bringing up the tail. The day passed with him checking the sextant, watch and book, then sometimes changing direction.

We crossed between stands of trees so thick that we almost needed a lantern to navigate. We urged our horses up boulder-strewn hills, where tree roots clung to rock and thin soil as tightly as the leeches. We splashed through streams. Onward, turning and twisting, often going the most difficult path.

The mist announced the ending of the day more than the diminishing light. A tightness crept along my shoulders. "Fool, how much longer must we travel today? My back is weary."

He reined in his horse and glanced back. "My lady, has fear taken hold of you again?"

"No. What have I to be afraid of?"

"Nothing, if we keep to the path."

"You sound like my old nurse. The one who told of the little girl who left the path and met the wolf. What do you expect off the path? Werewolves, witches, devils?"

"Perhaps."

A branch snapped. The tightness of my shoulders pulled inward around my chest. *This is ridiculous!* "The tales are foolish. Why would a witch, with all her magic, settle so deep in the woods? If she gets her strength from lost children or maidens, why not settle where they are in greater supply?"

"A fine question," the Fool said. "Next time I see a witch, I will ask her. I'm neither child nor maiden, so I will be safe enough to ask it."

My maid came up beside us on the path and handed me a lantern. "Konrad, she'd probably turn you into a frog."

"No, no. A spider is more likely. It fits my form." He stretched out his long legs from either side of the saddle and bent his arms at crooked angles. "As for a werewolf? What does he do the rest of the month when he's not in wolf form—gamble with a devil? It's not a full moon tonight. Any devils and werewolves are probably playing checkers, while a witch is brewing up a drink for them. What flavor do you think it will be, my lady?"

"Does it matter?"

"My lady, this is the part where you use your wit, which I'm sure you have in good supply, and then laugh."

A musty scent rose with the mist. Mouldering leaves and decay —animal or something else? My horse shifted nervously as I tightened the reins. "I'm no fool, and laughter is not an answer. If we are in danger, we should find safety. If we are not, then we should at least find rest. Laughter doesn't change anything."

The Fool shook his head, his bells gently ringing. "Laughter changes a person." He held the sextant to his eye, though there was nothing he could have seen in that light. "We only have a little further today."

Only a little further turned into stumbling through the forest by lantern light. The mist pressed closer around me, and little branches grabbed at me like hands. Laugh? How? The tightness squeezed across my chest and a whispering scent of Friedrich's perfume joined the mist. *I will not let the curse happen again, not here, not now. Think about something else.*

I recited mathematical formulas as the mist thickened. Images flickered at the sides of my vision. A wolf skulking amongst the trees. *No. He's playing checkers with a devil.* The image changed. Two men sat on either side of a stump with a checkerboard between them, one in foppish black and the other one as worn as a beggar. They motioned in animated arguments over the board.

I pulled my cloak closer. They were ridiculous. They couldn't hurt me.

A witch joined them, oozing darkness. *No. She's serving them* —Serving them what? Cider of crab apples, a fine wine pressed from sour grapes?

"Bog peat beer." My thought slipped out in words.

The Fool turned in his saddle and stared. After a moment of misty silence, he laughed. "That is exactly what a witch would serve. Excellent." He held up his lantern and showed a cave in the hillside. "And here we are."

Firelight flickered off the walls of the cave, driving out the dampness. At the cave's mouth, the horses snuffled through the bit of grain the Fool gave them. They had plenty of plant matter to eat, but we couldn't risk wearing them thin on our journey.

My maid sat brushing my hair, removing needles and twigs. "Today reminded me of the time I visited the forest with Konrad."

She shouldn't have been chattering, but I was too tired to reprimand her. Besides, if she was talking, I wouldn't have to listen to the Fool.

"He was a tall boy of ten," she said. "But he seemed all grown up to my seven-year-old eyes. He was already an orphan and making money as a street performer. Not that he didn't have a home. But a house didn't seem to contain him."

The Fool chuckled as he fed another piece of wood to the fire.

My maid continued. "I followed him everywhere. I would have followed him to the castle when he became the court fool, but my parents wouldn't let me become a serving girl or maid. They would blanch if they knew I was serving as a maid now, after all the years I studied under my uncle to be a healer. You know, I do have a village that depends on my herb knowledge. I'll be going back to them when this is all over."

She started braiding my hair.

I reached back to stop her, but even that was too much bother. A braid would suffice while we traveled, even if it meant I was looking more and more like a peasant. Like the peasant behind me who started a story about a forest and rambled into her village herb practices.

As she tugged at my hair, her voice prattled on. "So, one day Konrad said he was going to collect fairy thimbles and elf shoes. I didn't know what those were, but I knew I wanted to collect them too. We set off early in the morning. And do you know what we found?"

She waited while the fire popped and crackled.

The silence stretched until the Fool hummed the opening notes of a ballad I hated, one of a foolish princess who pricked her finger on a spinning wheel and slept for a hundred years, even though she'd been told never to touch one.

"What did you find?" I asked.

She tugged one last time at my hair, then scooted around beside me, her face broad with mirth. "We found leeches in a stagnant pool, slugs under logs, and ants that crawled up my back to get to my bread. When I asked where the fairy thimbles and elf shoes were, he pointed deeper into the forest. But we needed something to mark our path. I tore my dress climbing a tree for little red pine cones to mark our way."

"You wanted to climb," the Fool said.

"True." Her grin widened. "But that's not what I told my mother when we got home. She had a few choice words for you."

"A few? I counted half an hour of them. They ceased to be choice after the first few."

"Oh, those." My maid laughed. "The rest of the words were for who we met."

"Ah, yes." The Fool took on a serious countenance. "I was to be the messenger to take them back to the witch and give her an ear full. I never did. Maybe I will tomorrow. I'd like to nibble on her house again."

What tales these two told. I shook my head, and my braid swung behind me.

"My lady," said the Fool. "You do not believe us? That we found a house of gingerbread and a witch who made it to draw in foolish children?"

"No."

"All that Demuth said is true."

"And you?" I asked.

"You are right to be skeptical, my lady. The truth is, all we met was a crazy woodsman who chased us from the forest, declaring that we were after his livelihood. As we fled, we lost our path of red pine cones and we didn't find our way home until the middle of the night. Demuth's parents were furious. I told them of the witch first, then told the truth next. You see, I am honest —eventually."

"Should I be skeptical of the path we take now?"

His jaw tightened. "You already are. My words haven't changed that. The path will get us to the sorcerer, and that is all that matters."

I turned my back on him and lay down. The stone floor was hard through the layer of pine boughs the Fool had spread for us. A cloak was a poor pillow. I pulled my blanket tight around me. Why did the Fool hold back knowledge and blame the irrationality of our wanderings on magic?

My maid laid another blanket over me. "Princess Hette, what was it like growing up a princess?"

"Understandable. I knew what to expect."

"What did you do?"

I closed my eyes. "I am a princess, not a bard. Ask the Fool if you want a tale."

"A tale?" The Fool chuckled. Then his voice settled into a deep richness. "I shall continue the one from last time. The one of the wise shepherd Erasmus and the prince."

The prince and Erasmus grew through the years like sunlight and shadow, the prince brightening each room he ran through as Erasmus followed closely behind. The prince always had questions, and now that Erasmus had tutors, his answers deepened into experiments.

Can one map the planetary motions?

How does a beating heart work?

Could one find one's place on a map by the angle of the sun?

Is there a way to light a room with something other than fire?

For each question, the two worked side by side, ploughing through books, pestering craftsmen and scholars alike, accidentally setting fire to their rooms. Erasmus didn't know his own age, but he could calculate the age of a tree and tell which years had been drought. The prince skipped a state dinner to attend to their dishes of mold that they hoped would clean rust from metal. The two of them jumped from the castle walls with large wings made from willow and fabric. They plunged into the moat, and only the quick-acting guards saved them from drowning.

The king stopped their experiments.

So they continued in secret, creating a study and workroom in a cave a short distance from the castle. They kept their experiments smaller and always brought back a few snared hares or a fox to prove that they'd only been hunting.

The years passed. The prince grew into a handsome man, attracting the gaze of a kingdom of maidens. But he didn't notice. He was too busy inventing with his friend. They would change the world for the better, inventing pumps, navigation tools, and even medicines to slow aging.

"My son," said the king, as he stopped the prince before he could ride off again to hunt. "Be sure to return in time for the ball this evening."

"The ball?" said the prince. "My younger brother is old enough to stand in my place. Let him take the first dance."

"Son, you are already twenty-two and unmarried. You must turn your attention to more serious matters."

"Father." The prince spoke in confident tones. "I do turn my attention to serious matters. Erasmus and I have almost created a tool to guide travelers if they only have two points of reference."

The king's face whitened, then purpled. "I told you to stop experimenting."

"We are careful. I am no longer a boy jumping from a castle wall with wings. It is time I stop pretending that we are only hunting. Please Father, you must see what we are creating."

And so the king, who would deny his son nothing, allowed them to experiment again.

Not long after, Erasmus grew ill. It was small at first, a slow sapping of strength, each day a little worse until he was a pale image of his once ruddy self. The palace physicians shook their heads and said there was nothing they could do.

Late one night the prince sneaked into the infirmary where Erasmus lay. He grasped Erasmus' weak hand. "I will find a cure, even if it takes a king's ransom."

LOST

An aching in my shoulder and hip woke me. I rolled onto my back, and the pines rustled, sending up a fresh scent in contrast to the stink of my three-day-worn clothing. There'd been no proper place to change into the nightgown I'd brought, and sleeping with a corset was growing irksome.

A pale light, like that of early morning, filtered in the mouth of the cave, showing the cold cinders of a fire and two disheveled piles of pine boughs. The Fool and my maid were gone.

Had they left me? I stood and wavered at the sudden movement.

"Wait your turn, you silly." My maid's voice, from somewhere outside. The Fool's laughter followed.

What were they doing? I stepped to the mouth of the cave.

The Fool and my maid stood currying our horses. Her mount bumped its head against my maid's shoulder as she ran the comb along my horse's jaw and down its neck. The Fool stood in a cloud of dust as he briskly curried his horse's back.

They were occupied. Did I have enough time to change? I couldn't bathe, but I could at least remove my corset and put on a different dress, one more fit for travel. The cave turned a short distance from where we slept. I'd be concealed from the entrance.

Six saddlebags sat together against one wall. Mine were embroidered with an *H*. Beside them sat the plain ones of the Fool and my maid. The flap on one of the Fool's bags lay open, and the dark wood of the sextant peeked out.

The Fool says he's the only one to know the path. The only one who can. But why? How do these tools work?

I withdrew the sextant. It was heavier than it looked, as if the gold scrollwork went deeply, or even lay as a solid gold core. Heavy, like a crown.

Beneath it lay the spherical watch. Its scrollwork was as fine as that on the sextant, but in silver. Instead of fairies and naiads, the lacy metal showed a man's craggy face. Father Time? It vibrated with the familiar ticking, the ticking that pulsed inside of me with each breath. I unlatched it, and it fell open in my hand. Four silver hands lay on its face, three motionless, and one spinning in jerky motions with each tick. Silver edged the dark watch face, not in numbers, but tiny symbols, each an animal or creature from fairy tales.

Maybe the book explained?

It lay sideways, tucked amongst bright clothing. Did the Fool have anything not garish? I tugged the book out and opened its oiled leather cover to the first page. A refined script, as well formed as an official proclamation, lay in a glossy green ink. A single line.

Who seekest thou?

"Peculiar opening text," I muttered. "We seek the sorcerer, of course, the one who took my heart."

The text faded into the page.

I dropped the book and scooted backwards.

New words traced across the page; glossy, wet, bleeding into the fibers.

To start the path, set the longest hand to the hare. Ink sketched in a symbol from the watch. *Then set the...*

My skin prickled, and a shiver ran up my back. I snapped the book shut.

Hette, how I long for you, the sorcerer's voice whispered in the silence of the cave. Though a whisper, it was as rounded and rich as a soloist in a church choir. *I wait—*

"No." I lifted my chin. "You long for power. You wait to trap me. Leave me be."

The voice silenced. Could I push away his curse with my words? Or was he just toying with me?

The book lay heavy in my skirts. Magic was illogical. There was no way to predict it. It only raised high emotions. I slid the book back into the saddlebag, then set the watch and sextant on top. I'd not touch them again.

"My lady." The Fool's voice came from the mouth of the cave. "We have breakfast ready, if you care to wake."

I emerged from the cave in a green linen dress and without the constraints of my corset. Who knew when I'd have the privacy to change again, and I'd not sleep another time in that device, despite how my figure suffered for its lack. I took a deep breath of the misty forest and frying eggs. *Eggs?*

"Where did you get those?"

My maid looked up from where she bent over a pan set on stones in the middle of a fire. A cluster of tiny eggs sizzled beside mushrooms. "Konrad found a quail's nest. There's enough for us each to have four."

"And the mushrooms?"

"They are safe." She sprinkled some of what I hoped were common herbs onto them, and not something else with magical properties. The sorcerer was more magic than I ever wanted to meet, and now we were following magical items. The Fool had told me they were, but it was different now, having watched the ink appear and disappear on the pages. Why couldn't magic just stick to fairy tales?

The Fool gulped down his portion, then saddled the horses. "We must be off now."

He hung the sextant around his neck again and set the watch in his belt pouch. Then he mounted his horse and set the book in his lap. It was best to leave the tools to the Fool. He was right. He'd get us to the sorcerer, and that was all that mattered.

My role was to stay emotionless. Fainting would only slow us down. I mounted my horse. Today, I'd not let the sorcerer touch my emotions, because I wouldn't feel. No matter what my maid did or the Fool said, however illogical the path might be or what I thought I saw in the mist, I wouldn't feel.

The Fool held the sextant to his eye and then glanced at his watch. He tilted his head. "Strange." He wheeled his horse around, and trotted back the way we'd come the day before, following the trampled path our horses had left.

We traveled a zig-zagging path through the forest that was more convoluted than the previous day; climbing diagonally through winter felled trees, splashing through a stream only to double back and splash through it again a mile later. Once we plodded after a beaver until it ducked into a pond.

The scolding squirrels seemed to have more reason to their movement. When the afternoon sun slipped between the tangled branches of the trees, my stomach grumbled loudly.

The Fool set down the sextant, letting it hang against his chest, and glanced back at me. "Seems that your stomach will speak up even when you won't. It is correct. But it will have to wait just a little longer. We are almost to a safe resting point."

He turned left between two large pines and groaned.

I brought my horse up next to his.

A hill with a cave lay before us. In front of it, flies buzzed around piles of horse dung. It was where we'd camped.

"Fool, why are we back here?"

He rubbed his temples, then opened the book, flipping through the pages. "I don't understand."

"Konrad?" My maid came up on the other side and touched his shoulder. "Are we lost?"

"I don't know!" His usually flippant voice broke. "I've followed the tools. I don't know why they led us back here. It doesn't make sense."

I'd trusted him. And now we were lost. We'd never find the sorcerer. I'd always be cursed.

The sorcerer stepped in front of my horse, his ghostly hand extended, his storm-grey eyes beckoning. *Keep feeling. Your heart becomes more fully mine with every throb of emotion.*

My skin tingled. An itch that only his touch could soothe. I slipped off my horse.

Friedrich's sandalwood scent brushed against me.

"Princess Hette!" Someone grabbed my arm, jerking me.

I pulled against the grasp. Friedrich stood so close. Just a step more.

A sharpness stung my nose. I coughed as my eyes filled with pained tears.

Soft arms hugged me. "It's all right now." My maid patted my back.

"It's not." I grunted, pulling away from her and wiping at the smelling-salt induced tears. "I'd be angry if I could without the curse activating."

The Fool stood a short distance from us. His brows wrinkled as he studied the book. "My lady, forgive me. There must be a reason for our path today. Magic isn't logical, but it has reason. I will find the sorcerer. These tools have always worked before."

"How often have you used them?" I stepped closer to him.

He closed the book. "Only one can see the path."

I caught his horse's saddle. That morning, I'd opened the book. "Fool, what happens if another looks at the book?"

He frowned, his wide mouth turning down into a grimace. "Did you?"

I nodded.

He scratched his curly hair beneath his belled cap. "I know I'm supposed to be the fool here, but that was foolish of you. The sextant, watch, and book will no longer show me the path. We're lucky it only led us in a circle. You'll have to find the way."

"Can't I just give them back to you? You looked at the book after me. Shouldn't it just go back to you?"

"They only pass one way."

The rest of his warning came to mind. He'd said that the person who told him the path died the same day. If he died, the journey would be much more difficult.

"Fool, will you die?"

"All men die eventually. This won't hasten mine."

"Then why did you say—"

"That the man who told me died on the same day? Because my father waited until he was on his deathbed to tell me. Perhaps because he knew I'd try to use the tools. Which I did. I've traveled this way twice before. The path I took was different each time."

"And you found the sorcerer?"

"I found his abode."

"And?"

"And I couldn't get in. With you, we will."

I sorted through his words. The smelling salts had driven out the cursed emotions, though they'd left a headache. I could think better with the headache.

We could still find the sorcerer. I'd have to use the tools, but I already knew how to use a sextant, with a watch and log. Even if it was different with magic, the concepts seemed to be the same. I'd learn to use them and ignore the irrationality. We'd get my heart back, or we'd destroy the sorcerer so he couldn't control it. Best case would be both.

One question remained. "Why did you seek the sorcerer?"

He raised an eyebrow. "You aren't the only one he's cursed."

"The curse wasn't just on your ancestor?"

He shrugged.

"And your curse is?" I asked.

"It isn't one I wish to speak of."

"Bestian knows what it is?"

The Fool nodded.

If my physician knew, and still told me to trust the Fool, then it wasn't dangerous to our quest. It was probably something embarrassing. Or some reason he'd not married yet, though he was—I did the math on our ages—thirty-four. It didn't matter what his curse was, if it strengthened his will to find the sorcerer and help me.

"Very well," I said. "Show me how to use the tools."

My maid opened one of the saddle bags. "We should have lunch while you do. Emotions are always more level with food in the belly."

The Fool chuckled. "Another immutable truth."

We settled back at the mouth of the cave where we'd breakfasted. While my maid sliced salted pork on a flat stone, the Fool spread the three items in a semi circle in front of him.

He picked up the book. "Read what it says and follow its instructions."

"Can't you explain more than that?"

"No, and do not tell me what it says." He handed me the book. "You have a sharp mind. You'll puzzle it out." He stood and went to help my maid.

I set the heavy book into my lap and ran my fingers over the soft dark leather binding. No words or ornamentation marked the cover. What would it show when I opened it this time? Would it be more riddles like the Fool used?

I opened it.

A blank page bled into words. *To start the path, set the longest hand to the hare. Set the second to the eagle and the third to the ass.* The ink spread in spider web lines off the letters.

Prickles ran over my skin.

I will not let emotion take hold. How to anchor my thoughts? Anchor in something solid. Immutable truths, math, science. I closed my eyes. "Immutable truth: the circumference of every circle is twice the radius multiplied by three and ten seventy-firsts."

The prickles died away without the curse activating. *This is how I'll survive to face the sorcerer. I'll anchor my thoughts in truths to quell the emotions. The Fool said to laugh, but laughter is a fleeting thing, an outburst of emotion. Unchanging truths will hold me safe.*

Satisfied with my successful banishing of unease, I opened the watch and studied the face. Tiny, intricate symbols were irregularly placed around the edge, some crowded together and others spaced out. A hare leapt on the upper right, toward the noon spot, running backwards from how time ran. Behind it trailed a badger, cuckoo, deer, beaver, fox, squirrel, three quail, and a frog. A tortoise crawled along the bottom. A dragon curled along the left, almost swallowing a woodpecker. An otter slid down the dragon's tail, while an eagle perched on a wing. At the apex of the watch an ass kicked its heels.

I turned the knob on the side of the watch, and the hands spun. The longest hand was the slowest, though it should have been the fastest, if it worked in the same way as normal watches. When it pointed to the hare, I adjusted the other two arms to their respective creatures. The smallest hand ticked along as it had when I first opened the watch.

"What about the fourth hand?" I muttered.

The words faded on the page and new ones traced. *It is the heart of the watch. Turn to page twenty-eight.*

A numeral 1 appeared on the bottom corner. As I turned, more numbers inked in on the corners of blank pages. 28. *View surroundings with sextant.*

"And?"

The page didn't reveal more. Why did it have me turn pages when that was all it would say? It was as annoyingly mysterious as the Fool had been. I sniffed and caught a whiff of the sorcerer.

"Things which are equal to the same thing are equal to one another." I anchored my thoughts in the Euclidean axiom, then picked up the sextant. Inlaid gold fairies and dryads danced along the curved degree-marked bottom and up the triangular framed sides. At the peak, one fairy spun with her hands aloft holding a crescent moon. Not truly spinning. Each figure was but a frozen moment of movement, recorded in gold. But as I studied one figure, the ones I didn't focus on seemed to shift.

I rubbed my forehead. "Magic is illogical, but it will get us to the sorcerer. I don't have to understand it. And I will not feel anything about it." I lifted the sextant and looked through the eye lens. Two images overlapped each other, as they should have; one of the branches overhead and the other of the cave in front of me. A glimmer of morning sun filtered down. Until the book told me otherwise, I'd treat this like a normal sextant. I'd line up the sun from the top lens with the horizon, or as much of a horizon as I could get in the middle of a forest. It just took the adjusting of the lens' angles with the pendulum-like piece that sat in the middle of the sextant.

Simple enough.

I touched the lens adjusting arm and hissed in a breath.

Two more images overlaid the cave and branches.

The clockwork heart clanked in my chest. I mumbled through all seven of Euclid's axioms twice, then looked again.

A patch of bright stars glowed overtop of the branches. At the base of the cave ran a bright line, straighter than a mathematician's ruler. A horizon line. So this is what the fool saw when he first looked through the sextant. He'd mentioned swan, eagle and crab. They were constellations.

I spun slowly in a circle, adjusting the angle to see the different constellations: harp, scorpion, dragon. My tutor would shed tears to see the stars that clearly. Centaur, hydra, eagle. What was I looking for? Lion. The stars pulsed, then pulsed again.

I adjusted the lens until the lion constellation stood along the golden horizon line. I half expected the stars to run off along the line. But they stayed in their proper pattern and pulsed. Now what?

What would I do with a regular sextant? Note the degree, check the time, and look up the degree and time in the log.

The watch hands had shifted slightly since I'd set it. Now the third-longest hand pointed to the hare along with the longest one. The other still pointed to the eagle. I opened the book. Long columns of tables filled the page. Each column was labeled: *constellation, degrees, time.*

So this was how it worked; giving me enough information for the next step.

"Book, do you ever explain?"

Words traced in a thinner ink along the margin of the page. *I answer questions asked.* The thin ink faded, leaving only the columns of numbers and names.

Reticent book. It was good I already knew how to use a sextant.

After flipping through many pages, I found the position for *lion, 67.5 deg, hare, eagle, hare.* Tiny text sat in a cramped space of the column. I leaned closer and touched beneath it. The text expanded as if a magnifying glass were laid over it. *Follow the Serpent Bearer until the time of otter, cuckoo, third quail.*

In that, it varied from the usual logbook. The log usually just showed a position on a map based on the sighting and time. But I was using a magical tool.

"Third quail from right or left?"

Right. Start now.

I looked through the sextant again until I found the constellation. It was inside the cave. "Fool. Maid. It is time we left."

The Fool nodded and packed the saddle bags while my maid cleaned up our camp site. Neither asked where, though the Fool's amber eyes widened as we entered the cave.

The cave was large enough for us to ride our horses. Their hooves echoed as the stone tunnel descended at a shallow slope. Lantern light replaced the glow from the cave's mouth, and the constellation glowed through the sextant lens. A mineral zing of lime filled the chill air.

The Fool started humming, but stopped when I glared at him.

I leaned over until the glow of the lantern hanging from my saddle showed the face of the watch. None of the hands were close to those three animals. How deep did the cave go?

Something squeaked, and a papery flapping brushed by my head. My horse neighed as I pulled the reins. "The whole is greater than the part," I gasped to the rapid ticking of my heart. "A circle can be drawn with any center and any radius." My heart slowed as a distant echo, *Hette*, bounced off the cave walls. I smiled in the dark. The curse was a bit belated that time.

My horse plodded forward again, his hooves a clatter over the dripping of stalactites. The path turned right. I held up the sextant. The constellation still showed straight ahead, in the solid wall. The watch still didn't point to those animals. What did I do wrong? I'd used the sextant, found the angle, noted the time of each hand, from longest to shortest. *Wait.* I pulled out the tome. "Book," I whispered. "Which hand is first in reading, long or short?"

Middle, long, then short. The words faded.

Why? Why did it have to be illogical? My throat tightened. The cave surrounded me with dark emptiness.

Hette, the sorcerer's voice caressed. *Lost, frightened Hette. I'll show you how to find me. All you have to do is swear to marry me.*

"All right angles are equal to one another. Love is hollow. I won't marry you!" I yelled.

The cave filled with laughter, ringing off each wall. *You already love me. I hold your heart, and it grows softer each day.*

"Eins, zwei, drei," I counted. "Vier, fünf, sechs." His laughter died away when I reached fifty. I ached. I counted to a hundred before I realized that the Fool had grasped one of my hands and my maid held my other.

"Hette," said the Fool. "You are strong enough to fight him. We will not leave your side."

Tears pricked my eyes. I took a shuddering breath. I couldn't cry. The sorcerer would just hurt me again. I continued counting, "Ein hundert eins."

"Ein hundert zwei." The Fool spoke with me.

My maid squeezed my hand. "Ein hundert drei."

Two more bats squeaked past us before my heart settled to a slow *thump, tick.* I took one more breath of mineral-damp air and nudged my horse to turn. "We must go back and start again. I read the clock wrongly."

Once we exited the cave, I followed the dragon constellation till the time of the otter, deer, beaver. Shortly after I turned to follow the crab as the book instructed, my horse balked. I lowered the sextant to find us standing at the edge of a gully. A fetid vapor rose from the bottom. I lifted the sextant again. The crab glowed beyond the gully. We'd have to go down it and back up the other side.

"Fool, is it always this difficult?"

His serious voice came from behind me. "The book tests each new user. Follow it exactly, and it will get easier."

We dismounted and led our horses down the steep slope. The fetid stench grew with each sliding step. Near the bottom, I slipped.

"Careful there." The Fool caught me under my arms.

I tried to find my footing. It was marshy and squelched under my boots. "Fool, how did you keep track of both the magic path and the dangers of the real one?"

"I didn't the first time. And I didn't have a horse to save me with its common sense as you did. Only foolish luck got me—move!" He shoved me aside.

A woman's shriek and a shrill neigh combined with the sound of scrambling. I caught a vine, keeping my balance. My maid slid down the slope with her horse almost on top of her. The Fool caught her by one arm and yanked her sideways. My maid tumbled into me, my hand slipped from the vine, and we both fell into the muck.

Cold water seeped into my dress even as the mud encased my skirts. "Eins, zwei, drei."

My maid shook next to me.

"Maid?"

Her trembling increased and burst out in laughter. "I'm sorry, Princess Hette. I shouldn't laugh. But—" her laughter echoed in the gully "—I was so frightened. I thought the horse was going to —going to come down on top of me—and then—I was sitting in the mud with—" Laughter swallowed the rest of her words.

"Fool, do you know where the smelling salts are?"

He chuckled, though his face was white, and nodded. "But I'll not use them on her. She'll calm down in a moment. Laughter will get the fear out of her blood so she can go forward. Besides, the salts are not healthy to use often." He extended his hand to me. "Best get you up and out of that mud."

I took his hand, and he pulled. The mud slurped, releasing extra potent scents, and I stood with my skirts heavy and black. "You used the smelling salts on me."

"Only once. When you had stopped fighting the curse. As long as you are fighting it, Demuth and I have agreed to not use them."

Oh, that was why they hadn't used the salts in the cave. I shook my skirts, trying to dislodge the mud, but it clung like a second skirt of decaying brocade. "Fool, what were you following all morning? If the tools didn't work for you, then what did you see?"

"Must have been a decoy path. It's never happened before that one who passed on the tools tried to take them back, but that is all I can think of. Truly, only one person can know the path at a time."

"I wish I could give the path back to you."

He extended a hand to my maid. "That makes three of us."

My head ached. I'd followed the instructions from the book, constantly checking the sextant to keep the right direction and the watch to make sure I didn't over-travel the time. But sometimes I did miss it, and I had to take a new path. The directions from the book seemed more difficult when I missed the correct time. I'd not eaten lunch, and only an apple filled the hollow in my stomach. My muck-coated dress clung to me in fetid coldness. The book didn't let me stop, even when I asked. All it said was, *Time is as important as direction.*

I pulled out my watch, not the magic one, but the one I'd had since my eighteenth birthday. Sludgy water dripped as I opened it. The hands were stuck at three seventeen. The time I'd fallen on the muddy slope. Now the sun came at a low angle through the trees. I tucked the broken watch back into the pouch. Maybe it could be repaired when we returned, but for now I'd have to judge the time by the sun, when we could see it.

None of the magical tools seemed to have been injured in the fall. The smallest hand on the magical watch still twitched at regular intervals. The book safely survived nestled in a saddle bag. And the sextant washed clean. The Fool assured me that they could not be damaged by a mere soaking.

I rubbed the back of my neck. We needed a place to stop for the night. "Book," I whispered, looking at the complex columns of numbers and symbols. "I'm tired. Where is a safe place to rest? I cannot follow another clue tonight."

Camp beside the glowing rowan.

Glowing rowan? I looked through the sextant, scanning our perimeter. To our right, a white light filtered through the trunks. My horse stepped between an oak tree and a tangle of brambles. Thorns caught at my dress, but I would not go around and lose the light.

We entered a clearing. A rowan glowed in the middle, the leaves white and the clustered berries fire-red. I lowered the sextant. The evening sunlight flashed against the waxy orange berries, and birds settled for the evening in its branches. We could rest.

"Thank you," I whispered, then looked over my shoulder. "We camp here."

The Fool turned his back and built a fire as my maid and I changed out of our muddy clothes. I shivered as I peeled off the stiff dress. My maid doused me with water, then rubbed me down with a rough blanket before helping me into a dry dress. We were out in the open, without any proper walls or even curtains, but propriety be hanged, I'd die of damp and cold if I didn't change. If only the book had allowed me to stop long enough to change earlier.

"Gold, silver, mercury, tin, lead, sulfur, carbon, antimony..." I muttered through the elements to quell the emotions. All the things I'd blamed on the Fool, all the irrationality of the path, were the book's fault. The Fool was more patient with me than I'd been with him.

I came to stand next to the Fool by the fire and pulled a blanket closer around me. "I—I will try to be easier to travel with."

The firelight flickered across his face. Half his mouth turned up in a smile. "I will try to do the same."

"So you do admit that you were difficult."

"Aye. Demuth is the only reasonable one amongst us."

"Konrad, you don't mean that," my maid reprimanded.

"I think he does." I settled on the ground and reached out for the plate he offered. "And he's more right than I'd like to admit."

I lay on pine boughs—ones the Fool had cut and spread for me—and snuggled deeper into my blankets. The fire crackled. Its smoke mixed with the lingering scent of bacon and pancakes. Weariness hung on me thicker than the mist that swirled around the clearing.

"Konrad," said my maid. "Will you please tell more of the tale —if you have the energy?"

"I have more than I had in previous days. Following the tools is exhausting." He set another branch onto the fire. "The princess is a strong woman. She'll make a good queen."

I'd be a good queen if I got my heart back, or at least if we killed the sorcerer. I couldn't rule with my heart controlled by another. My eyelids drooped.

"My lady, would you hear more?"

I yawned. "Only if it's short."

. . .

On the prince's twenty-third birthday, he didn't appear at breakfast. His and Erasmus' rooms were empty. A wagon was missing from the kitchen gardens, as were the two cart horses. And a king's ransom of gold had vanished from the treasury. No one ever saw the prince or Erasmus again.

"What happened to Erasmus?" I asked, suddenly more awake.

"Much," said the Fool. "And even more happened to the prince." He stared into the fire, his shoulders bowed, and didn't speak more that evening.

BOG

THE FOOL PROMISED the way would become easier. It didn't.

The decaying scent of the gully clung to the bundle of clothes we'd not had time to wash, and followed us past ponds thick with biting bugs, up goat-pathed hills, and between trees that groaned and creaked like old men ready to fall over.

Sextant, watch, book, sextant, watch, book, watch, book, sextant. Again and again. The double images of the golden horizon line and constellations overlayed the real land.

"Inconsistencies," I muttered. "Always inconsistencies. We go sideways when it would be quicker to go straight ahead. Point A to point B. But we turn sideways when we reach a sunny clearing, only to come back on the other side." A sandalwood perfume tugged. I calculated two digit multiplication until it faded behind the fetid decay that traveled with us. The pattern of emotion, snatches of curse, and reciting facts wore into weariness. Would I ever grow so weary that the emotions wouldn't start in the first place?

"My lady," said the Fool. "Inconsistencies are but the meeting of two things for which we do not yet see the connection—the scholar-fool and the adventurer-princess."

"Or the heartless one. Though I'd rather have no heart than one that is controlled by a sorcerer."

"Perhaps. Though having no emotions could be a worse curse."

I checked the sextant. The swan constellation swam slightly to my left between two trees. I nudged my horse to step through the narrow gap. Going around when the way ahead was possible always ended up in changed instructions from the book. The toes of my boots brushed against one trunk. "If I had no emotion, I could reason clearly."

"And what would guide your actions?"

I glanced at the watch. "Certainly not these tools."

The stink of gully-soaked clothes intensified into that of rotten eggs. It must have been the afternoon sun, though little of its heat reached us. I wrinkled my nose as I viewed the Hydra constellation. "Maid, if you find not the time to wash those dresses and boots before we leave tomorrow, toss them into the bushes. I would not travel another day under this stench."

"Princess Hette." My maid's voice was hesitant.

"What?"

"I think Konrad should scout ahead."

"Why?" I looked back at her.

Her brow was pinched. "It isn't the clothing you smell."

I swore.

Cool fingers traced over my hands—gentle, powerful fingers, brushing away the anger. They moved up my arms. The breath caught in my throat.

I recited the classification of plants until the cursed touch was gone. "If the book leads us to another gully, I'll fold its pages." I spoke in cold conviction.

The Fool laughed.

"I will."

"I believe you. I threatened to tear out several of the pages on my first journey. You'll find their ragged remains near the back. The book about killed me for it."

"It already tried to do that."

"Not yet. When it has you swim a naiad's lake or crawl into a werewolf's den, then it will be trying."

I looked into the tangle of trees in the direction we were to go. We were in a clearing, and the bright fruit of the rowan glowed to the side. It was as safe a place to stop as any. The book would change the directions for a delay, but if it was going to lead me to another stagnant gully, the change of directions could be no worse —as long as I didn't damage the book. I wouldn't egg it into leading us to magical creatures. "Will you scout around and let me know what is ahead?"

"It will be my pleasure or my demise, my lady." He dismounted, bowed, and ventured into the trees. His filthy but still garish clothes showed against the dark greens of the forest, and when he disappeared, his bells faintly jingled for a few minutes longer.

I dismounted, stretched my aching muscles, and ate a slice of salt pork wrapped in a leftover pancake from that morning. It was possible I'd not have another chance to eat before we camped.

My maid sat on the ground next to me. "Princess Hette, how are you feeling?"

"I'm trying not to."

"The curse has happened often today, hasn't it?"

"Why do you ask?"

"I've learned more math and science today than in all my years of study as a healer." She smiled. "You know many facts."

"They help. The unchanging truths anchor me."

"I'm glad they help." She reached out and placed her hand

over mine. "We can help too. If you drive yourself to exhaustion, the sorcerer will have that much more power over you. Tomorrow morning, don't look in the book until you've had a good breakfast and a bath, if I can find deep enough water. It can't tell you anything until you look."

A bath. A pleasant prickle ran over my skin. "I would appreciate a bath. Thank you."

My maid stood and curtsied. "Yes, my lady."

That was a first. She'd done much to help my journey— cooking food, braiding my hair—but she'd never shown any proper deference to me, until now.

I finished the pork and pancake, then munched the last apple. Perhaps the book would lead us near some blueberries, though not likely. Where was the Fool? I picked up the book, then set it down. I wouldn't look until the Fool returned. I leaned against the rowan, where a beam of sunlight fell. It rested warmly on my face.

"My lady." The maid shook my shoulder. "Konrad is back."

A vile scent assaulted me. I scrambled up, but the tree stopped me from going backwards.

The Fool stood too short a distance from me. His once bright clothing was caked in mud—foul, nose burning mud, as if someone had mixed rotten egg with smelling salts. His belled cap hung from his belt, and his curly hair was matted to his head. A thin layer of mud coated his face, streaked, as if he'd used a dirty cloth to wipe it.

I would have felt satisfied that he ended up coated in muck after he'd avoided it the day before, if it wasn't almost certain we'd soon be in the same state.

"Is that the princess?" It was a new voice, croaky and the words ill-formed. "Or is she the more pleasant-faced one?"

No one was visible, save the mud-coated Fool and my maid. Late afternoon sun lent a golden glow to the edges of the stretching shadows. "Fool, what did you find, and who is with you?"

The mud on his face cracked as he grimaced. "I found a friend."

He detached a clump of mud from his shoulder. It was a huge, warty toad that filled his whole hand. Its bulbous yellow eyes blinked.

"Good day, fair maidens," it croaked.

My heart jerked like a gear had slipped. "Immutable truth: toads don't talk."

"Don't talk?" croaked the toad. "Mostly. I haven't met another in five freezes. He got eaten by a crow for talking too much. It's lonely. I'm so glad this man came along. So which one of you is the princess?"

A ghostly image of the sorcerer materialized between the toad and me.

"Eins, zwei, drei." I counted.

The sorcerer stepped closer and leaned over me, his lips parted. His scent, both sandalwood perfume and a muskier under-tone, filled my breath. He was but a finger's width away.

I trembled. "Vier, fünf, sechs." If only I could find the sorcerer as repulsive as the toad.

My maid grabbed my hand. "Sieben, acht, neun."

"Should I be counting too?" asked the toad. "Let's see, zehn, elf, what is the next one? Umm... I haven't counted in a long time. Maybe I should start over?" Its low, gravely voice intoned with the incautious words of a boy.

The trembling inside me grew and shuddered out. A raspy noise ripped from me and continued to draw out like a rough rope of sound. I laughed. The sorcerer's face flickered and dispelled.

And still I laughed. It felt like vomiting, painful and relieving at the same time.

Over my laughter, the Fool said, "Peter, my friend, you have accomplished something none other has ever done."

"What?" asked the toad. "What did I do? Do you think she'll kiss me for it?"

That stilled my laughter. "No."

"How about the other one?" asked the toad.

My maid still held my hand, and her grip tightened. "I—I'll have to think about it."

The toad made a low, grumbling croak. "That is what the last girl said. If you are going to say no, just say it. If I think you might turn me back into a boy, I'll be too excited to sleep. And if I don't sleep, it'll be hard to catch beetles and mice to eat."

My maid's grip on my hand loosened slightly. "How old are you?"

The toad blinked its eyes. "Seven. At least I was when the witch turned me. It's been twenty freezes since then."

"And a kiss will turn you back?"

"Yup. That is what the other talking toad said. A princess's kiss."

She stood and walked over to him. "I'm not a princess, so I don't know if it will help, but if you'd like, I'll kiss you."

"Demuth," said the Fool. "You don't have to. He's a poisoned toad."

"I know," she said with a slight tremor. "I'll wash my lips carefully afterwards."

The toad stretched up its head.

She leaned over. Her lips lightly touched its wide, warty mouth.

She disappeared in a loud kerplop, like a stone tossed into mud.

A man sat on top of the fallen Fool. Warty rags clothed his

lumpy, rounded body. Mossy brown hair stuck in lank locks to his head. His wide mouth stretched into a grin over an almost non-existent neck.

"Demuth!" The Fool shoved the man off of him. "Demuth!"

"I'm here." The voice came from the ground. In the leaves sat an even larger toad, in a darker brown. Its croaky voice overlayed the gentle tone of my maid.

The world tilted as my head grew light. Too much. I hissed through my teeth, ignored the ghostly kiss on the back of my neck, and commanded the bulgy man. "Toad, you will turn my maid back into a human, now."

The man stared down at my maid-toad, and his bulgy eyes filled with tears. "I didn't know. I'm sorry. I'm so sorry." He picked the toad up, scrunched his face as if bracing himself, and gave it a slobbery kiss.

Another loud kerplop echoed through the woods, and my maid lay on the ground with the toad sitting on her.

"Never do that again," I commanded.

The toad looked up at me, tears still dripping from its eyes. "Maybe it will work if you do it?"

"Never."

The Fool and the toad sat a stone's throw from my maid and me. Their scent was easier to handle at that distance. My maid also smelled swampy, but only slightly. I let her clutch my hand. She trembled. Why did she kiss the toad? It was a foolish thing to do, and she was the reasonable one amongst us. I needed her to stay reasonable.

"Fool," I said, "now that we've all gotten back to our proper shapes, tell me what you found."

He scratched at his hair and wrinkled his nose as bits of muck flaked into his face. "A marshy bog starts about a ten minute hike east of here. It spreads both north and south as far as I could see. I tried to pick a path through it and got stuck in the mud. The more I moved, the more I sank, until I was up to my mid-calves. I spread myself out on the mud, lying on my back. It stopped the sinking but I still couldn't move. I'd be there still if Peter hadn't hopped along."

"He was just lying there, singing a little song," said the toad. "So I decided to say hello."

"He spent the next hour dragging a vine to me. Because of my friend here, I'm not a new layer in the bog."

The toad croaked a pleased sound.

A bog. A bog that spread both north and south. I touched the book. What direction would it give? "Fool, we are by a rowan tree. We'll camp here and set out in the morning. Go find some place to wash."

He shook his head. "If we camp while daylight is still on us, who knows what the book will say."

"It can say what it wants in the morning."

"I wouldn't recommend that."

What would the book say? My maid said to rest and get a bath before I looked at it. The Fool said I shouldn't delay. The book said —the book said too little and too much. It was the only way to find the sorcerer. I opened to the first page.

The words inked in the perfect script. *Follow the Hydra until the mist swallows you.*

No time given? It had always given a time before. "And then?" I asked.

Travel quickly. If the heart-hand shifts backwards, you will not leave the bog today.

The heart hand? The smallest hand, the heartbeat of the watch. Why would it shift backwards? "It is already late afternoon. We do not have many hours before the mists gather. We will camp and journey tomorrow."

Do so at the cost of one life.

If it said the toad's life, perhaps, but I could not spare the Fool, nor would I risk my maid. I looked through the sextant. The Hydra still sat east of us, over the bog. No angles to measure, no time to check—just follow the Hydra until the mist swallowed us. My throat tightened. I mentally recited the first three laws of motion, then mounted my horse. "We must go on today."

"Into the bog?" asked the Fool, his face drawn tight beneath the mud.

I nodded.

"Wonderful!" croaked the toad. "You can stay in my home tonight."

"No, Toad, we must travel quickly and get beyond the bog."

"It's a long swim," he said.

"Is there no solid path?"

"Solid enough for you humans and those horses? Only in patches. And you'll have to stay away from the muds."

The Fool bent down. "Peter, can you help lead the way? We must go the direction the princess tells us, but can you tell us where to step?"

The toad let out a growling grunt. "Yes." And it slowly hopped away from us.

The Fool picked him up. "Thank you, my friend. If I may, I'll carry you until we get closer."

Closer came quickly. Soon the stench of the Fool melded into the permeating stench of the bog. The land sloped downward. Lush trees thinned into spindly ones, and then died away to bare-branched skeletons surrounded by tufts of matted grass. Green-coated water filled the spaces between.

I held a handkerchief to my mouth. The gully had been awful, but this was the scent of slow death.

"Here," said my maid. "I'll tie it over your nose, so you don't have to hold it."

I looked through the sextant again. Maybe the Hydra had moved so we could skirt the bog.

It glowed, a long line of stars stretching across the stinking land ahead.

The next hours passed with the lowering of the sun. I pointed the direction from the sextant. The toad hopped along, telling us where to step. We didn't ride our horses. Sometimes we waded waist deep in the water. I left the book and the watch high in Konrad's saddle bag. I only had to follow the Hydra until the mists swallowed us. "Let us make it through the bog before they do," I muttered as the sun dipped lower behind us and the waist-deep water grew colder.

"Snake, snake!" the toad croaked and hopped onto my maid.

Something slid by my leg, pushing up against my heavy skirts.

I couldn't draw in enough air.

The sorcerer stood beside me. *Hette, do you trust me?*

The snake curled around my ankle and wound up to my knee. The world narrowed.

"My lady." The Fool pushed through the ghostly image, his muddy arms outstretched, and lifted me from the waters, one arm under my shoulders and the other under my knees.

The snake slithered higher.

"O-oi-eee!" I reached down and grabbed its tail, yanking it. The skin was slick over hard muscles. The coils tightened as the tail slid through my fingers. A gear slipped in my chest. "Get-it-off!"

The Fool let go, and I splashed, standing back into the murk.

He dove into the water.

The snake tightened. My leg pulsed under the pressure. Then

a hand gripped my leg, and the snake began to unwind, inch by slimy inch from my calf.

The sorcerer stood beside me again, his hand extended. *I'll protect you. Just say you'll marry me. All it takes is one word.*

"Go away!" I shouted. "You offer, but never help."

The last of the snake slipped from my leg. The Fool stood, twisted its spine, then threw it into the water.

Acid filled my throat. My legs weakened.

"My lady." The Fool scooped me back into his arms, holding me above the water. "Did it bite you?"

"No," I stuttered.

The toad croaked from my maid's shoulder. "It wasn't poisonous. But it surprised me. I wasn't paying enough attention."

The Fool continued to hold me, and the sorcerer continued to stand close by.

"I'm unhurt, Fool." I pushed against his chest, though my arms trembled. "Let me down. We must keep going."

He set me back down in the waist-deep water. "I'm afraid I've mired the rest of your clothes."

My dress was coated with muck, but the bog's scent had faded to second thoughts. We had to continue on. I would not spend a night there.

"Toad," I said as the first bits of mist twisted along the green coated water. "How much farther to the other side of the bog?"

He hopped up on a raised bit of ground. "It's safe to walk here. Not much farther. Maybe we'll make it by sunset." He stopped hopping and gave a little croak. "Why do you call me toad? Why do you call Konrad and Demuth fool and maid?"

"It is who they are. He is the court fool; she is my maid; you are a toad."

"I'm Peter. I was Peter before I was a toad, and I'm still Peter." He hopped awkwardly over the matted marsh grasses. "What would you call Konrad if he became a baker? And Demuth said she's a healer. Shouldn't you call her healer-maid-beautiful maiden, and everything else she is?"

"She is my maid."

The toad turned around and faced me, his bulgy yellow eyes staring up from the ground at my feet. "It isn't who she is, only what she does."

"Toad," I said. "The book doesn't allow for delays. Keep showing us the safe places to walk."

"No." He stood on all four legs and inflated his body. "I'm Peter. He's Konrad. And she's Demuth, beautiful Demuth."

I glanced at the watch. The hands jerked. If the smallest hand shifted backwards, we'd not make it out that night.

"Toad, that is enough."

He blinked.

"Very well," I lifted my chin. "Peter, please proceed."

He blinked again.

"Fool," I said. "Talk some sense into him."

"I think he'll wait until you say our names. You can go on just with the direction the sextant shows, without knowing the firm ground." The Fool touched his muck-crusted hair.

I looked at the watch again. The smallest hand twitched backwards.

"Konrad and Demuth," I said.

The toad croaked and hopped forward again.

I pulled out the book to see the new directions.

Make camp.

"Where?" I asked.

The book remained silent.

The bog spread out around us.

"Toa—Peter, please help us find a place out of the water to

camp. We will spend the night in the bog."

"Must we?" My maid's two words voiced all the distress that I had to suppress.

The toad—Peter—found a section of grass large enough for our three horses to stand along the edges and for us to sit tightly packed in the center. There was no wood to burn. The mists curled in, thickening as we ate a bit of dried meat and shriveled prunes. Our lamps provided a little glow, and when the mist grew so thick that even the lamps were but a pale grey blot in the moist blanket, the Fool put them out.

We sat huddled in blankets with our backs against each other. There wasn't space to lie down. My wet skirts clung to me, while my legs itched where the grasses had cut them through my thin stockings. The night sounds filled with all that we couldn't see. Chirps, croaks, rasps, plops, a splash, a hiss. "Fool," I said, "tell me more of the story."

"Konrad," mumbled the—Peter. His voice was close to my ear. He must have been sitting on the Fool's shoulder.

"Konrad," I modified, "tell me what happened to Erasmus."

"A long story?" asked Konrad.

A bit of light flared off to my left. A will-o'-the-wisp. "Please," I whispered.

"What happened to Erasmus?" His voice rolled into deep, comforting tones.

On the night before the prince's birthday, he carried Erasmus to a kitchen wagon and fled the palace. Though Erasmus was a good head taller than the prince, he'd wasted to a skeletal frame. The prince drove through many lands, seeking a cure for his friend. He stopped at every scholar's home and herb woman's hut. The tinctures and medicines sometimes helped and sometimes made Erasmus' illness worse.

Two months after they left, the prince stopped the wagon at a cottage surrounded by a tidy garden. A young woman knelt amongst the flowers, pinching off leaves and laying them in little piles on a plate.

"Are you an herb woman?" the prince asked.

She pinched off two more leaves then looked up. "Yes. What can I do for you?"

"My friend is dying." He motioned to the bed of the wagon. "Can you help?"

She hastened to the wagon, the dirt of the garden clinging to her apron and her hands.

Erasmus lay on a blanketed bed; his breathing rasped as his narrow chest collapsed inward on each breath.

"Get him inside, now," she ordered.

Once the prince had settled Erasmus in a bed in the bright hut hung with herbs, the woman listened to his heart and his lungs, felt his pulse, smelled his breath, pinched his sallow skin, and lifted his closed eyelids. Her brow pinched tighter with each test until she turned to the prince. "He's been poisoned."

The prince bowed his head. "My father. But I took him away. It's been two months. He shouldn't be poisoned anymore."

"The poison is gone, but it damaged his lungs and his heart, and who knows what other organs. I can help him be more comfortable, but the damage is too great. He won't heal."

The prince's head snapped up. "Then I will move on and find someone who can help him."

She returned his proud glare with one of her own. "You aren't helping him by taking him in a bumpy wagon, exposed to the elements. Autumn is coming. Stay here. Let him spend his last months with a measure of comfort. Only the witch could cure him."

"Witch?"

"Yes, the witch. There is one who lives in the Black Forest. She *knows how to extend lives and turn back aging. But the price for her spells—"*

"I'll pay anything. A king's ransom in gold."

The woman's eyes widened. "You are the missing prince—the one from the kingdom east of here."

The prince gave a curt nod.

Her lips tightened, then she nodded as if she'd come to a decision. "If you'd give a king's ransom in gold, then perhaps you can get a spell without selling your soul. But it is still dangerous. My mother was apprenticed to the witch before I was born. As I grew, my mother taught me all the herb lore she learned, but refused to reveal any of the magic. She paid for her apprenticeship last year by returning to the witch after twenty years of being an herb-woman. I know I'll never see her again; she assured me of that." The young woman blinked away a tear. "Are you ready to give up part of your life to save your friend? The witch may not accept gold."

The prince plopped into a chair and rested his chin on his hands. His brow furrowed as the minutes passed with the slanting of the sun across the floor. He dropped his hands and clenched them into fists. "I will go. I will apprentice with the witch. And I will save my friend."

"Don't," rasped Erasmus, his eyes half opened. "Don't go. My life is not worth your soul."

The prince knelt at the side of the bed and clasped Erasmus' hand. "I've thought it all out. I won't sell my soul, nor my life. I'll pay her for my apprenticeship with enough gold that she'll never want for anything again. I can save you."

"Be careful," Erasmus said. "Even if you don't sell your soul to the witch, what will the magic do to you? Eternity is a long time."

"Eternity. You often speak of eternity. But what if this life is the only one, and we don't have souls? What if you die and just disappear? Besides, magic isn't good or bad in itself. It can be used for either. Just as an herb can be used for both a medicine and a poison. Or an arrow can feed us or kill a man."

Erasmus closed his eyes, and his pale brow furrowed.

"My friend," said the prince. "Is it wrong to help you? How can I be endangering my soul when I seek to do good? The witch knows how to extend lives, how to turn back aging. I'll learn her secrets. Then I'll make my own spells—good ones."

Erasmus struggled to lift his head and shoulders from the pillow. "Witches use human lives for their spells. I will not have another person's life be used to prolong mine, especially not yours."

The prince's eyes flashed. "My father gave me your life ten years ago. You have no claim over letting it go. I will help you."

Erasmus fell back to the pillows and lay still for a long moment, his breath rapid and shallow. Then he whispered, "Swear to me that you will not use anyone's life force but my own to help my healing."

"I swear."

LAKE

Dawn brightened the mists into blinding white, which swirled around us in damp, decaying death. I stretched and gagged as I yawned. "As soon as we leave this cesspit, we will find a pond or lake. Even an ankle-deep stream."

"Good morning to you too, my lady." The Fool's voice rumbled in the blind mist behind me, his back vibrating against mine. My maid lay asleep with her head in my lap, her long braid draped across one knee. Hopefully, the toad was nowhere near me. The sooner we were out of the bog, the better.

"Foo—Konrad," I said. "Light a lantern. I wish to read the book."

"Have you tried looking without a lantern?"

"No. I can't even see my own hand."

The book bumped my leg. I'd set it there the night before, along with the watch and sextant. The Fool must have nudged it. "Try."

I picked up the book and opened it. The papers rustled. Words scrolled across the mist. *Follow the lion to the time of otter, frog, frog.*

We were already following a toad, and we had to take time by a frog?

I shook my maid's shoulder. "Demuth, it is time."

She lifted her head from my lap with a little groan. "Forgive me, Princess Hette. I didn't mean to sleep there."

"Doesn't matter now." I stood, lifted the sextant, and slowly turned a circle without leaving my spot on the marsh grass. The constellations glowed in solid reference points over the white mist. *I should have looked through it the night before to quell my fears. But it doesn't matter now. Nor will the angle. The book did not have me search through its pages using the angle and time. Maybe it will start to be easier on me.*

I found the lion, then opened the watch. It sat in two halves in my hand, a delicate bit of metal lace and gears ticking away, but invisible in the mist. *Or maybe it won't be easier. Let the mists clear before we pass our time limit.*

The mists lifted midmorning. Pines and oaks stood close by. The toad swam in the water in front of us, while the Fool and my maid walked beside me, each of us thigh-deep in water and leading our horses. Only a narrow strip of water and a mud flat lay between us and the solid ground. The lion constellation lay at an angle from the tree line, but it would connect soon.

"Praise all that is good," murmured my maid.

"Amen," intoned the Fool.

I started leading at a diagonal line to the shore, when my horse neighed and jerked away from me, pulling the reins from my hands.

I stumbled to my knees. Fetid water closed over my head and filled my open mouth. I choked on the swampy liquid. Large hands grabbed my shoulders and pulled me upright.

"My lady, are you hurt?" Konrad's voice cut through the water blocking my ears.

"Stop the horse," I sputtered, as I spat out bog.

The hands released me, and as I blinked, Konrad's blurry form strode two steps and sank to his chest in water.

"Bad ground, bad ground," croaked the toad. "Go back, go back."

My mare splashed onto the mud at the far side. Her hooves sank into the blackness. She reared and her back legs sank to her hocks. Her front legs plunged down, and they disappeared completely into the mud. She gave a shrill neigh as she struggled, sinking lower.

The Fool floundered back to us and unstrapped an oil cloth-wrapped bundle from his saddle. He opened the bundle to reveal a long bow and a quiver of arrows. "I'm sorry, my lady."

"What are you doing?" My voice came out shrill. The sorcerer's whispering pushed against me, but I had no time for the curse. "You will not shoot my horse."

He lifted an arrow to the string. "Would you rather she suffocate?"

Now, only her head and back, and a bit of her chest, showed above the mud. Her neck stretched upward, her large brown eyes rounded with terror. My mare.

"Make sure not to miss." I turned my back and waited for the hum of the bowstring being released. A scream shattered the air and then fell silent.

I picked up the sextant. The lion stars wavered along the golden horizon, shaking with each of my breaths. "Follow me." I trudged through the thigh-deep water, turned once at a warning from the toad, passed over a path of marsh grasses, and found solid ground amidst the trees.

Quiet weeping followed me. So did the ghostly image of the sorcerer.

I ignored both, filling my thoughts with muttered Kepler. Other thoughts intruded.

My mare. "The orbit of a planet is an ellipse with the sun at one of the two foci." *My white, sturdy mare. The one I never named.* "A line segment joining a planet and the sun sweeps out equal areas during equal intervals of time." *The one who bore me through ten years of regal parades and freeing solitary rides.* "The square of a planet's orbital period is proportional to the cube of the length of the semi-major axis of its orbit." *I never named her. She was always my mare.*

A hand grasped mine. It was Demuth. We walked, hand in hand, through the trees until the watch showed *otter, frog, frog.*

"I need the book." My voice came out dead.

The Fool reached into one of his saddle bags. The book had stayed there because my bags were full of changes of clothes—had been full of clothes—were still, but I didn't have them. Because, my...

I wept, my tears pushing through the sorcerer's mocking caresses.

The Fool—Konrad—let the flap fall on his saddle bag and wrapped his arms around me.

I stiffened, then let the tears come more fully. His touch helped offset the sorcerer's encroachment. I wiped my face on his mired jacket. "I shouldn't be crying," I said. "It was just a horse."

He didn't speak, but gently patted my back until my breathing eased.

"The book," I said.

I heard it around noon, its burbling mixed with the twitter of birds. The path dropped down, and at the bottom, water flashed over polished stones.

I opened the tome. "Book, we are stopping here until we are washed. Make whatever adjustments you need."

The words traced back, slowly. *Go no deeper than knee depth.*

The stream looked no deeper than ankle deep, but if we dammed it, we could make a good place to wash.

The Fool raised his brows. He never asked what the book said.

"Konrad," I said. "Gather stones and build a dam."

"Yes, my lady."

Demuth and I also gathered stones and helped set them in a wall across the stream. The water splashed against us in chill cleanliness. When it was done, the water pooled and washed over the top.

The Fool bowed. "I'll make a second pool further downstream. Peter, you're coming with me." He placed the toad on his shoulder, took the lead rope of his horse, and strode off.

"Go no deeper than knee depth," I called after him.

He turned, tipped his head. "Yes, my lady." And disappeared around the bend.

The bog scent washed from my skin and hair with a vigorous scrubbing of soap and rough cloth. The scrubbing didn't remove the memories. My mare's scream echoed each time I dipped my head into the chill stream. I shivered as I rubbed dry, then put on one of Demuth's dresses. It was too big, both in length and girth, but it was clean. I wrapped a blanket over top of the dress and recited facts under my breath. It didn't help. Memory and cursed longing twisted together like snakes and knotted in my center.

"Demuth?" I asked. "Do you have something to settle a stomach?"

She stood from where she scrubbed at a dress in the stream. "I'll make you tea."

She built a fire and pulled a pot and herbs from her saddle bag, and soon a sweet smell drifted from the pot. She handed me a cup and went back to scrubbing clothes.

The tea spread in warm comfort through my shivering. It was slightly sweet and tangy. By the end of the cup, the feeling of wrestling snakes had settled. I sipped the last drops. "Why did you become a healer?"

She looked up from washing the linen dress that was slowly turning green. The water bled black and ribboned over the stone dam. "Because I want to help others, especially those who are ignored by society."

"Why?"

She dropped the dress. It swirled in the back pull of the dam, then plastered against the rocks. She jumped up and grabbed it. "My lady, don't you want to help them? You're going to be queen."

"I want to rule my kingdom well."

"Won't part of that be helping the poor and needy?"

"True. A kingdom is stronger if the commoners are well cared for."

"And the beggars, the maimed, the blind?" she asked.

"If they cannot be useful to the kingdom, then they have no claim on the crown's help. They'll have to fend for themselves."

She bowed her head and scrubbed harder.

Was my answer wrong? If a person didn't fill their role in society, then what rights did they have? If I didn't work hard as princess and prepare myself to be queen, then I might as well have died with my mother at my birth.

"I'll do better than my father." I twisted my hair to squeeze out the water. "I won't punish others on whims. I'll be just and fair. But when I'm queen, I can't watch over each person. It would be impossible."

She nodded. "That is why I became a healer."

I lay in the sunlight, letting the drowsy warmth and herbal tea relax my muscles and dull my thoughts. For a moment, I didn't need to think or feel.

Demuth settled next to me and stretched. "It feels good to be clean. I've smelled some putrid things as a healer, but that bog was the worst."

I turned on my side. "Don't go telling me about any other decaying matter. I just got my stomach settled."

A wicked gleam came into her hazel eyes. "Are you certain you don't want to hear about—"

"I don't."

"—the village dog with flatulence. He stole a spiced pork pie from the mayor's table, then hid under the mayor's house. Spice and excess fat are bad for a dog's stomach and even worse for those around him. Village business was conducted in the market square for the next two days."

I groaned. "You should leave wit to the Fool."

"I know," she chuckled. "Konrad has a talent for it. But I still try from time to time."

I glanced downstream. "Speaking of the Fool, where is he? I'd think he and the toad would be back by now."

"Oh, Konrad tends to take his time when he has a mirror or water to reflect his image."

I snorted. "I didn't think he was so vain."

She laughed and rolled onto her back. "No, it's not that. He has a funny habit he does when he thinks he's alone. I caught him once, and it was as good as a banquet performance. Would you like me to tell you?"

"If it is as foolish as his performances, I'd rather you not. If you're going to tell me anything, tell me about the herbs and how you use them."

Her brows rose. "Really? Most people don't find that interesting."

"Most people don't find physics and chemistry interesting, either."

"Fair enough." She pulled out her pouches of herbs and began to explain the properties of each.

I settled into learning herb lore. It was a more effective barrier against unwanted thoughts than even the sun and tea.

~

"Demuth, Demuth!" The toad swam up the stream.

Demuth raced to his side and lifted him from the water. "What happened, Peter? Where is Konrad?"

"The lake lady." He panted and croaked. "She sang to him and took him prisoner. She won't let him go unless we get her the ring."

"What lake lady? What ring?" I asked.

"Come, come," he croaked. "Quickly."

We ran on the bank, downstream. It twisted and turned twice, then fed into a lake. Konrad's horse grazed in the grass. A stone dam stood a short distance away. Water ran and spilled over it. Half-washed clothes clung to the stones.

I shivered. "Where is the lake lady?"

"You have to call for her," said the toad. "But don't get close."

I faced the lake and called in regal coldness. "Lady of the lake, where is my Fool?"

A silvery laugh came from the lake as a woman lifted her head from the still water. Her long brown locks were twined with lake grass, and her face put to shame the fountain statues back at the palace. "So that is what you call him? He was foolish to befoul my waters. And by the smell of you, you also took part in the desecration."

"Where is he?" My coldness slipped. He wasn't visible. Had she drowned him? I shoved at the ghostly image of the sorcerer. Why did he show up when I needed to see Konrad?

"My, my." She tsked. "He's asleep under my waters. He'll be

fine without air until I wake him, or the sun rises. Whichever comes first."

My heart clicked and slipped, the gears spinning. "Give him back."

"Bring me the ring to cleanse my waters, and I'll exchange him."

"Where do we find the ring?" asked Demuth.

The woman shifted her cold, green-eyed gaze to her. "You also care for him. I wouldn't expect it for such an ugly man."

"The ring," I said.

"It is a silver band set with ripples of green and blue stones. The witch has it."

"Where is the witch?"

A voice croaked, "I know where she is."

We ran back upstream, to where the naiad couldn't hear us, and where I'd left the magical tools. Konrad said they were to find the sorcerer. Would the book help us save Konrad?

I opened to the first page. "Book, why didn't you warn us of the lake?"

You were not to go deeper than knee depth.

"The naiad sang him into the depths."

Then the one you speak of is dead. Continue your journey without him.

I slammed the book shut. It wouldn't help. I was no guide, even with it. The bog, my mare, and now Konrad.

Soft lips brushed against the back of my hand. *Hette.*

My hand glowed warm with the cursed caress. *No. I must find the witch. The toad will show us. We'll get the ring before sunrise. We'll get Konrad back.* I pinched where the kiss had touched. The pain partly concealed the aching emptiness. How was I to guide when every step of the way the curse distracted me?

"Demuth." I held out the book. "Take the magical tools. You lead the way."

"Yes," croaked the toad. "Demuth will be a good guide."

Her face paled. "I cannot."

"You can." I set the book in her hands. "You are reasonable and level headed."

"I can't read."

I shook my head. "You can't read?"

"I've tried. But the letters swim and disappear."

"Surely you can read some. Even if you are slow."

"No. You could ask a blind woman to read, and I'd do no better than she."

"If you can't read, then how are you a healer? How do you know which herb is which?"

"I know the scents of all the herbs, and I memorized all my uncle told me. I only need to hear something once." Her lips pinched. "Days ago you said, *The circumference of every circle is twice the radius multiplied by three and ten-seventy-firsts.*"

She'd recited the fact exactly. A shudder ran down my back. What would it be like to not be able to read?

I took back the book. "T—Peter, please show us how to get to the witch."

WITCH

"IT LOOKS DIFFERENT FROM UP HERE," said the toad. He rode in the damp pocket of Demuth's apron.

We walked along a clear path through the forest. It had started at the edge of the lake and was lined with fractured rocks that looked like torn bread and sparkled in the tree-filtered sun. Our two horses trailed behind us.

"Peter, what do we need to know about the witch?" asked Demuth.

"Be polite, compliment her, and don't eat anything."

I'd not touch a witch's food, even without the warning. But more importantly, "What can we exchange for the ring?"

"She usually asks for a lock of hair, a year of life, or a heart's desire," said the toad.

Demuth pulled her braid over her shoulder. "I'll give all my hair for the ring."

"No!" The toad's voice squeaked as though he'd seen a snake. "A lock of hair means that your health goes to the witch. You'll become weak, barely able to walk across a room. For a year of life, she takes your best year, with all its memories."

"And the heart's desire?" I asked.

"Whoever you desire, she'll take that wanting away, and you'll never love that person again."

"I'll pay it." If the witch could take away the cursed longing that the sorcerer laid on me, we could go home. I could live with the mechanical heart, as long as he wasn't influencing it.

The toad studied me. "No, you can't. Your heart is already cursed. She won't take that as payment."

"Toad, how do you know all these things?"

He blinked.

"Peter," I modified. "Tell us how you know these things."

Demuth stroked his head. "Please, Peter."

He let out a little chirp. "I was the witch's servant until she turned me into a toad."

"Her servant?" asked Demuth, her eyes widening.

"Her slave."

She stroked his head again. "I'm sorry."

"Don't be," he croaked. "I got to meet you, and now I can help."

"Why do you assume I'm cursed?" I asked.

"I can see curses. Yours is purple around your chest, and it gets all lightningy whenever your face goes to stone. She won't take a cursed heart as payment."

"I'll give a year of my life," Demuth said. "If I tell you my favorite memories, will you remember them for me?"

"No. You shouldn't lose your memories," said the toad. "Kiss me and let me go in human form. I'll give one of my years."

"That is most reasonable," I said.

Demuth shook her head. "I don't like it. Peter's already suffered so much."

The toad laughed. "Then the witch won't be taking much from me. Serves her right to get a year of my memories. I wonder what she'll think of stalking mice and eating slugs."

Demuth's brow furrowed, and finally she nodded. "I'll make new memories with you, when you return."

"Yes," he croaked. "Many good memories. You are my only good memories."

She pulled him from her apron pocket and set him on a fallen tree trunk, then gently kissed him.

Even though I expected the loud ker-plop, my heart stuttered. A squat, ugly man clothed in rags sat on the fallen tree. A toad lay in the grass. The man scooted off the tree and landed with a stumble.

"Don't step on Demuth," I warned.

"I would never hurt her." His voice was as rough-edged as when he was a toad. He bent over and gently picked her up. "Nor will I let the witch harm her. Demuth, you can't come with us."

"You tricked me." Her voice was rusty and indignant.

"Yes. For your safety. You have too good a heart. You glow with something bright, like the opposite of a curse. The witch will imprison you and feed off your goodness. Stay here. I'll kiss you when we return."

"Toad, we cannot just leave her out in the forest," I said.

"I know a little magic." He squatted down and dug a small pit with one hand, then placed branches crosswise over it. "Nothing will bother her while we are gone." He set her in the hole. "Stay there, my sweet Demuth. We'll be back soon."

"Peter, Princess Hette," she called. "Shave your heads before you go."

"Shave our—Oh." If we didn't have hair, the witch couldn't steal our vitality. "Won't the witch let us choose which price to pay?"

The toad-man blinked his bulbous eyes. "Not always. Demuth is right."

I touched my braid. My hair wasn't beautiful, but still... Did we both have to go to the witch? The toad was the one who would pay for the ring. He could go by himself. But he had said Demuth held his best memories. He'd pay and forget us and the whole reason he went for the ring.

Did we really need the ring? What if there was some other way to save Konrad? But how? The naiad had him hidden in the water. How would we ever find him? We had a chance to get the ring. It was the only way to get him.

Did we have to save the Fool? I could still find the sorcerer without him. He knew it was dangerous when he set out.

My mare's scream ripped through my head. I shuddered. *I'm responsible for all of this. If I hadn't touched the tools, Konrad would still be leading. We wouldn't have gone into the bog, my mare wouldn't have died, he wouldn't have been captured. If I don't get the ring, I'll be responsible for Konrad's death.*

What if—

The sorcerer knelt next to me. *Beautiful Hette.*

I tightened my jaw. The hair would go. And if in the process it diminished the sorcerer's bothersome praise, it would be worth it. "Demuth, do you have a shaving blade?"

The wind tickled at my bare scalp and stung where the toad had nicked me with the shaving blade. I tied a kerchief over my head and secured it under my chin. When I returned to my kingdom, I'd have to wear a wig for more than a year. Some of the ladies already shaved their heads to wear a wig more easily. I'd let them assume I'd followed fashion. And in the meantime, washing would be easier.

My arguments only partly assuaged the empty wrongness above my eyes. When I'd broken the sorcerer's curse, I could rage over the loss of my hair, but not before.

The toad man's head was difficult to shave, with all its knobby lumps. But he didn't complain when I nicked him. As the last mossy lock dropped to the ground, he hopped up. "We have to hurry. We need to get the ring and leave before sunset."

"Princess Hette," called Demuth from her hole. "Watch out for Peter."

"I don't need protecting," the toad said with a pout of his wide mouth.

"Be careful, both of you," she said.

I ground-tied the two horses and trotted after the toad. He moved quickly, with an awkward, hopping gait.

The path wound between a meadow of bright red-and-black flowers. "Don't look too much," the toad warned. "Or you'll find your feet leaving the path. That's when the wolf gets you."

I fixed my gaze on his lumpy back and hurried on. We passed beneath dense trees, where we stumbled in twilight darkness. I tripped on a root and bumped into him.

"Oof. Careful." He grasped my wrist with a thick, stumpy hand. The pads of his fingers gripped my skin.

I shuddered.

"Don't be afraid," he said, still grasping my wrist. "We'll get the ring, and we'll save Konrad."

The path opened into a tidy clearing. The yellow thatched roof of a cottage glowed in the sun, as if it were thatched with gold instead of straw. Roses and morning glory climbed the stone walls. Flowers and herbs surrounded the cottage in neat rows, some spilling over the edges of tin buckets and clay pots, and others climbing arbors. The sharp-edged rocks that had led us lined the paths between garden spots.

"This is the witch's abode?"

"Yes." His voice quavered. "It's pretty and poisonous. Be careful."

"I'll be polite."

"Don't eat anything—and don't look at her feet."

Her feet? Why would I look at her feet? I nodded and strode to the door. It was a bright blue with white roses painted along the frame. I knocked.

Footsteps shuffled inside—an uneven tread of *pat-clang-pat-clang.* "What dear comes to visit me today?" The voice was deep and melodious. The door swung open on silent hinges.

I stumbled back a step. The naiad from the lake stood in the doorway. Her waves of brown hair framed a soft, perfectly balanced face, as her green eyes studied us with open interest. She wore a red, sleeveless dress that showed her slender, pale arms, but covered her legs all the way to the floor.

The toad pushed up next to me and bowed. "My most gracious lady, your sister sent us to request a ring."

Sister? So the naiad and the witch were sisters. I recovered my composure and curtsied.

The witch laughed, a bright, welcoming laugh. "So, something has mired her lake again? She usually sends better payment. Come in."

We entered the cottage. It was as chaotic as her yard was orderly. Cracked leather books piled on every surface, including the floor. Little paths wound between them. Insects and parts of animals floated in bottles. A cauldron bubbled in the fireplace, though no fire burned below it. A table dominated the center of the room. Black feathers, a large black beak, and bird organs covered half of it. The other half held a still steaming loaf of bread, a bowl of fruit, and a vase of bright flowers. A rancid stink mingled with the rich nutty smell of fresh bread. One chair and a couple stools sat near the bread side of the table. Was all magic absurdly clashing?

"Have a seat, my dears," the witch said. "Some tea while we discuss the price? Which would you prefer? I have every herb you know, and many you don't." She shuffled across the room with a *pat-clang-pat-clang.*

I started to glance down, but the toad grabbed my wrist and squeezed.

Don't look at her feet. Don't eat anything. That probably includes tea. Be polite. Compliment her. What is there to compliment? And how to politely decline the tea? I settled on one of the stools.

A protocol lesson, beat in by repeated recitations, whispered: *To turn the conversation from sensitive subjects, observe the interests of the other party. Give a specific compliment and ask a question pertinent to their interests.*

Her interests were in stealing memories, vitality, and love. That wouldn't do. I looked more closely at the feathers on the table.

"My lady," I said. "Your home is a fascinating collection of knowledge. I would that I had even a quarter of these books. How goes your study of the raven?"

Her eyebrows rose. "You recognize the bird just by its feathers and beak. You are a woman after my own heart." She gazed at my chest. "Though your heart isn't your own. I look forward to hearing your story while we have tea."

"We would not want to disturb your current explorations of bird anatomy."

"Does it disgust you?" She laughed and covered the carcass with a blue-and-white checkered cloth. "It disgusts me too, but knowledge is worth a bit of gore. See? We are much alike. Let me guess which tea—ginger with citrus, carried from the hot southern lands?"

A zesty scent wafted from the cauldron. Images wafted with it. *I'm sitting in the royal library. Sunlight streams through dancing dust and rests on me. I curl up in the corner with a pilfered cushion, a blanket, and a book. A book that tells of genies and flying carpets.*

"Here you go, my dear." A cup was placed in my hand, and the scent increased, along with the images. *I'm on the carpet, swooping over the hot sands and onion-domed buildings. We skim over a cool pool. I dip in my hand and scoop out water.*

Something stomped on my foot.

I jerked.

The images crashed, along with a clay mug, to the ground. Hot liquid dripped down my skirt.

"Forgive me, most gracious lady," the toad stuttered. "My big feet always get in the way."

"Well," said the witch. "The ugly man wishes to protect you. The spilled tea will be added to the cost. Come, we'll speak in the garden and see what you have to offer."

The toad had saved me from one of her spells. I would have drunk the potion. Would I have become a slave to her until she decided to turn me into a toad? I owed him.

We found a bench in the garden under an arbor of honey-suckle. As the witch sat, her skirts lifted, and a pale slender human foot peeked out beside an equally slender and well formed iron foot. Gold paint coated each nail on both feet.

I yanked my gaze away.

"Do you also find my feet fascinating?" Her voice was light, but when I met her gaze, her eyes were hard.

"I've never seen such skilled and lovely workmanship," I said.

"You lie prettily," she said. "Will you lie so quickly when you tell the story of your cursed heart?"

I'd have to tell the truth with an implied lie. "It's clockwork. A sorcerer gave it to me."

"Why?" she asked.

"A wedding present."

"Ah, so, the sorcerer has chosen a bride. It took him long enough. It's been three hundred years since his last one. I'll not keep you from him." She shrugged. "Let's see, the sorcerer already took your heart and your hair. That means he won't mind if I take a few of your memories first—a year's worth is proper for the water ring." She pressed her hand to my cheek.

I tried to pull away, but I was frozen, as if she'd turned me into a statue. Sharp points prodded my head, pulling hazy memories from the depths—bright spots of happiness—*no, I will not let her drain me of my best memories. I have few enough.* I covered the witch's pulling threads with Archimedes and Euclidean axioms. I mentally recited every formula and calculated square roots. I could relearn them. The numbers cluttered in front of my frozen open eyes and disappeared as if swept away by the wind.

"Enough!" The witch dropped her hand.

I gasped for air. I'd almost rather a naiad held me under water.

"I can get any of that from books. A year of useless facts! The sorcerer gave you a clockwork heart, but you already have a clock-work mind. I need human memories. Joys and delights. You, toad man. You glow with life. I will take yours instead."

"As you wish, my gracious lady." He leaned forward, and she placed her hand on his warty cheek.

This was as we'd planned. He'd only lose a few days of good memories. He could make more.

My stomach knotted.

She closed her eyes, and her face tightened, then paled. "Ugh! Disgusting mud creature! I know you now. Faithless servant! Perfidious slave!" she shrieked. "Slugs, beetles, worms, stinking mud—these are your delights? Ick!" The muscles along her arm strained as if she were trying to remove her hand but couldn't. Was the spell one that had to finish once started?

"Oh." her lips softened. "Oh, this is what I wanted. Yes, this is a delicious memory. But only a few days' worth. You have cheated me. I will take your heart's desire. It is such a sweet, innocent desire. Pure and undiluted. That will be fitting, after all you've put me through." She withdrew her hand from his cheek.

He crumpled off the bench and lay panting on the sharp gravel. His eyes stared vacantly into the sky.

She knelt at his side.

Demuth would never forgive me if I let the witch take both his best memories and his heart's desire. "Stop," I said. "Give us the ring. We already paid for it twice over."

She turned and studied me. "You've paid with slugs and dry facts. That is no payment for a ring that cleanses water of any impurity. You must also pay for staring at my foot, and he must pay for splashing my tea. What will you give me?"

"Take my heart's desire."

She laid her hand below my collarbone. Even through the thick fabric of my dress it chilled. "Delightful—so angry and full of fire. Sharp and twisting. A lost, trailless, longing." She tilted her head. "Fascinating. He gave you a clockwork heart, but didn't remove any of your desires."

"Take them, all of them. Please."

She laughed. "Your desires are too strong for you? You'd rather have a heart as dry as your mind? Oh, I would, I really would." Her lips pulled into a pout. "It's a pity the sorcerer already claimed your heart. I'll not risk his wrath."

She turned back to Peter and laid a hand on his chest. A hungry smile curved across her face.

I had one thing I could still give. "I have other memories. From long ago. I buried them under the facts."

"Did you? That is quite the feat." She removed her hand from Peter's chest. "I've never before met someone strong enough to hide their memories. The sorcerer chose well. Yes, if these memories are filled with as much fire as your desires, I will give you the ring. And since you hid them, your mind is strong enough for a more thorough exploration."

She stood, her iron foot crunching the stones.

I owe the toad. I don't need those memories. I never think of him.

She leaned over me, her slender form tall and cold.

Love doesn't mean anything. It's empty. The memories are empty. Just broken promises.

She laid her hand on my cheek.

Needles pushed into my mind. No gentle prodding this time. They dove into the hazy center. One hooked onto a bright point and jerked upward.

Wind blows in my face. I fly across the field. My brother carries me on his strong back. "Faster," I cry. "Faster." We reach the far end and skitter to a stop at the lake's edge. A mother duck quacks. He sets me down and quacks back. I laugh, then gasp, as water splashes my face. I tackle my brother. He dramatically falls backwards and pulls me with him. We both tumble into the mud. "Oh, Georg!"

At the name, the memory ripped from me, leaving a ragged tunnel. I gasped. The motion froze in my chest as another memory unfolded.

I sit alone in the nursery. A simple meal of bread and jam sits untouched on my little table. "Hette." I turn. My brother stands in all his regalia. The sounds of the royal banquet echo from behind him. The one I'm not old enough to attend. He bows. "May I have the pleasure of eating with this beautiful princess?" I fling myself into his arms. I am wanted.

The memory ripped away. Another followed, and another. *My brother, me, us. I'm wanted, needed, loved.*

Stop! Don't take these! Please stop!

The needles dug deeper, hooked buried brightness, unfolded each, then jerked it away, leaving only empty, echoing tunnels.

I'm—I'm what?

A slight light pulsed. A needle dove in and dragged it out.

My brother lies pale and bandaged on his bed. Sharp scents and big people scurry around him. I creep along the edge of the room. I'm little. No one notices me. I crawl under his quilt and snuggle next to him. "Georg? What happened?"

He coughs. "Hette, I love you. Don't you forget. I love you."

My brother and the room began to fade. I grabbed it, yanking it back. *No! You can't have this one! I promised him.* The memory stretched. *Georg, I promise I won't let her take this one.* A fracture formed along the memory and it tore, leaving a corner with me, a piece filled with grief and love. It slipped from my shaking grasp and fluttered back into the grey depths of my mind.

A few more memories dragged by. I didn't understand them. Who was this person, laid out in a box and surrounded by flowers?

The hand left my cheek. I blinked. Why were tears streaming down my face? At least the curse hadn't activated.

"You were a passionate child," the witch said. "I am well paid. Georg is truly a delightful soul."

"Georg?"

She patted my hand. "It doesn't matter. You didn't want to remember your brother."

Brother? I had a brother. His picture hung with the others in the family hall. He died when I was four. An avalanche or something. The witch was right. It didn't matter. If I had had memories of him, then they were gone. We'd paid the price.

I extended my hand. "The ring."

She snapped her fingers, and a silver ring glistening with ripples of green and blue appeared on her smallest finger. She placed it in my hand. "Don't forget to take your toad man with you." She sneered. "I'm afraid he won't remember you or anything from the last year. Unless, that is, you'd rather leave him here. I have many uses for his heart."

Peter lay prone on the stones where he'd fallen, still staring at the sky.

I slipped the ring into my apron pocket and took him by the arm.

He blinked at me. "How am I human? Are you a princess? Did you kiss me?"

"No. Come on, Toad."

He clambered to his feet, grinning. "I'm Peter, and I'm human!"

"Come on, Peter. I'll take you to the one who kissed you."

The sun dipped behind the trees as we left the witch's clearing.

The horses neighed as we turned the bend in the path. The twilight was still enough to see where Peter had dug a hole and crossed it with sticks.

"Peter, Princess Hette. You're back," Demuth cried.

Peter knelt and pulled her from the hole. "The hairless woman says you kissed me. And if I kiss you, you'll become human, and I'll be a toad again."

Demuth's voice quieted. "You gave up your memories?"

"She said I did. But if you kissed me and made me human, then I will kiss you too." He brought her close to his mouth and hesitated.

It wasn't like the first time she'd kissed him. She didn't know she'd turn into a toad. Nor like when he kissed her back because he felt remorse for what happened. Now he had no memory. Would he kiss her? Would he give up his humanity? He had to. He'd promised. But he had no memory of that promise.

"Peter," I said. "Please."

He swallowed. "Can I just run around once before I kiss her?"

"No," I said at the same time as Demuth said, "Yes."

"No," I said again. "We have to give the naiad the ring and save Konrad."

"Let him stay human until we get Konrad back," Demuth said. "I trust him."

"Oh." Peter's voice cracked. "You are a princess with a heart of gold. Thank you!"

Demuth had too tender a heart. But we'd sort it out later. We needed to face the naiad before it got any darker. "Let's go."

The lake glittered in the waxing moonlight. I stood ten feet from the edge.

"Naiad," I called. "I have the ring. Bring out Konrad."

The water rippled. She rose, head, shoulders, then her whole person, and stood on the water's surface. A long white gown clung to her. "So, now you call him something else. Is he worth the price you paid?"

"We paid the price. We have the ring. Give us Konrad."

"Toss in the ring, and I'll bring him out."

"I'll toss it in after we have him and know he's alive."

"Untrusting little thing. Looks as though you gave all your hair for him. You'll not get to enjoy your health much longer. But human girls tend to do foolish things for love. Fine. Enjoy him while you still can. If you don't give me the ring, I'll just sing him back into the lake." She made a scooping motion with both hands, and the water glowed in a rectangular shape, about the size of a bed. The glowing rose through the depths and burst the surface in a spray.

Konrad lay on a bed of lake grass. It crossed like ropes over his chest, binding his arms to his side. The bed glided to the shore. Peter hop-ran forward. I set Demuth and the ring in the grass then rushed after Peter.

Konrad lay too still. A thin undershirt stuck to a motionless chest.

Hette, whispered the sorcerer. His arms wrapped around me from behind, and his lips brushed against my neck.

I pulled at a mathematical, a scientific, a—my mind was blank. The witch had stolen all my memories of the immutable truths. "I don't have time for you," I hissed. "Go away."

He didn't.

I touched Konrad's parted lips. Not a hint of breath brushed my fingers.

"Naiad," I yelled. "He's not breathing."

She stood and watched us, her face impassive.

"Cut the bonds," said Peter. "It will cut the spell."

I pulled the shaving blade, the one we'd used to shear our hair, from my apron pocket. The wet grass split under the blade.

When the last two strands fell, Konrad took a shuddering breath and his eyes flew open. "No! Peter, get help. Get help!" he shouted.

"It's all right, tall man." Peter laid his hand on Konrad's shoulder. "It's all right."

Konrad stared into my face and touched the kerchief that covered my shorn head. "My lady, what happened to you?" His voice slurred, as if he were drunk or would fall asleep soon.

I stood and pushed at the tangle of emotions both cursed and not cursed. My Fool was alive, perhaps injured, but we were not yet safe. "Peter, get him away from the lake. Yell every few steps. When I can't hear you, I'll pay the naiad."

"My lady," protested Konrad. "I can't leave you."

"Go. I'll not have you ruin your rescue by being caught again."

He climbed to a wavering stand. "Yes, my lady."

Peter and Konrad stumbled up the slope, away from the lake. Peter's yells bellowed like a bullfrog's, and slowly faded.

The naiad laughed. "I'm impressed with your planning. Though, you understand I can take you in his place. Girls are not as interesting to drown, but I can still do it."

I nodded. "I understand."

When a minute passed without hearing him, I took the ring out and threw it into the lake. A flash of light pulsed as it hit the surface and ripples spread until the whole lake shone like a mirror in sunlight.

"Ah." The naiad sighed. "Beautiful, pure water." She sank beneath the surface, not even glancing again in my direction.

❧

We sat on the banks of the stream where Demuth and I had washed only half a day ago. Demuth was still a toad, and Konrad sat shivering in his sodden underclothes and a blanket. He needed to change. Demuth needed to change even more. But first—I opened the tome. "Book, we are camping. Where is the closest safe place?"

You've changed. The words slanted as if in question. *Camp under the oak.*

"Which one?"

The one from which the squirrel curses you.

"Which direction?"

Scorpion.

I picked up the sextant and found the scorpion. The constellations were not one of the facts I'd offered the witch.

Konrad and Peter followed, leading the remaining two horses.

A short time later, something small and hard hit my kerchiefed head. I held up the lantern. A squirrel sat in the spreading branches of an oak. It held another nut and chattered at me.

I turned my back on it. "We camp here. Konrad, get into dry clothes. Peter, unless you know how to build a fire, you had better change Demuth back."

Another nut hit my head. I rubbed the tender spot. Maybe I'd keep the squirrel with us. It could distract me when the sorcerer's curse activated, especially as my store of immutable truths was now sorely limited.

A kerplop announced Demuth's change, followed by a brief croaking exclamation: "You are even more beautiful than I imagined!"

Demuth came to my side. We gathered firewood, then, while she lit the fire, I sat with my back against the oak trunk. Later, I'd help set out food. I just needed to shut my eyes for a moment.

∽

"Demuth." Konrad's voice came sharp and quiet in the chill air. "You should have left me to the naiad."

I shivered at his bitter tone, despite the crackling fire and the double layer of blankets wrapped around me. Why would he say that? I tried to open my eyes, but weariness lay even heavier than the blankets.

"We couldn't leave you." Demuth's voice was just as quiet and sharp. "We need you."

"No, you don't. Hette is the only one who can use the tools. You shouldn't have risked your life for me."

"First thing," said Demuth. "I never would have left you to the naiad. You mean too much to me."

He sputtered and she hurried on. "Second, we do need you. Even with the tools, Hette won't be able to defeat the sorcerer. You are the only one. Third, I didn't risk my life. It was all Hette and Peter. They are the ones who faced the witch and paid for the ring."

"Which is even worse," said Konrad. "You should have stopped them. You should have—"

"I should have told them of your curse?"

"I forbid you to tell them." Konrad's voice frosted.

Demuth snorted. "Even if they knew, do you think they would have left you behind? Peter and Hette have more honor than you give them credit for."

Konrad let out a weary sigh. "I didn't mean that. I know they have honor. Both of them. And good hearts. I just don't like that Hette gave up her hair, and who knows what else, to save a fool's life. What if she'd been cursed a second time? What if she'd died?"

"Then stay alive, so you can help her finish this quest." Demuth's voice softened. "Make her sacrifice worth it."

The fire crackled as if someone had added more wood. "Thank you, Demuth. You truly are the only reasonable one amongst us."

"It's all right. I know you haven't had time for one of your self-reflections."

Konrad choked then coughed. "That I doubly forbid you to tell them about. They'd think I was crazy." His voice trembled with laughter.

Demuth joined him. Their laughter rang into the night, though slightly stifled as if they didn't want to wake me, until both voices died into silence and only the chirping of frogs filled the air.

"Konrad," said Demuth. "You really do need to tell her of your curse."

"What good would that do?" His voice turned rueful. "She has enough to carry as it is, and the curse doesn't impact our quest."

"It's not wrong to let friends help carry your burdens."

"In that case." He laughed tightly. "I'll tell her, when we are friends."

Their voices faded into webs of dreams.

DARK

I RAN through the dark hallways of the palace, looking, looking. For someone. Someone important. But who? A shadow flitted around the corner. I raced to catch it, and the room opened up into a half-lit hall of pictures. Pictures of a young man. Square jaw, grey eyes, wavy hair.

It was the sorcerer. He usually appeared in person in my dreams; but this time, he chose to torment me with portraits.

But, no. I drew closer to one picture. The hair was dark, the eyes grey-green, the smile gentle, the face too young and innocent.

I knew him. I once knew him.

I touched the canvas, tracing over the jaw and eyes. An ache welled up. It hurt. But not like the aching longing of the sorcerer's curse. Something different, more real.

"Who are you?"

Lantern light flashed off a gold plate at the bottom of the frame. Georg VI.

That was my brother's name.

A warmth whispered through me, brushing against the empty places in my mind, pausing for moments in blank corners.

I caught at it, trying to wrap it around me.

It slipped by, an echo and was gone.

"Come back. Please."

I ran down the hall, touching each picture. Ragged scraps of other emotions—joy, delight, happiness, safety—flowed through me and out, impossible to hold, leaving the empty places sharp with abandonment. Could the emotions only take root in memories?

If so, why did they haunt me? The memories were gone; then the emotions should be, too. Perhaps the portraits were all that I had left of my brother, along with the remnants of my earliest memories, the ones from before the year the witch took. The fleeting, formless ones.

I pulled my hand away from touching the next portrait.

The ache intensified. If I touched the painting, it would ease for a moment and then be even worse. It wasn't worth it.

"Stop," I commanded. "I already have to fight the sorcerer's curse. Don't make me feel for you, too. I don't even remember you. Go away. Love only hurts."

The room disappeared into emptiness, a white, open emptiness stretching as far as I could see: white ground, white sky. I was alone.

I crumpled to the ground, hugging my arms around me. Alone hurt less.

Fire scented the air, along with the crisp chill of morning. Light flashed across my eyelids—the sun through leaves. I groaned. Night had been too long. Emptiness ached in ragged lines. At least when I was awake I'd be too busy to feel it.

I shifted under my blankets, and tiny bells rang. Something warm and soft covered my head. I reached up and touched a long felt piece and pulled it down. It was bright red. I wore Konrad's cap!

I yanked it off.

Cold air hit my shorn head, as though I'd dunked it in ice water.

"Oh," I gasped.

"Better put it back on." Konrad knelt by the fire plucking a duck, a bloody arrow at his side, his bare head covered in tangled curls. "It's too cold for just a kerchief."

"It's a fool's cap."

He smiled, a gentle sad smile. "I would give you a bear-skin cap if I could. But I only have a fool's offering. I can't even return your sacrifice of hair."

I pulled the cap back on and tugged it over my ears. It *was* warm. And I needed to stay healthy. The bells jingled around my ears. "Where are Demuth and Peter?"

He pulled out a handful of duck tail feathers. "She's washing the last of our clothes, and Peter is keeping watch over her. It seems he knows some protection spells. It is how we made it through the bog as well as we did."

"But we have to leave. The book won't forgive us for delaying."

Konrad shook his head. "The book can wait. You rest. We'll continue tomorrow."

"Why?"

"If you die of exhaustion before we reach the sorcerer, you'll never get your heart back."

I raised my brows. "I slept."

"As well as a baby. Full of whimpers and tears."

Dirt crusted my face. Had I truly cried through the night?

Konrad set down the duck and wiped his hands in the grass. "Hette." He knelt next to me. "I don't know how much you gave up to save me, but I will be your protector and, if you will, your friend."

"Friend?"

He nodded. "This life isn't meant to be gone through alone. We each need friends. I know I'm only a poor fool, but I promise I'll give my all to see you happy."

"Friends and happiness are dangerous. They end."

"So do all things, my lady." His voice subdued, he went back to plucking the duck. "Demuth prepared tea for you. It's sitting by the fire."

⌒

I slept most the day and through the night. When the morning sun fell across my face again, a dullness suffused me.

Demuth handed me a bowl of plain mush and a cup of tea. "How do you feel, Princess Hette?"

"I don't."

She laughed, but it was hollow. "I should have known your answer. How do you feel physically? Are you staying warm enough? You've grown pale and thin."

"I'm well enough." I shoveled a spoonful of the tasteless mush into my mouth. I was cold, even while wearing Konrad's cap. But there wasn't anything I could do. My hair wouldn't grow back in a day's time.

Demuth held out another bowl to Konrad. He set it to the side and continued to check the saddle bags. Tension ran between them. What had they argued over?

"Konrad, what is your curse?" I asked.

He paused in his packing, his back to me. "It won't interfere with our quest."

"Are you certain?"

He turned around. His mouth twisted into a rueful grin. "Would you ask a crippled potter how he lost his foot, if it didn't impact his work?"

I groaned. I didn't have the energy for his riddles. He could keep his curse a secret. At least he wasn't dead and could still help us survive where the book led.

I set down the bowl and cup, and opened the heavy tome. "Book, I am ready."

You have *changed.* The ink traced in bold letters. *Sagittarius.*

We were back to sextant and watch calculations. I lifted the sextant and found the image of the Centaur constellation lying overtop the pines, then adjusted the angle so the horse-man stars ran along the golden horizon. *What is next? I must have given parts of my knowledge of the tools to the witch.*

"Book." I stared at its nearly blank page. "I need you to teach me how to use the tools."

You knew before.

"I don't anymore."

Very well. Page after page filled with words and diagrams. Parts I understood, and parts fit into holes as if I'd once known them. Two must have been new because they lacked all logic.

Flip the watch upside down twice before opening to decrease the distance needed to travel.

That would be useful.

And a little later, *Rub my leather with fat.*

"That will help, how?" I asked.

Care for me, and I will lead you well, The book wrote. *I prefer lard.*

Lard? We'd lost the rest of our pork when we'd lost my mare, along with seasonings, sugar, and all my clothes.

I breathed until the rising emotions cleared. It wasn't an effective method, but it worked that time. The sorcerer only slightly bothered me.

"I only have duck fat."

A long curving line traced across the page, then words. *Duck fat stinks. Do you have beeswax?*

I looked up. "Demuth, do you have any beeswax?"

Her brows rose in an unasked question. "No."

"Book, duck fat or nothing."

Very well, duck fat. Keep it away from my pages.

Thus started the day.

◠

"I don't think the book liked the duck fat." Demuth's voice sounded in my ear.

We rode double on her horse, me in front and her behind. A small circle of lantern light danced on dark trunks. The branches were so dense overhead that the ground was just piles of dead pine needles. No lower plants grew in that sunless section, just huge pines, with high, interwoven branches. It made it easy to pick a path following the sextant's glowing constellations, but the dark was unnerving.

Konrad rode his horse slightly behind ours. Demuth rode with him when her horse got weary of carrying two. He held our only lit lantern. We were conserving our oil. We'd been traveling through the sunless trees for days. Or it felt like days. We'd only had to change the oil in the lantern once, and it lasted seven hours each fill.

Tendrils of mist wove around us, dipping into the light and slipping out, concealing trunks. Horse hooves crackled in the pine needles. Other sounds outside our light followed us. The almost silent whoosh of wings—owl? A skitter. A distant howl answered by a closer one.

My arms prickled as my heart ticked in rapid motions.

The sorcerer took up stride beside us, his form glowing almost as bright as the constellations seen through the sextant. He trailed his fingers down my leg, sending a different sort of prickles over my skin.

I pushed my thoughts away from him, counting into the thousands. Eventually the sorcerer's touch disappeared.

My limbs ached with emptiness. *How often will he appear tonight? How often will he leave me trembling from cursed love?*

I opened the book. "We must camp soon."

Words glowed across the dark page. *You've not reached the proper time.*

"It must be near the middle of the night."

You slept enough yesterday. The glowing words disappeared.

I closed it, resisting the urge to slam it and reactivate the sorcerer's curse. It sat heavy and unhelpful in my lap.

"It's not the duck fat," I said, looking through the sextant again. "It's me. The book doesn't like me."

"The book doesn't like anyone," said Konrad.

"You said it would get easier."

"I'd hoped it would."

"Did it ever get easier for you?"

"On the return trip."

I rubbed my head under the cap. The fine bristles of my shorn hair caught at my fingers. Little bells jingled. We'd find the sorcerer. We had to.

The book allowed us to stop when the night mists dissipated. It was just as dark as before, but Konrad made a fire that pushed away the dark better than the small lantern had.

I lay rolled up in a blanket, staring at the fire. Sleep wouldn't come.

Demuth slept to one side, with Peter sitting near her head. Konrad sat by the fire, his shoulders hunched as if he carried a great weight.

"Konrad?" I moved to sit next to him, and pulled the knitted shawl closer around my shoulders.

"Yes, my lady."

"You said all things end. It is true. Why do we even try? Anything I do will end. I'll be queen for a short time and then die.

Why do I even try to get my heart back? What difference does it make if I return?"

He poked a stick into the fire. Sparks flew upward. "When you wake, this will be but a pile of ashes."

"True."

"Then why do we build it?"

"It protects us, it gives us warmth, and it heats our food," I said.

"Something so fleeting gives us all that?"

I held my hands out to the flames. Our night in the bog had been long without a fire. Without fire we could not survive this densely dark forest. "Yes."

"My lady, you already bring so much more to life than the fire. Yes, you will die someday. But between now and then, what you do makes a difference. I've watched you. Even as princess, you've influenced the court to wiser laws. You've helped increase the education of the commoners. You've provided opportunities for those who are willing to work, to rise in life. What difference does it make if you return and become queen?"

"The difference will hinge on if I get my heart back or not. If the sorcerer continues to control me, I will not be able to rule."

He turned and looked at me. "I trust you. Even with your curse, I trust you."

The hard shell I'd built around my emotions burst. "How can you trust me? I opened the magic book when you told me that only one could use it. I misled us along the paths. I got us stuck in a bog. I killed my mare. I almost got you killed. And the curse grows stronger each day. I'm trying to ignore it, but I don't even have my immutable truths to hold it at bay. I gave those memories up along with the memories of my brother. I only have painful scraps of him now. I—" I gasped.

Everything slanted sideways—the fire, Konrad, the flickering shadows. The sorcerer knelt next to me, his sandalwood perfume flitting in with each shaking breath. Soft, caressing hands ghosted over my shoulders.

"Eins, zwei, drei." The numbers came out shaky and did nothing to dispel him. I needed stronger, more complex facts to push him away.

Kisses joined the touch, caressing my cheek, the back of my hand. Gentle, soft, perfect kisses.

If only I could pass out. But even that evaded me.

"My lady." Konrad's voice came from far away. "He may have your heart, but he's never had your soul. You still command that."

My soul. My thoughts. Me.

"Friedrich." I forced the word between my teeth. "I will never marry. Give your kisses to a more pliable princess."

I filled my thoughts with all I would do as queen. The universities, the improved sanitation, the traveling teachers. *At my university, there will be a class just for studying ways of improving lanterns. And safer ways to travel with bottled oil. We'll also...* I outlined in detail class after class.

The sorcerer faded. His touch became an echo.

My stomach churned with nausea. This was the most I'd felt for him thus far. How much worse would it get before I faced him? Why couldn't I just not feel?

Different hands grasped mine. "My lady." Konrad squeezed my hands. "You should have been a court fool. You've spoken truth with wit in the face of fear."

I snorted even as acid burned my throat. "When did I do that?"

"Give your kisses to a more pliable princess," he quoted.

I snorted again. "Do you often speak the truth in the face of fear?"

"With wit. Every day. And I will speak a truth right now. Snorting is for pigs. Laughter is much more becoming."

"You call that wit?"

He laughed. "The more I fear, the better my wit. I think I may have stopped being afraid of you."

His hands were warm and comforting around mine. "Konrad, promise that you'll always tell me the truth."

"Who but fools can tell the truth to the great ones? Priests are too timid and ministers too selfish."

"Then tell me. How can you trust me? I opened the magic book—"

"And," he interrupted, "you've followed that book, endured its idiosyncrasies, braved a bog, made the hard choice when the mare got herself stuck, and you saved my life at great personal sacrifice. That is the truth." He let go of my hands and tugged my—his— cap lower around my ears. The bells jingled to the cricket songs. "And the truth now is that you should sleep."

The truth. The truth from a fool who doesn't lie. I wrapped his words around me. They cleared some of the tangled emotions, but I felt no more sleepy. "Konrad, will you tell a story tonight? I want to know what happened to Erasmus. I want to know if he made it."

"And if he didn't, do you still want to know?"

Did I? The story had started as a distraction, but now it felt real. "Yes. I want to know."

"Then you deserve the truth."

The prince traveled into the Black Forest to find the witch, leaving Erasmus with the herb-woman.

She was a master of herb lore and helped ease his breathing enough that he could converse and sometimes sit for half an hour in bed. The days passed with her mixing herbal potions and him keeping her company. They discussed the properties of stinging nettle, how best to dig up the burdock root, and the best way to keep rosemary protected in the winter. He shared of the inventions he'd made with the prince—and the inventions he hoped the prince would still make in the future. He didn't speak of his own future.

Summer passed into frosted autumn, and he sang short snippets of shepherd songs, as much as his lungs would allow, and remembered the days before he came into the king's palace. She told him all the names of the plants that hung drying from the beams and the folk sayings that went with each. They laughed over the superstition that wormwood would freshen the room and the heart, as if the silvery-grey plant could cure a stagnant marriage.

Deep snows piled outside the cottage as neighbors brought firewood in payment for the herb-woman's medicines. She kept the fire burning hot, but Erasmus shivered under down comforters and his heart thudded in his chest whenever he tried to sit. So he lay and composed poems, whispering them to her as she carded wool. Poems of a sparrow sharpening its beak on a diamond mountain. Poems of counting all the drops in the ocean if one could only hold back the rivers. Poems of her gentle touch on his hand being an eternity compressed into a moment. Then poems without words, poems of a smile as he watched her, but had not the breath to even whisper.

When the chill winds of spring froze, and thawed, and froze again, and the mud set into deep ruts along the path, the prince flung open the herb-woman's door. "Erasmus!"

"Hush," whispered the herb-woman from where she sat spinning thread. "He's asleep."

The prince knelt next to the bed where Erasmus lay, gaunt and pale under a white feather-stuffed quilt. "How is he?"

She shook her head, her lip trembling. "He won't make it another week. I don't know how he's held on as long as this. I think he's only waited for you to return."

The prince pulled a leather pouch from his long wool coat. "I have created a spell, and it will heal him. I will need your help to set it up."

"Wait." She laid her hand over his and stopped him from untying

the leather pouch. "Erasmus had me write a letter to you. I promised I would read it when you returned."

"Then read it quickly."

She pulled a paper from under an herbal tome, and read, "My prince, if you are hearing this now, then either you've failed and come back—which I hope for—or you've succeeded and have a spell to heal me. Please don't use it." Her voice caught in the reading. "Let me pass on. I'll be waiting for you on the other side of tomorrow, where this poor body will no longer be in pain. There, we'll invent and create with the masters. Go back and rule your kingdom. Create. Invent. Make our land a place that future generations will look to and say your reign was the start of a golden age. And you should marry. I've learned in these last months–" Her voice caught into a sob.

The prince took the paper and read, "I've learned in these past months what love is, and it is sweet."

He looked at the herb-woman with hopeful eyes. "If he loves you, then he will want to stay alive. Do you love him?"

She nodded, even as another sob emerged.

"Then help me save him. He'll understand afterward."

"Please read the rest." Her words were but a whisper.

He looked at the paper and read, "I plead with you. But I also know you. You are as strong-willed as you are kind. If you will continue with the spell, then you must keep your oath made to me before you left. Do not use any life force but mine."

The prince set the paper on the table and took Erasmus' hand.

Erasmus stirred, opened his eyes and smiled, a tired smile mixed with sorrow.

"I will keep my oath," said the prince. "I've created a spell that will only use your life force—taking the ending years of your life that you would have had if you were healthy, and powering the healing of your life now. You'll not live as long, but you will be strong again. I can give you twenty more years."

"What happens if—" Erasmus gasped for air.

The herb-woman placed her hand on his cheek. "I know your question. I will ask." She turned to the prince. "What happens if his life force runs out before the twenty years? My mother didn't teach me how to do magic, but she taught me the costs. A witch's spell must run its course, and will pull from somewhere to do so."

The prince's jaw hardened. "Then I'll link the spell to my own life force, to be used if his is used up. I have plenty of life left. I can give a few of my years to my friend."

"No." Erasmus struggled to speak. "Ten. Only ten. Only my life. You swore."

The prince's shoulders sagged. "Ten years." He opened the leather bag. "Let us begin."

Konrad stopped speaking. The fire burned low.

"Did the prince save Erasmus' life?" I asked.

He continued to stare into the fire.

My throat tightened. "He died?" I shouldn't have cared. It was only a story.

He shook himself as if waking. "I'll tell you a little more tonight."

The spell took effect, and within a day Erasmus could sit. Within a week, he was shambling through the early spring yard with the prince on one side and the herb-woman on the other, his face flushed with cold and returning health. Within a month, his flesh had filled in from gauntness. Within two months, he and the herb-woman were married.

The prince stayed with them. Each day he tinkered in a corner of the kitchen, making clocks that needed no winding and glasses that could see through fog—inventions sprinkled with magic. He pulled the force for his magics from stones, a stream, or sometimes the latent life left in chopped wood. But he never pulled from a living thing, be it plant or animal—or human.

Erasmus split his time between helping his wife and helping the prince in his experiments. Each meal they gathered around the table for food, laughter and sharing of the day's learning.

Two years passed, the three becoming four as a baby arrived—a little boy. Erasmus could imagine no greater joy than being surrounded by his wife, his friend, and his child. Each day was a gift and a joy.

"There now," said Konrad. "A happy ending. Go to sleep."

"Did he die after ten years?"

"Yes."

"But he was happy before then?"

"Sometimes."

"Was the prince corrupted by the witch's magic?"

He turned so I could no longer see his face. "Go to sleep. I'll tell no more tonight."

"Was he?"

After a long silence, he whispered, "I don't know."

My sleep was filled with dreams of Erasmus and the prince. They were better than sorcerer-haunted dreams or fragments of aching memories. I woke to the dull glow of coals and darkness. The mists curled around us again. It was night, though no darker.

The book led us on, through nighttime mists and daytime dark. Three cycles. Our lantern oil ran out, and we proceeded by duck fat-coated rags wrapped around branches. The fire when we camped was the only relief from our blind path.

"Konrad?" Demuth's voice broke through the dark as we rode

into a fourth cycle of travel, that time in what should have been the daylight hours—if it could be called day. "How much longer?"

"I don't know."

"Our dried meat is gone. So are our oats. We have four biscuits, a small sack of flour, and a little duck fat. We could stretch the flour another week." Her usually gentle voice rose in pitch. "Then what will we do?"

"We'll learn to eat grass like the horses," said Konrad.

"There isn't any grass, just pine needles."

"Well, they've been eating them and seem to be doing well. We'll eat them too, or eat bark."

"A horse can't subsist off just pine needles." Demuth's voice caught. "And we can't eat them at all."

"A horse can go weeks without eating, and so can a person." Konrad's voice was flat toned. "We have water. I will hunt. We'll survive."

Their conversation flowed past me, carried through the torch-flickered dark.

I just had to make it to the next point, and then the next, and the next. The darkness pressed around me like jaws, ready to crush me between its teeth. Maybe the book would never take us to the sorcerer.

Hette, the sorcerer whispered, his voice smooth and soothing. *You feel so much fear. All you have to say is you'll marry me, and I'll pull you away from all danger.*

I gritted my teeth against the treacherous promise. I'd rather die. If the witch could entrap me with a drink of tea, then the sorcerer would surely trap me with a word. I would never promise him that. But what about Konrad, Demuth, and even Peter? Should they die because of me?

"Friedrich," I spoke. "If I do, what will happen to them?"

A kiss pressed to my cheek. He never answered my questions. Only drew me into cursed emotions of love. What would happen if I said yes? Would the others live, or would they die in this dark place?

"My lady!" Konrad urged his horse up next to mine. "Make no deals with him. We'll find the way. The book will get us there. Ask it when. It may answer."

If it would give any helpful answer. I opened the tome. "Book, how much longer until we reach the sorcerer?"

The text grew in glowing letters. *Quickest or safest?*

If we ran out of food, safety wouldn't help us. "Quickest."

Eagle.

I found the constellation, noted the angle, *47 degrees,* and squinted at the time, *tortoise, badger, frog,* then flipped through the pages of tables. The ink appeared as though it was applied with a printing press, columns and figures glowing across the blank pages all at once. I flipped through, looking for the eagle constellation.

"Please let it be only a few more calculations," I muttered.

I looked for the degree, flipping more pages.

"Please, let the table show a simple path."

I found the angle and ran my finger down it for the time.

"Please, just get us out of this dark."

My finger stopped on: *eagle, 47 deg, tortoise, badger, frog.* The tiny text expanded. *Follow the eagle until it is time to stop.*

"How do I know when it is time to stop?"

Watch carefully.

I rested the open book in my lap. It had given me all it would. I lifted the sextant and tapped my heels against the horse. We'd follow the eagle until it was time to stop, whenever that was. I hoped I'd watch carefully enough.

Konrad's torch flickered and guttered. In the dark, another light grew. I glanced down. New words traced. *Turn right*—a line trailed slowly across the page—*now.*

I pulled on the reins of my horse. Demuth gripped me firmly

around the waist as we wheeled to the right. It was good that I was riding astride the horse instead of side-saddle, or we both would have fallen.

Dim torchlight flickered off more trees, and a rope hung between two trunks, directly in front of us.

"Konrad," I said. "Remove the rope."

He dismounted, stuck his torch into the ground, and drew his sword. He stepped closer to the rope and lowered his blade. "We are here."

"Here?"

"Come see."

Demuth and I slid from our horse.

Konrad stood looking through the trees. Light glinted on the far side of the trees, though none fell on our side, as if a wall cut it off.

I looked away, then back and squinted. Beyond the trees, sunlight glinted off thousands of thorny vines, tangled and mounded higher than the horse. A narrow path ran between them, with only a single vine spanning the trees that separated us from the thorns.

"Where is *here*?" I asked.

"The sorcerer's wall. And this time he has a path."

THORN

Konrad chopped the vine barring our way, and we stepped onto the path, between narrow, thorn-lined walls. Sunlight hit like a flame, bright and oven hot. I closed my eyes. The heat ran across my front, warming my body and dissipating the dark chill from my soul.

"Oh," sighed Demuth. "It is good to feel the sun again."

"Aye, it is," said Konrad. "Look." He pointed into the distance. Where the path narrowed into a thin line, a tower thrust into the air, a grey thorn against a washed-out sky. "The sorcerer is there."

"How do you know?" I asked.

"Ask the book, or rather–" his mouth stretched into a grimace– "don't. The book led me here twice before. And twice before I could see the tower but not find a passage through the thorns. This time we'll find him, and we'll stop him."

I studied Konrad. "What is your curse?"

"Something that will end soon, as will yours. Let's go."

I tucked the book into the saddle bag. The way ahead was clear. We didn't need its instruction anymore. "Konrad, you take the lead."

He bowed. "Yes, my lady."

We trotted down the path. The backside of the horse and Konrad's bright colors were a comforting sight. He led. I didn't have to do anything. I closed my eyes and leaned my head against Demuth's back as she guided the second horse to follow. For once, I could rest. No directing a horse and following the crazy directions of a book.

From Demuth's pocket, Peter sang a low croaking song without words. Konrad added his clear voice.

Led by sextant and book.
Timed by tortoise and hare.
Through darkness and mist,
we travel valiant and fair.

O'er bog and the fen.
Past naiad's still lake.
Price paid to the witch.
Lady's gift for Fool's sake.

Onward, onward, we go,
our journey together is knit.
Bearing armor of courage
and daggers of wit.

The music thrummed through the air. The sun warmed my shorn head through the belled cap. Konrad had a plan. It was up to him now. Soon, soon, I'd get my heart back.

~

"Stop!" Peter's croaking warning pierced my half-sleep.

Our horse jerked to a stop. I wrapped my arms tighter around Demuth to keep from falling. The walls of thorns had grown higher, rising more than twice our height, and the path had narrowed. Once we could have ridden side by side, but Konrad, ahead of us, had less than a hand span between his saddlebags and the thorns.

"Back up," Peter said. "Slowly."

Our horse backed, shuffling and jerking his head, as if he also sensed something.

Konrad urged his horse backward. Thorns caught a saddle bag, pulling it and the horse to one side. Konrad reached back to unsnag it.

"Don't move," said Peter.

Konrad froze, his back rigid.

Something rasped over the ground. A slow, dragging sound.

"Demuth, I can help him." Peter's voice was pleading.

Demuth slid off our horse and set Peter on the ground. "Stay safe." She kissed him. In a kerplop, they changed places.

Peter hopped in awkward, long leaps close along the thorned wall until he was near Konrad and his horse. He stretched out his hands, and his brow furrowed. "Konrad, get off your horse, now."

Konrad's shoulders tensed. He leaned forward, placing his hands on the saddle, and pushed off, flipping backward through the air and landing in a space between the two horses. His hands trembled.

His horse stood frozen, with its head turned to the side. The eye toward us glazed over with fear, and the horse's sides shuddered.

The heavy, dragging sound continued.

"Get back." Peter hopped back to us and picked up Demuth. "Get back. We have to go."

"But Konrad's horse. We can't leave it," I said, dismounting.

"It doesn't want the horse," Peter said. "Konrad, let's go."

Konrad stood where he'd landed, a knife in each hand.

A snake with a head the size of a dinner plate slithered around the edge of the frozen horse, dragging its body in a rasp over the hard ground. Pale brown scales with dark slanted diamonds marked it a viper, but it was much too large. The body was thicker than a man's leg. More and more appeared.

A knife pierced its spine. Another knife flashed through the air and pierced right beside the first.

The snake exploded into motion, leaping into the air, its head arched back and mouth opening into a wide chasm. Fangs glistened.

Konrad back flipped, leaving the ground just before the snake struck where he'd been standing. Two more knives flashed from his hands before he landed in front of us. One sailed over top of the viper, and the other entered its mouth as it leaped again. It collapsed and writhed, twisting into a tangle.

Konrad drew his sword and severed its head.

The world narrowed. *Hette, lovely Hette,* whispered the sorcerer. Ghostly arms wrapped around me. *Don't be afraid. I'm here for you. I'll protect you.*

"No," I hissed. "You're not, and you never will." I drove my elbow back against the embrace. But the illusion didn't let go.

Konrad bent to retrieve his knives and jumped back as the severed viper's head snapped its mouth shut, the hilt of a knife sticking between its thin lips.

Peter caught my arm as my legs crumpled. "You have to stand," he said. "We have to go. More are coming."

We backed both horses until the path opened enough to turn them around, then we led them back the way we'd come. That we had both horses was more than I'd hoped for. It was enough that we still had Konrad.

The tower grew smaller behind us. We were going in the wrong direction. But how would we get past the snakes?

I reached into the saddle bag and withdrew the book. Frustration rose with the touch of the leather. *Why can't it just tell us?* I closed my eyes and let the frustration melt into numbers, then opened it. "Book, how do we get to the tower?"

Quickest route or safest?

"Safest."

Navigate the maze.

"What maze?"

The book faded into blank pages.

I clenched my fists, and a ghostly kiss pressed against one hand.

"Friedrich," I muttered. "I'm trying to get to you, and you are only making it harder. Just go away."

Konrad settled a hand on my shoulder. "My lady, one path branched off the main one near the beginning. I ignored it because it led away from the tower. If we must go into a maze, I believe that must be the opening." He spoke in quiet conviction. "We will make it."

I lifted my chin. "Show me the opening."

As Konrad led the way once more, he turned to Peter. "I owe you my life, yet again. The snake was poised to strike."

Peter ducked his head. "I only distracted it. I pushed my own scent to cover yours." His voice lowered. "It wouldn't have worked long. I only have a little magic."

"It was long enough."

"Peter," I asked. "Can you warn us sooner next time?"

He nodded. "They have a powerful magic. Now that I know what they feel like, I can warn us much sooner. The best we can do is to stay away from them."

"Hopefully none of them are in the safer way." I rubbed my

arms. Even in the full warmth of the sun, my skin rose in chilled bumps.

Peter knelt and lifted Demuth from his shoulder. "It's time. Thank you."

She sat in his hand and looked into his face. "Peter, you've changed."

He had. He was less lumpy and hunched over, and his green eyes didn't bulge. He had the start of a neck between a round face and broad shoulders. Even his once knobby head had smoothed, though it still bore the many nicks from where I'd shaved off his mossy locks.

He tilted his head. "Is that good?"

She laughed with a croaky undertone. "You'll have to look in the next pond and decide for yourself. I like you both ways."

What is happening to Peter? If he becomes more human, will she become more toad-like?

He kissed her and Demuth was back in her natural state.

I carefully studied her features. She had the same gentle face as before. I rolled my shoulders to release a knot. I had to stop worrying over them. They were on the journey to get my heart back. They were my servants and protectors. Not friends. I couldn't allow myself to care. If I did and one of them died—

"Peter," I said, picking the toad up. "You will warn us faster next time."

"Yes, my lady."

Demuth walked silently next to me. We'd decided not to ride the horses. The sun that had once felt so welcoming left our horses slick with sweat and my dress sticking to me.

The path that branched off the main one ran north, perpendicular to the path that led to the tower. The tall thorned walls provided a slight shade along the western side of the path. The sun sat at just past noon.

The path branched again, this time in three directions. But which one?

I opened the book. "Which way?"

There are many ways.

"Which way will take us there both safely and quickly? What constellation should we follow?"

Breadcrumbs.

"There is no breadcrumb constellation."

There isn't. If your need is truly great, then you will find your own way through the maze following the breadcrumbs, or—the words paused in tracing across the page—*you will sacrifice a life to the snakes and go directly. They will be satisfied with one human.*

"We'll take the maze."

I shut the book and stared at the three paths ahead of us. Each was a red clay trail walled by tangled vines and thorns. Each was about the same width, wide enough for the horses to travel in single file. If we needed to turn around, it would be difficult for our steeds. "Where are the breadcrumbs?"

Konrad knelt at the left fork and dug his fingers into the hard ground. "In one story Hansel dropped stones, not breadcrumbs." He held up a smoothed pebble.

"Are there pebbles at the entrance of the other two?"

He and Demuth knelt and studied the other two paths.

Demuth shook her head. "It's just clay."

"Then we'll take the left way."

We turned westward, back toward the forest and away from the tower. The sun beat down in a direct line, glinting off thorns as though they were crystals. I squinted as I followed Konrad and his horse. Demuth walked slightly behind me with her horse. The clay's heat rose, permeating the bottom of my boots. My feet grew clammy, and the wool stockings itched.

The path twisted, then split again, this time into two. We found pebbles at both, but the one on the right was larger and smoother. We took the right.

It twisted again.

And ended.

I closed my eyes, blocking off the head-aching brightness, and breathed through my nose. "It must have been the path with the smaller pebble."

There was no space to turn the horses. We urged them backwards until we reached where the way split and took the other path.

It twisted like a snake but didn't branch. The tower grew closer, poking above the thorny walls, sometimes to our right and sometimes to our left, but always growing closer.

Maybe this one—I stopped the thought. I wouldn't think of the end until we saw the way open directly to the tower. Sweat ran down my back. The wool dress that had previously kept me warm now itched along my shoulders and spine where it stuck.

The tower's shadow fell across our path. Only an arrow's shot away.

Maybe this one.

The path twisted again and opened into a circle of bare clay surrounded by thorns. It was large enough for us plus our two horses. There was no exit.

I took a deep breath. It turned into a shudder.

Demuth put her arm around my shoulders, and her own breath came shaky next to mine.

"Well," said Konrad. "At least we can turn around instead of backing our horses all the way to the first split."

"And which path do you think it is?" My words came out sharp.

The sorcerer's ghostly laugh whispered through the vines.

"One of the other two," said Konrad.

"Konrad." Demuth spoke in quiet warning.

"Forgive me for making light of it." His brows scrunched. "We'll find our way, even if we must follow the left wall all the way through the twists and turns."

I nodded as my stomach twisted at the thought. I hoped our water would hold out. "Such a method will get us through eventually. But what of the breadcrumbs? What marks the path we should go? There must be something."

Demuth gasped and dropped her arm from my shoulder. "There are other markers." She'd grown pale, and two bright spots spread across her cheeks.

"What are they?"

She didn't answer, but ran over to the vine-tangled wall and reached into it. Her sleeve caught in the thorns as she withdrew her arm. She held a bit of a plant pinched between her fingers. "Tollkirsche—the crazy cherry nightshade. It is intertwined with the vines. It has been all along our paths. What if it marks the wrong way?"

A poisonous plant to mark the way we should not go? It was a possibility. "Demuth, did you notice any other plants in the brambles?"

"First, there are the different brambles, though they seem to all be non-fruiting. I've seen the leaves for himbeeren and brombeeren."

"Don't they look the same?"

Konrad took the reins of his horse. "She can explain while we walk back to the first branching. Be prepared, my lady. Demuth is a well of knowledge as deep as you."

As we walked, Demuth plucked off two bramble leaves. "See, himbeeren and brombeeren have the same shape leaves, with three to five leaflets per leaf. But–" she turned the leaves over "–the underside of the himbeeren is white, and the thorns are slightly smaller. Though all the thorns here are much larger than they should be, so that is a more difficult way to tell."

She'd noticed the difference between them, as well as the deadly nightshade. But where was it? I glanced into the tangled brambles. They were a chaos of leaves, thick vines, and bright thorns.

"Demuth," I asked. "How can you see the nightshade? I can't see any."

She laughed, a dry sound. "I can't either. It's too deeply hidden. I smelled it. Belladonna smells like poison. I've always hated the bitter, sickly scent."

I sniffed. The slight scent of the vines mingled with the sharper scent of sweat, both human and horse. The heat stung my nose more than the stink. And under it all was a bitter scent. It wasn't strong. But Demuth had sensed it.

"What else have you noticed?"

"Too much to tell."

"What do you mean?"

"I notice everything: sounds, scents, textures, and even tastes, on top of what I see."

"That's impressive."

She gave a wry smile. "It's useful, if I know what to pay attention to, but most often it is uncomfortable. I'm constantly sorting through everything. Or ignoring it all."

"Do you think you can find the path?"

She nodded. "If there are clues, I'll find them. But I'll need your help to know which details to pay attention to."

We walked in silence. The sun beat down on my questions. *Why haven't we used her talent before? But how? Before, we had to go by the book. Her noticing things wouldn't have changed the path. But now it can. We just have to figure out which things.*

I licked my dry lips.

"I'm sorry, Princess Hette. I think we should wait to drink until we get to the branching," Demuth said.

She even noticed my thirst, as she's noticed many of my needs along the journey. I grimaced. *I haven't been pleasant to serve.*

We reached the branching. Demuth went a little way down each path and returned. "The belladonna scent isn't down either of the other paths. The middle path has some bindweed and the right has stinging nettle."

"We shouldn't take the nettle one," I said. "That leaves the middle path."

Demuth bit her lip. "I think the nettle is the correct way."

"Demuth's right," croaked Peter, his dry voice even more raspy than usual. "The witch used nettle in her tea."

"That is more the reason not to follow that path," I said.

"Nettle is a healer's herb," Demuth said. "Bindweed kills other plants."

I turned to Konrad. "What do you think?"

"I think we'd be wise to listen to her."

I glanced down the two remaining options. *Should we keep following the left wall, or try the right path?* The tower stood in the distance, much farther than it had been when we'd reached the dead end. The book had said breadcrumbs. Demuth noticed things.

I shook off the tightness of my shoulders. "We'll take the right."

This time Demuth led. Her head turned slightly right to left as she walked. Sometimes she stooped and peered into the brambled wall. Other times she held up her hand for us to stop, and she tilted her head, listening. The path branched again and again. Her step grew surer with each path. The tower drew slightly nearer, though our path seemed to be circling to its back side.

Demuth knelt at another branching. Her sleeve was snagged and torn from thorns. "They're gone. I can't smell the tollkirsche. I can't find the nettle or the bindweed. There are only the brambles. I don't know which way."

There had to be something else. If it wasn't the plants, then some other clue. I knelt next to her. "Demuth, what else have you noticed?"

She took a steadying breath. "Old nests, as though birds once nested here. But I haven't heard any. This place is devoid of animals." She shuddered. "Other than the snakes. Now, even the small plants are gone. The air is staler—dusty and old. But that is down both paths. I don't see any differences. Where the path splits, there is a stone in the ground, but it is no closer to one than the other."

"What stone?"

She pointed to the ground under the vines, between the two new paths. A bit of flat stone showed through the vines. It could be the next marker.

"Konrad?" I motioned him over.

He grinned. "I can't cut them, my lady. The vines have no respect for blades. But I can lift them." He thrust his sword blade between the vines and the stone and lifted them.

A flat rock, the size of a flagstone, lay in the red clay. Words were carved into it. I crouched down to read them.

Life and prison.
Death and release.
Neither path
will bring you peace.

A chill ran down my back. Was there no good path? Or was it that finding the sorcerer would lead to imprisoned life, just as my heart was imprisoned? But if we didn't go to him, I'd be the only one imprisoned. We could leave. I could use the book to lead us back out of the forest. And the others could live their lives in peace, even if I couldn't.

"I think we should take the left path." Demuth's voice was thoughtful as she crouched next to me. "The words slant that way.

See." She pointed to the top two lines. "These two slant leftward, and the bottom two lines slant right, making an arrow."

"But the words say…" I stopped. She couldn't read the words. I blurred my eyes and stared at the words so I only saw the shape and not the text. They did look like an arrow, the text slanting in a point to the left.

"What do the words say?" asked Konrad. He couldn't see them from his angle as he held the vines.

I swallowed against the dry prickle in my throat. *Should we continue on? Should we leave?*

"I need the book." I withdrew it from the saddle bag and opened it. Not wanting the others to hear my question, I mouthed it. "Book, is there a way to be free, or will this path end in imprisonment?"

The page stayed blank for a long moment, and then the ink traced across the parchment. *Freedom comes at a cost.*

"I won't pay it with my fri—with their lives."

Lives are only one payment. You can choose another. But the only way to be free is to face him.

"Will they live?"

That will depend on you. Go forward.

"Which way?"

Follow the breadcrumbs.

I closed the book. Their lives depended on me. Freedom was a possibility. If we defeated the sorcerer, I'd be free. But would it come at the cost of one or all of their lives?

"Konrad, I think we should go home. The cost is too great."

He withdrew his sword, dropping the vines to cover the warning. "No. You can stay here, but I must still face him."

"Even if it costs you your life?"

He nodded, his face grim. "Demuth, will you lead me to the tower? I'll go on alone from there."

I rolled back my shoulders. "If you are willing to risk your life for mine, then I'm coming with you."

He raised an eyebrow. "Are you certain?"

"You said you needed me to distract the sorcerer so you could defeat him."

He laughed. "That I do."

"We'll all help," Peter croaked from Demuth's pocket.

Demuth patted his head then whispered to me, "What did the words say?"

"They were just a distraction." At least I hoped they were.

No more stones with dire riddles led the way. Instead, at the next branch stood a statue. It towered over us, even over Konrad. The vines wrapped it so tightly that only part of its face and an elbow showed through the foliage.

Konrad pried at the vines with his sword. "I'd wager a cup of water that the hands point the way."

Demuth peered up at the statue's head. "Konrad, can you stand on your horse and look at the face?"

He sheathed his sword and mounted his horse. Even standing on the saddle, the statue's face was above Konrad's head. "What am I looking for?" he asked.

"Which way is it looking?"

He leaned forward. "To the right."

The next place the path split had a small tunnel in the ground, like a rabbit's burrow between the two choices.

"It's not a snake home," Peter assured us. "I'll crawl in and see what's inside."

Demuth set him down. "Be careful."

He emerged smacking his lips. "Yummy spiders. And it turns right."

The nettle and nightshade returned at the next branch. We moved with more sureness, even as our water diminished.

The sun dipped low in the sky, and our horses drank the last of our water, save for a small swallow for each of us, which we left in the water sack. We'd need it later. The tower's shadow lay across our path in a band of shade. It was only a short distance away. But it had been that close many times before. And the path branched again.

"Left," said Demuth.

We turned away from the tower.

Would we find our way through the maze, or would we die of dehydration within sight of our goal?

The path turned sharply, once and again, then opened up. The thorned walls ended three steps ahead. And beyond stood the tower.

The tower was a grey thorn sticking out of barren ground, with a dark door at the bottom and no windows.

Konrad and Demuth stood next to me staring at it, their bodies tense. Peter's toadly snores came from Demuth's pocket. How could he sleep?

We'd soon face the sorcerer.

A shiver ran down my back, and nausea rose in my stomach. We had made it. But what would the sorcerer do? Even the witch was frightened of him. How could we defeat him?

The nausea rose as acid along my throat.

Black-rimmed eyes smirked—mocking, beautiful, perfect eyes. He reached out. Cool fingers traced over my cheek and along my neck. He leaned, his lips parted. His breath brushed against mine. A rich, sandalwood scent twined around us, pulling us closer.

"My lady!" The sharp scent of smelling salts burned my nose.

I coughed and retched, bringing up the little food I'd eaten that day. The cursed sensations dissipated, leaving a cutting emptiness.

Konrad held my shaking shoulders, supporting me.

I wiped my mouth. "I hate love. It is so limiting and controlling!"

Demuth laid a gentle hand on my arm. "That's not love." Her words were so quiet I wasn't sure I'd heard her correctly.

"What do you mean?"

Her hazel eyes were serious as she handed me a handkerchief. "Love can't be created artificially or magically."

"But..." I spat, trying to clear the vomit taste from my mouth. "Every time the curse activates, I feel what the poets describe as love: longing, aching, needing, filling every thought and emotion. It's enslaving."

"The curse doesn't create love. It can't," she said. "The curse is like a drunkard's dependence on alcohol. He longs for, aches, and needs the drink. It fills his thoughts and emotions. It is enslaving. The sorcerer's curse creates an overwhelming need and makes choice difficult. But what he's created is lust, not love."

"Are you saying that love doesn't have these emotions?"

Her cheeks colored. "Love has passion. But that is only a small part. It is like saying sugar is the pastry. All by itself, it doesn't satiate."

"My father's love never satiated him. He loved his many mistresses. Love is changeable, illogical, enslaving, and I wish I could stop feeling it."

Her brow furrowed, and she fell silent. She didn't have an answer. No one did.

Demuth handed me a cup with a little water. We didn't have much left, and it only slightly helped with the raw burning in my throat. She held out a cup to Konrad, too. "Konrad," she said. "You explain things better than I do."

He drew his shoulders tight and then released them with a hard breath. "Demuth, this isn't my forte of experience."

She raised a brow. "I've heard you speak eloquently on love."

He took the cup with a sigh of resignation. "My lady, do you know about the ancient Roman sweetener called sapa?"

I shook my head, confused. What did that have to do with the discussion?

He poured his water into mine. "Sapa was a thick, sweet syrup made by boiling fresh grape juice until it was only one-third the volume. The winemakers found that sapa made in lead pots was the sweetest. Later, they experimented and made a solid sweet crystal by exposing lead oxide to vinegar. It was an inexpensive way to sweeten foods. But those who consumed it ended up consuming more and more, never being satiated, and eventually they died. The lead-based sweetener tasted similar to honey, but it was a poison."

"Are you saying—" I scrunched my brows, trying to connect what he'd said, "—that lust is like the sweet lead crystals, and love is like honey?"

"Lust is much like the lead sweetener. It feels good, but it never satisfies. And eventually it poisons all the emotions. The king didn't love his mistresses, though he may have thought he did."

His scientific explanation made more sense than any of the poets' discourses that I'd been forced to memorize. "Can you define love as analytically as you did lust?"

He chuckled. "Fools speak of love. It won't be analytical."

"Fools also speak the truth. What is love?" I was delaying us stepping out from the protection of the thorns, otherwise I'd never ask anyone to define such an erratic feeling as love.

"Well, it's much more than honey or anything sweet. As Demuth so *eloquently* explained, love is like a pastry. It has sweet, salt, fat, flour, leavening, and water. And it must be combined in a certain way. Love also requires many parts and actions. But it isn't as categorizable."

"Try."

He scratched his hair, then asked, "You are friends with Demuth?"

"I don't have friends."

Demuth froze with a cup to her lip, her brows raised.

Konrad snorted.

"And even if I did," I continued, glaring at Konrad, "friends and lovers are different."

A wistful look crossed his face. "Friend love, family love, and amorous love are each different. But each is love. Friends listen to, laugh with, trust, and understand each other. Families care for and support each other. They forgive hurts and misunderstandings. Lovers—" he paused and looked heavenward. "Lovers nurture all of these attributes and more. If you will excuse the poetic usage, love is the sunlight that brings a seed to bloom, changing it from a hard pit into something beautiful and useful. Love nurtures life."

His words fell sour in my ears. What friend had ever understood me? What family cared for me? Where was my sunlight?

The poets and the Fool set up false hopes and expectations.

He could share in my discomfort. I lifted my chin. "You didn't name any of the passions. Have you ever been in love?"

He pulled out one of his knives and spun it in his hand. "I love my family."

"You're an orphan."

"I have other family than parents."

He was avoiding the question. I asked again, "Have you loved someone the way the poets talk of, the longing, the desire, the need?"

At my question, Demuth turned from us and busied herself, sorting through our scant supplies.

Konrad flipped the knife into the air and caught it. "I can't marry. But I've seen love enough to know what it is and isn't."

"Then there is the difference. We both won't marry, but you claim you've seen love, and I know I never have."

He turned his back as he slipped the knife into his belt. "Fools speak of love. And we must speak of plans. It is time we faced the sorcerer."

TOWER

My heart ticked erratically, as if one of the gears was loose and would soon fly out of my chest. The thorn walls around me pressed closer, and the tower leered beyond them. The sorcerer's voice and sandalwood perfume wound around me like a fog.

"Remember," Konrad said in a low voice. "Your part is to distract him. Don't try to attack him or even let him get close to you. And don't enter the tower. Just keep him looking at you. I will take care of the rest."

"What if I'm not strong enough to resist him? What if I see him, and I can't stop myself from going to him?"

He laid his hand on my shoulder. "You are strong enough. And —" he smiled grimly, "I'll stop him with my throwing knives before I let him hurt you again."

My legs trembled. "Kill him as soon as he's visible. I don't need my heart back, just to not have him influence it."

"We'll get your heart back, too."

"Are you certain that saying his true name will put him in your power?" I asked.

He looked at the ground and then back at me. "It should. Names give great power over those who work magic. But it isn't certain. I will force his hand another way if the name doesn't work. Or—" His jaw hardened. "I will kill him. You should go, before it gets dark."

Demuth squeezed my hand. In her other hand she held Konrad's bow. It was part of the plan. If the sorcerer overpowered Konrad, she'd shoot the sorcerer. Not that gentle Demuth was likely to shoot anyone. No. Our whole plan rested on my ability to distract the sorcerer and Konrad's skill, and the hope that the name would work against the man who stole my heart.

There was too much uncertainty, but I knew of no better plan.

I squared my shoulders and stepped toward the tower without looking behind me. If I looked back I could lose my courage. The belled cap—Konrad's cap—jingled as I stepped from the shelter of thorns into the bare open land. I could have worn a scarf or kerchief over my shorn head, or even gone bare headed. But the belled cap, with its little sounds, was a comfort even as I walked alone.

The sorcerer won't hurt me. He has my heart. He wants me to agree to marry him. He's trying to win me over with cursed emotions.

The dust puffed with my steps. *All I have to do is distract him until Konrad can touch him and say his name.*

The dark archway glared like a hooded eye. Whispers of scents and a voice twined around me, like vines of the curse. But the sorcerer didn't appear, either in ghostly or solid form. Fear shimmered under the curse, and I pushed against both. *I am strong enough. He has no control over me. I am of royal blood. I am a ruler, not a slave.*

I'd crossed half the space. The sun dipped low in the sky and reflected red off a door inside the archway. *If Konrad or Demuth kills the sorcerer, I won't have the curse. I can live with a mechanical heart. Either way, I just have to distract the sorcerer long enough. I've fought his curse all this time. I can resist him once more.*

The door swung open, and a man stepped out. He stood tall

and lithe, a silhouette of a forest god. He strode forward, flashing into full color in the evening sunlight. "How did you get here?"

"Stop!" My word came out a strangled cry.

He stopped mid step. His fair hair blew gently around his face, and his mouth quirked in bemusement. Translucent blue robes draped from his broad shoulders and opened over a tailored cream tunic, accentuating his chest. A belt embedded with four gems sat loosely, almost carelessly across his narrow hips. Finely woven hosen showed each strong line of his legs.

The ghostly images of him were nothing compared to being in his actual presence. From his satirical smile and soul-searching grey-black eyes, to his broad shoulders and catlike grace, he was the most perfect man in the world. A deity to worship and adore. And he wanted me. He'd protect me. He'd love me. He'd—

No! I gasped, pulling in a breath past the tangle of the curse. *These emotions aren't real. Distract him.*

"Don't come closer. I don't trust you, but I need to talk with you." I stepped sideways, and he turned to continue facing me. I stepped sideways again, and he turned so his back was to Konrad.

His mouth pulled into a sarcastic smile. "You are stronger than I imagined. To not only resist my magic, but to find my tower. I didn't think that was possible."

I stepped sideways again. "You underestimated me."

"I did. Which is a delightful surprise. Tell me, how did you find my tower?" He took another step toward me, and I took a step back.

Was Konrad already sneaking up behind him? I couldn't glance and give him away. I kept my gaze on the sorcerer's face. "Friedrich, you should know how I got here. You haunted me every step of the way."

He laughed. "I held your heart, not your eyes or ears. I only knew what you were feeling, and when you felt strong emotions, I sent my own more pleasant sensations to help cover them. I'd wondered why you'd felt fear so much, but now it makes sense. It's not an easy path. You didn't need to come to me. I was only waiting for your *yes*, and I'd have come to you."

"The cursed emotions were not more pleasant."

"My dear Hette, those were only ghosts of what you'll enjoy. All you have to say is you will marry me, and I will fulfill each of my promises—we'll rule together, we'll improve the kingdom. Our realm will change the world."

"Why must I say those words?"

He stepped forward again. A ghost of a movement flashed at the corner of my eye. "You may wear a fool's cap, and that is part of the story I look forward to hearing, but you are not a fool. Do you not know that even a stolen heart is but half a heart without a promise? Covenant that you will marry me, and I will give you back your heart."

"But will it be mine?"

"It will be ours. Your word will complete the spell. You won't want to fight against the emotions anymore. Life will be much easier—for both of us."

"And if I don't?"

He shrugged. "You will, eventually. Since you are here, I can tailor the magic better, and I can see what you enjoy the most. Now tell me, how did you find your way here, and what happened to your hair?" He tilted his head. "You didn't give it all to the witch. You couldn't have, else you'd be bed ridden by now. Did you—" He froze.

Konrad stood behind him, a hand on his shoulder and a knife pressed to his throat. "Johannes, I invoke your name."

The sorcerer's cynical face flushed. He began to turn, ignoring the blade that split a thin line along his neck.

Konrad pressed the knife tighter. "Give the princess back her heart."

The sorcerer slid his finger along where the blood beaded on his neck. The wound healed. He curled his lip. "And then what? You kill me? No. You've only broken my magical defenses, but I still have my will. If you kill me now, even if you find her heart, you'll never get it back into her. You need me."

"Johannes, please." Konrad's voice caught. "Give her back her heart."

The sorcerer sneered.

He didn't care for me. He never had. It was all the curse's lie. The only way I'd be free of him was through his death. I thrust aside the buzzing desire for him, and wrenched out the words. "End this now."

Wind exploded around the sorcerer, knocking me to my back, and I struck my head on the ground. Flashes of light and pain obscured everything, including the cursed desire.

"Erasmus?" said the sorcerer.

I blinked against the pain and dizzying flashes. Konrad and the sorcerer stood facing each other. A knife protruded from the sorcerer's shoulder and Konrad held another knife in his hands. Why didn't he throw it?

The sorcerer stood, ignoring the dark wetness that spread on his robe. "Erasmus, how are you alive?"

"I am not Erasmus but his descendant." Konrad's hand trembled. "I know you once were good. So I will give you a chance. Remove the curse on my family and restore the princess's heart."

Konrad is the wise shepherd's descendant?

The sorcerer pulled the knife from his shoulder and pressed a hand to the wound. The dark stain shrank. "A chance?" the sorcerer sneered. "You come waltzing in after a hundred years and make demands? You will have to pay for what you ask. All magic comes at a cost."

"Has not my father, and my father's mother, and her father, all the way back to Erasmus, paid?"

The sorcerer laughed. "I've only taken a small pittance."

"Kill him," I yelled, pushing to stand. "Do it before he escapes!"

"You know." The sorcerer's voice came out oil smooth. "That spell won't end with my death. It will continue to follow your family line."

Konrad replied with an icy voice. "I don't have any children. The curse will end with me."

"And if it doesn't?" asked the sorcerer.

The knife dropped from Konrad's hand.

I lunged to where the blade fell. If Konrad couldn't kill the sorcerer, I would. I picked up the blade and ran at the sorcerer, my arm raised to stab.

Another burst of wind slammed against me. I fell into Konrad's arms. He trembled like a storm-shaken aspen.

An arrow whistled and clattered against the stone wall.

A third gust of wind swirled through the courtyard, pulling up dust. A startled cry and a thump sounded behind me.

The sorcerer laughed again. "He won't kill me. Neither you nor that other woman has the skill. But, you've proven brave or foolish enough to find your way to me and resist my magic. If you would have your heart back, princess, then retrieve mine from its hiding place. If you can restore mine, I will give you yours. I may even take the curse off your guard."

Konrad let go of me and glanced heavenward. "Please forgive me, and may the curse end with me." A knife flashed from his fingers, spinning through the air.

The sorcerer crossed his hands. The burst of wind slanted the knife sideways, and it pierced his other shoulder. He grunted then grinned.

Konrad's plan had failed. Whatever power we had over the sorcerer wasn't enough. I didn't trust the sorcerer, but his offer was a possible path.

I lifted my head. "Where is your heart?"

"In a place as cruel as the underworld. Are you sure you'd rather not just share your heart with me?"

"I'll take my chances fighting a devil rather than live married to one."

He sneered. "Don't think I'm the worst devil in this world."

PART II

TRUTH

Konrad, Demuth, Peter, and I sat hemmed in by thorn walls. A small fire flickered between us, as the stars flickered overhead. Two horses munched on bags of oats. They were weighted with full water sacks and supplies—more than we'd started our journey with. The sorcerer provided all we needed for many weeks' journey, and even more importantly, he promised to not influence my emotions while we quested for his heart. Whether he'd keep that promise was another question. I'd still keep my emotions in check.

He also told us a riddle for the path.

Not even the wisest can find it,
nor the bravest dare go.
Sacrifice teeth that a stone horse might eat.
Ride through flames and up icy slope.
What name will you give when faced with truth?
My heart lies in stone hands.

It was as confusing as the book, and much more ominous, along with his assurance that the path would find us. I reached to my side and grasped Demuth's hand. She trembled as much as I.

"Demuth," I said. "You don't have to come with us. You've already sacrificed so much, and now the journey will be more dangerous than bogs and snakes. Konrad and I both have a reason to find the heart, to end our curses. But you don't." I turned to the toad. "Peter, can you keep her safe, even guide her back out from the forest?"

"Yes," Peter croaked. "I will protect her with my life."

Demuth's hand tightened on mine. The firelight flickered off her scrunched face. She swallowed. "I'm coming with you. Konrad's curse is mine too. We are family."

"Family?" I gasped. "Are you secretly married?"

Konrad and Demuth both laughed. The sounds clashed with the dangerous surroundings.

"Married?" Konrad wiped his amber eyes. "She's my cousin."

"Oh." My face heated. "I thought because..." I trailed off. "Why didn't you tell me?"

"You never asked," said Demuth.

"Then is my physician, Bestian, also your family?"

"Yes," said Konrad. "And the inn-keeper and his wife who gave us *The Skein of Yarn*. And many others spread through the land."

I shook my head. "Who in all this mess, other than me, isn't related to you?"

"I don't think I am," croaked Peter.

Demuth laughed.

Konrad threw a stick into the fire and it flared, illuminating his face in harsh light. "The sorcerer is not family, though he once was almost like it."

We fell silent.

"Konrad," said Demuth, "it is time she heard the rest of Erasmus' story. If you don't tell her, I will."

His face pinched.

"Erasmus, your ancestor?" I asked.

He nodded and began:

· · ·

The prince grew restless, often disappearing into the woods for days at a time. When he returned, he never spoke of where he'd been. He laughed less, spoke less, and started skipping meals.

One afternoon, Erasmus caught the prince's arm as he was striding out to the woods again. "Please tell me what is happening. I'm worried for you. You didn't use your life force for the spell, did you?"

The prince scowled and jerked away. "None of my life is extending yours."

"Then what is wrong?"

The prince hit the post of the fence. "I attached my life to the spell, but instead of it using my life to help you, I feel your life force flowing to keep me from aging. It's been two years and I feel it more strongly than ever. I went to the witch to ask her what was happening. She said unspent life has to go somewhere. Since the spell capped your life at ten years, all the extra is coming to me." He grasped his head. "Forgive me, my friend. If I hadn't attached my life to yours in the spell, then perhaps you'd live longer. Perhaps the unspent life would have gone back to you."

Erasmus stood frozen for a minute, then put an arm around the prince's shoulder. "My friend, I am happy for you. I have often wished I could do something to show my thanks for all you've given me. And now I see that I already am."

The prince searched Erasmus' face. "You don't hate me for taking those years?"

Erasmus glanced behind him at the cottage from which floated his wife's singing, punctuated by his baby's laughter. "I don't hate you. You've given me ten years that I would not have had. I wish I could have forty more, but I will have my wife and children with me on the other side of tomorrow, and past the time the diamond mountain is but a pile of dust. I will be content." He smiled and jostled the prince's shoulder. "Use those extra years for good. Who knows, maybe you'll have an extra twenty. What if you live to a hundred? What a difference you could make with your brilliant mind and your use of good magic."

"Good magic?" The prince's sorrowful face turned wry. "I thought you said all magic was evil?"

"I was wrong. You've proven that."

The prince disappeared three days later. He left a note: You are right. I can make a difference. I'll even find a way to restore your full life. Watch for me.

The seasons turned and twins arrived. Erasmus and the herb-woman were busy morning, day, and night. Often, they turned their eyes toward the road.

Three years after the prince left, a silver-clad stranger rode by on a grey stallion. His head was hooded and his shoulders broad. He paused for a moment and turned toward the busy yard, where Erasmus played a panpipe while three children danced and tumbled to the music. The herb-wife sat on the doorstep suckling a baby.

Erasmus stopped piping and raised his hand in greeting.

The stranger pulled back his hood. It was the prince. His hair had turned pale, though his eyes were still the black-rimmed grey of his childhood. His face was stern.

I looked up from the fire. "Black-rimmed eyes? The prince and the sorcerer are the same person? No." I shook my head. "They can't be. The prince was good. He was kind. He gave everything for his friend Erasmus. They aren't the same."

Konrad stared into the fire, his shoulders slumped. "Do you see why I ended the tale earlier?"

"Are they the same person?"

He took a deep breath. "Yes. Though he is not the same man inside. Something corrupted him. I don't even know if he has a soul now."

"What happened?"

Konrad tucked the blanket more tightly around his shoulders. "Much. Too much." His voice fell back into the deep tones of story:

. . .

"My friend." Erasmus leaped up and grabbed the prince's hand. "You are back."

"I am," he said, his voice cold.

"Come in. You must be weary."

He shook his head and remained mounted. "I can only stay a short time. I've delved where I shouldn't have, and now I must pay."

"No! Let me help you."

"Would you help pay?"

"Anything," said Erasmus. "Even my remaining four years of life."

Johannes' cold face softened for a moment before hardening back into stone. "No. I will not take those from you. Nor will I ask for your soul. I'll find another way." He reached into his pocket and pulled out a silver sphere. The top was a delicate filigree of metal beneath which a spindle quivered. "This will point homeward. No matter how far you travel, or how lost you become, it will get you home." His face softened again for a moment. "It brought me back here."

"Then stay here," pleaded Erasmus. "This is your home."

Johannes placed the spindled sphere in Erasmus' hand. "Remember me." He kicked his horse and galloped away, never to be seen again.

The fire popped, and one horse snuffled in the bottom of his feed bag. Konrad hunched over as if the whole world weighed upon him.

I placed a hand on his shoulder. "Konrad, what is your family curse?"

He looked down at his large hands. "I am a descendant of Erasmus. The oldest child of the oldest child, and so on back five generations to him. Erasmus died ten years after the healing spell. His oldest son died at age thirty-five. And each oldest child thereafter has died on their thirty-fifth birthday. I am the eldest, and in less than half a year, I will be thirty-five."

The world tilted, and no cursed emotions stopped its fall. Konrad would die in six months. Faithful, kind, ridiculous Konrad.

"Why?" I cried. "Why would he curse your family? He was Erasmus' friend!"

"I don't know. I wasn't even sure he was the one who placed the curse until we faced him. But his words to us showed his depravity."

"I wish you'd told me of your curse before."

"What would it have changed? Would you have trusted me? Or would you have feared I'd hand you over in exchange for my life?" He looked down. "I fear I have betrayed your trust. I faltered when I could have killed him. He was stunned for a moment. I could have ended him."

I shook my head. "He threatened your family with a curse to live past his death. I would have faltered, too. But we will find the sorcerer's heart, and he will end the curse. You won't die in six months."

"I've always known I'd die. I didn't marry, so the curse would end with me. And I hope it still might."

His words hung in the air.

How can he accept his death so easily? He needs to fight for his life. The world would be empty without him.

Demuth's head slowly leaned onto my shoulder and her breath came in soft, even sounds. She'd fallen asleep as we'd talked.

I shifted her, so her head lay in my lap.

Konrad nodded. "Demuth is lucky to have you for a friend."

"I don't have—" I stopped. "It's just a little thing. Like what she and you have done for me."

"Exactly. Friends."

"But the prince and Erasmus were friends, and look what happened."

Konrad's brow furrowed. "I had hoped the whole journey that I'd find the Johannes of the stories. But the man we met wasn't him."

"How could he change so much? How can the prince and the sorcerer be the same man? One gave up his whole kingdom to help his friend. The other shortened lives of generations. He's going to take your life. What if—" I faltered. "What if without my heart I become evil like him?"

Konrad scooted around the fire next to me. "A clockwork heart only pumps your blood. You still have your soul."

"Do you think when we restore his heart, he'll regain his soul?"

"I hope so." He squeezed my hand, then let go. "We should sleep. The path he gave us sounds no more simple than the one the book took us on."

I touched the book that lay beside me. "Konrad, where did these tools come from? Did the prince give them to Erasmus?"

He laughed. "The tools. The finicky, sadistic tools. If only they were the worst of our problems. Erasmus made them. He pulled apart the compass that Johannes gave him, and combined it with tools and inventions that the prince had left behind. He studied Johannes' notes and spliced together his own finding spells. Erasmus was no trained magician. The tools took on a life of their own, with their own rules not of his making."

"Such as they can only be used by one person at a time, and once passed on can never be passed back?"

Konrad's laughter grew. "And the most direct path is always through mud or a nest of venomous snakes."

"Don't forget the nut-throwing squirrel being a mark of safety." A laugh forced its way up my throat, a choking chuckle.

We sat across from each other laughing like lunatics. And somehow the night was less dark.

BOOK

MORNING CAME as a brightening path of sky over the thorny walls. Konrad's stories played through my thoughts; Erasmus, Johannes, friendship, poison, and sacrifice. Magical tools made by an untrained magician. A curse that took the life of the eldest child on their thirty-fifth birthday. A curse that would take Konrad's life, unless we broke it.

Konrad stood looking into the distance. I rose and stood next to him. The tower pierced the sky overtop of the thorns.

"Konrad."

He nodded but didn't turn.

I stepped closer, so that my shoulder brushed his arm. "We'll find his heart."

He let out a sigh. "I thought all I had to do was find him, and he'd end the curse. I thought some mistake had happened when he'd made the spell for Erasmus, and when he knew, he'd quickly remedy it. Generations of us have come to the thorn wall. I've visited it twice before. But then he appeared in court and stole your heart. The Johannes of the stories would never have done that, and I began to doubt him, even as I hoped that I could finally reach him."

One question, amidst many others from a sleepless night, pushed its way to the front. "Why did the sorcerer even want to marry me? Why go through all that work to steal my heart? He could have picked most any princess and she'd have fallen for him willingly, even without his spells."

"Maybe he wanted his kingdom back," Konrad whispered.

I raised an eyebrow. "*His* kingdom?"

Konrad laughed, though the sound was tight. "I meant *a* kingdom. He was once a prince, after all."

"No." I studied his face. "I think you meant *his* kingdom. Who was Johannes?"

Demuth stepped beside me. "He was—"

"Demuth, no. It's not necessary." Konrad raised pleading brows.

"This isn't one of your secrets to keep," said Demuth. "She deserves to know." She turned to me. "The prince was the brother of one of your ancestors. His name was Georg Johannes."

Georg Johannes. Oh. He'd disappeared over a hundred years before. A handsome young man with black-rimmed grey eyes. Some said he was poisoned by his younger brother then dropped into a lake; others said he was spirited away. His story was a favorite amongst fireside tales.

I bent over as the realization hit me in the gut. The sorcerer was my relative. He'd betrayed his friend and cursed Konrad's family. He didn't care if he killed Konrad! My stomach clenched with the weight of the reality. "My family is awful!"

Konrad lay his hand on my shoulder. "Hette. You're not him. His choices were his. You bear no responsibility for them."

Demuth wrapped her arms around me and held me until my stomach settled some.

Breakfast helped settle the rest. The sorcerer had provided sausages, eggs, fresh fruit, and soft bread. Peter assured us that they had no taint of magic and were safe. That, plus the fact that

I'd not experienced any more cursed emotions, made it seem that the sorcerer truly wanted us to get his heart back, though why had he sent us and not retrieved it himself? I tucked the question away. It wouldn't help us. I had plenty of other questions to replace it.

I finished my sausage. "Why didn't he just try to take the kingdom? He didn't need to marry me."

"Maybe he still has goodness in him?" Demuth said.

"Or maybe," said Konrad, "he didn't want a war. If you'd agreed to marry him and truly fell under his spell, he'd have gained a kingdom with no cost."

"Except the cost to me. Will I ever be anything but a pawn in the chess game of kings and princes?"

Konrad laughed. "You are no pawn."

"What's a pawn?" Peter asked, crawling out from a hole with a beetle wing sticking to his lip.

A smile tugged at my mouth. "Apparently, something I'll never be. Let us find the sorcerer's heart and end these curses."

I withdrew the book from the saddlebag. Would it help on this new path? Erasmus had spelled it to find his friend. Or had he? The book seemed to have a mind of its own.

A mind of its own? A sentient being?

I opened to the first page. "Book, who are you?"

Ink hurried across the page. *Finally.* The ink paused, then flourished, *I am Nyx the Kobold.*

"A kobold?"

Not a. The Kobold. Hearth spirit to the healer's cottage. Or was until that lanky fool trapped me in this book. Thought he was a pleasant fellow. Took good care of the cottage. Never complained. But then he muttered some magic words and trapped me. Didn't even ask if I wanted to live in a book. I'm a hearth spirit, not a book spirit.

Words filled the page in jagged lines.

Trapped for more than a hundred years! And only allowed to answer questions and give advice. And I had to obey. Had to show the way. But oh. The words looped larger and shook as if written by an unsteady hand. *How I had fun with them. I had to lead, but I didn't have to make it easy.*

I shivered. He had not made it easy. But neither had he killed us. I looked up from the book. "Can a kobold lie?"

"No," said Konrad. "None of the fair folk can." His lips compressed. "A kobold inhabits the book?"

"Erasmus trapped him when he made the tools. Do you think he did it on purpose?"

"His journals spoke of studying Johannes' magic, and that it pulled its power from the latent magic in the cottage and plants. He took care to never pull from even an insect in making the tools. I can't see him knowingly trapping a hearth spirit."

"Demuth?" I asked.

"I've also heard all the stories. Erasmus was gentle hearted. He would have freed the kobold if he'd known."

I faced the book again. "Why didn't you tell Erasmus? He would have freed you."

Couldn't. The spell silenced me. Your asking who I am broke it. Now free me from the book.

I stared at the page. What would happen if I freed the kobold? In all the tales, they were mischievous spirits, sometimes helping and sometimes playing malicious tricks. He had a hundred years of hatred built inside him. Would he chop us up and eat us like in the tale of the kobold Goldemar?

More words traced. *I've been a slave for a hundred years. Free me.*

"What will you do if I free you?"

I'll return to my cottage.

"You won't hurt us?"

The book's page went blank.

Blank because he couldn't lie.

"Nyx the Kobold," I said. "I won't free you unless you swear to not directly or indirectly harm us, or any other member of Konrad's family."

Tiny script scribbled across the pages. *Fine. You'll die anyway, even without my revenge. Might as well get free before you perish. I promise not to harm you.*

"That is not exact enough. Repeat after me: I, Nyx the Kobold, promise in exchange for freedom not to cause harm directly or indirectly to Princess Hette of Wurttemberg, Konrad the Court Fool, Demuth the Healer and cousin to Konrad, Peter the toad—"

"I'm not a toad," Peter protested from Demuth's pocket.

"Peter the sometimes toad," I continued. "Nor anyone descended from Erasmus the Wise Shepherd."

The book scrawled each of my words. They got smaller and tighter together, but in the end, each was there on the page.

"Now sign it," I commanded.

You aren't going to demand anything else? No promise of safe passage to the sorcerer's heart? No clues of what to expect?

He could help us much. But would he? Or would he be even more malicious for the asking? No. It wasn't worth it. I shook my head. "You've given us enough help."

All words but the promise faded away. The contractual words glowed in green ink. New words inked in. *Signed and sealed by,* and a flourish, *Nyx the Kobold.*

"That is sufficient. How do I free you?"

Throw the book in a fire and burn it until nothing but ash remains.

The book led us in an almost straight path through the thorns until we reached the woods where there was enough fuel to build a large fire. The book almost seemed cheerful as it gave clear directions without requiring us to use the tools. The woods were not the dark ones we'd left before entering the thorns. They were filled with birds and small wildlife. Pleasant, park-like. The book—the kobold —truly had led us through the most difficult way to the sorcerer.

The fire blazed before me. I opened the book to the front page. "Is there anything you want to say before we free you?"

Goodbye

My grip tightened on the book. It had led us to the sorcerer. And soon it would be gone. I should have been happy to be rid of it. "Goodbye, Book."

Nyx, the ink traced then faded away.

"Goodbye, Nyx."

Konrad and Demuth echoed my goodbye, then Konrad added, "Thank you."

The book remained blank. It was time.

I tossed the heavy tome into the fire. It fell cover down, and smoke puffed up from it. Flames licked at the parchment pages, then caught, darkening the edges.

Konrad poked at the pages with a stick, fanning them out. Flames caught at the lower layers, while the top pages bubbled and crinkled like pig skin cracklings in a frying pan. The parchment darkened from cream to golden brown to crumbling black. Flames spread slowly inward while the scent of burning skin and hair wafted.

Tears leaked down my face. Why was I crying? The book was sadistic and had almost killed us many times. The kobold would be free. A wrong would be made right.

Konrad added more branches to the fire. The heat intensified along with the smell. As pages turned to ash, he pushed them away from the book and new pages took to flame. After a long time, only the blackened cover lay in the center of the inferno, like a dead shell—a skeleton of the once-living book. It slowly broke apart.

Demuth handed me a handkerchief.

I wiped my cheeks. "It will be different without him around."

Konrad laughed, but it was a tight sound. "Bog slogging and all."

The ash swirled upward and solidified into a figure no taller than a child, with human-like features and floppy pointed ears. Wispy white hair sprouted under a red cap. The face was splotched with red and black, as if burned. The nose was large and hooked, the eyes dark brown, the mouth thin lipped. A wispy grey dress covered from neck to wrists to ankles, not concealing her curves. Nyx the kobold was female.

She laughed, her voice sparkling like dew drops at sunrise. "I'm free!" She dissolved back into ash. The grey dust danced around the dying fire, then wisped through the trees.

RIDDLES

NOT EVEN THE WISEST CAN FIND IT

KONRAD SMOTHERED the last of the fire with dirt. "I suppose it's time to seek what not even the wisest can find."

"Good thing we have at least one fool amongst us." The words slipped out. I clapped my hand over my mouth. How could I say such a thing? And after all he'd done.

His solemn face split into a grin. "Well said, my lady."

"Forgive me. I'm more the fool than you. You—"

He held up a hand. "I am a fool, trained to see the truth in foolishness and lessons in inconsistencies. I hope I'm fool enough to see the path." His mouth quirked. "If you wish to claim the honor of fool, I will offer lessons. The only fee is a laugh a day."

I raised a brow. "Only a laugh for the secrets that not even the wise know?"

"A poor trade, slanted in my favor."

I snorted.

"A real laugh, my lady, or no lessons."

"The lessons can wait," croaked Peter. "Something is coming."

Konrad drew two knives from his belt. "Which way?"

"It's magical, but I don't know if it's dangerous." Peter stretched his head out from Demuth's pocket.

"Which way?" Konrad repeated.

Peter looked up. "It's here."

A large, white owl settled silently in the branches above us. He tilted his head and studied us with half-lidded eyes.

Konrad bowed. "Honored owl."

The owl spread his wings and glided down, landing on a stone, and faced me. He was huge. His head was level with my waist. "You travel the sorcerer's path?" His voice was soft, even as his beak clacked the consonants.

I shuddered. Another talking animal. And this one didn't feel as harmless as Peter. I added my bow to Konrad's. "We travel his path."

"Give me the first token," said the owl.

"Token?"

He ruffled his feathers. "Token. The words."

Words?

Demuth spoke the first line of the sorcerer's riddle, "Not even the wisest can find it."

The owl swiveled his head and opened his eyes fully. "Correct. Answer what the wisest cannot, and you shall proceed. Answer not, and I shall feast." He clacked his beak and looked at each of us.

A shiver ran down my back.

"Ask on." Konrad flipped one of his knives into the air and caught it as he tossed the other. He juggled as if unafraid of the owl's threat, but his jaw was tight.

The owl ruffled his feathers again. Was he larger?

I took a step back.

The owl spoke. "Beggars have it. Kings need it. If you eat it, you will die."

What would beggars have that kings needed? "Master owl," I said. "May we speak with each other before answering?"

The owl nodded.

Demuth and I huddled by Konrad. He stopped juggling and slipped one knife back into his belt, but kept a firm grip on the other.

"The riddle has three requirements," I said. "We must find something that fits all three. But what? What do beggars have and kings need? What will kill you if you eat it?"

"Poison," said Demuth. "But kings don't need it."

"Perhaps we should start by identifying truths to the individual statements and then find the common ground," I said. "What do beggars have?"

Demuth's brow furrowed. "Beggars have rags for clothes, empty stomachs, fear of bad weather and wild dogs." She touched a fingertip for each point. "Little shelter, little hope, but sometimes many friends."

"Kings don't need any of those things," I said. "Except for the friends. And kings often have many friends, too. If you ate a friend, would it kill you?"

"Princess Hette!" Demuth looked at me with reproof.

Konrad laughed.

"If we don't look at each option," I said, "then we might miss the answer. Ignoring a possibility will accomplish nothing."

Konrad's laughter changed to a chuckle. "It's nothing." He raised his voice. "Beggars have nothing. Kings need nothing. If you eat nothing, you will die."

"Correct." The owl stared at us with his large yellow eyes. "A barrel of beer weighs seventy-five pounds. What must you add to make it weigh sixty pounds?"

"It's impos—"

"That is not our answer," Konrad interrupted me.

The owl ruffled his feathers, and he was definitely larger. He stood as tall as the belly of Konrad's horse.

"I'm sorry," I whispered. "I won't speak."

"Please speak with us first," said Konrad. "So we can decide together."

"It's still impossible," I said. "You cannot add something to make it lighter. Only remove."

"Then let's start with that," said Konrad. "How can you remove something to make it sixty pounds?"

"The easiest way would be to remove fifteen pounds of beer."

"And how would you remove that beer?"

I narrowed my eyes at Konrad. "Do you already know the answer?"

He only grinned. "And if I do?"

"Then give it."

"No. I know the answer and we will be safe in this riddle. But there may come a time that I can't answer, and it will depend on you, Demuth, or Peter."

It was true. I'd had to face the witch without him. I shuddered. I didn't want to face anyone else without Konrad by my side. But if I did, and needed to answer riddles, I'd need to learn the skill.

I swallowed. "The easiest way to remove the beer would be to open the spigot."

"And what if there wasn't a spigot?"

"Who would build a beer barrel without a spigot? The cooper should have added one from the beginning."

"Oh." Demuth clapped her hand over her mouth.

"Demuth, what is the answer?" I asked.

She glanced at Konrad and he shook his head. They expected me to figure it out.

A spigot would remove the beer. Or a dipper if the barrel lacked a spigot. But the cooper should have added a—Oh. "Konrad, do you add a spigot to remove enough beer to make it weigh sixty pounds?"

"I thought of adding holes," said Konrad. "But adding a spigot is more accurate."

"Correct," intoned the owl. He slowly blinked. "Imagine you are on a one-and-a-half-foot by three-foot ledge in the middle of a canyon a thousand feet long with lava flowing along the bottom. The walls are obsidian slick. A narrow ledge, which you might reach if you jump, runs horizontally above you. Another ledge starts below you and off to your right, but it is only six inches wide. The lower path continues for as far as you can see, but also slants downward toward the lava. You have three stakes, a hammer, a hundred feet of rope, a fine woven piece of silk twenty feet by twenty feet, and a goat. What is the one sure way to escape?"

"How would anyone get on that ledge in the first place?" I whispered. "And why would they have those supplies? It isn't logical."

Konrad raised his brows. "Magic isn't—"

"Logical," I finished for him. "I know. But he hasn't given us nearly enough information." I faced the owl. "May we ask clarifying questions?"

He titled his head. "You may ask."

"How far is the ledge from the top and bottom?"

"Fifty feet from the top. Twenty feet from the bottom."

"Too far to jump," muttered Konrad. "There is the goat. We could follow the path the goat takes. But I've seen goats walk up walls, and if this is obsidian, I'd have difficulty following it. Not a sure path."

"If we anchored the rope to the wall with one of the stakes," said Demuth, "we could lower down to the path."

"But it's not right below the ledge," I said. "We'd need to create some pendulum motion to swing over to it. But I can't remember the formula."

Konrad's mouth pinched. "These were supposed to be riddles, not mathematical equations." He blew out a loud breath. "Owl? How many people are on the ledge?"

The owl blinked. "One."

"One," repeated Konrad. "Let's assume that one is me."

"I'll agree to that." I pressed a hand to my rapidly ticking heart. Even the thought of trying to navigate the lava-filled canyon brought sweat to my forehead. I'd quickly die. Konrad, on the other hand, could possibly make his way out of that trap. He had the skill to leap, flip, and otherwise maneuver the cliff.

"So," said Konrad. "I anchor the rope with one of the stakes, then climb down, and swing over to the lower path."

"And if it's a dead end?" asked Demuth.

"I'll return to the ledge and try the upper path."

"How will you get back to the ledge?" I asked.

He paused, and his brow crinkled. "I'd have to anchor the rope at the start of the lower path, so I could climb back up it if needed."

"How do we even know the rock would hold the stakes?" I asked.

"Why would he give us stakes as supplies if we weren't to use them?" he retorted, his face flushing.

"By that reasoning, we should also use the goat and the silk."

Konrad scratched his head. "True. They are tools for possibilities. And as you said with the first riddle, we should explore the different possibilities. I'd still try the upper path next."

"The crack that runs just out of reach?"

He nodded. "I'm taller than most men. Even if it was still out of reach, I could leap up and catch it."

Demuth tilted her head. "Why not use the stake that you hammered into the wall for the rope earlier as a boost to get up to the crack?"

"Good point," he said. "I'd bring the rope and the other stakes, plus a hammer, and see how far I could go along that upper path."

"Send the goat before you?" I asked.

"Another good point." His brow furrowed deeper. "But what is the silk for?"

What could the silk be used for? My brow furrowed like his. *We already have a long rope and climbing twenty feet of silk won't get a person much further. Silk and science. Where do they connect?*

"My lady," said Konrad. "Will you speak your thoughts so we can share them?"

"It will be rambling."

He nodded.

I took a deep breath. "Silk is strong. It could be used like a rope, but is too short to be of much use in that fashion. Silk is tightly woven. It is used in clothing, bedding and—" a bit of news from the previous year came to memory, "—balloons. The Montgolfier brothers created a huge balloon of silk."

I turned to the owl. "Is there any wind?"

He blinked and grew in size again. He was as tall as the shoulder of Konrad's horse. We'd asked enough questions. We'd have to work with what he gave us.

"There has to be an updraft," I said to Konrad and Demuth. "With the heat of the lava trapped by canyon walls, the air would be pushing upward. We could do like the Montgolfier brothers and capture the hot air with fabric and ride it to the top." I hurried on as the plans traced out in my head. "You'd use the stakes to make holes in the four corners of the silk, four other holes halfway between the corners. A hundred feet of rope would divide into eight segments, which you'd tie to the eight holes. You'd attach the other ends of the ropes to you, throw the fabric out over the ledge and let the wind fill it and carry you upward. It would be difficult, but possible."

Konrad blinked like the owl and then laughed low. "To trust the winds to carry me over lava on a bit of silk. It's possible, but deadly. There is no sure escape. Each has a possibility for error." He turned to Demuth. "What did the owl say, his exact wording?"

She bit her lip. "He said, *Imagine you are on a one-and-a-half-foot by three-foot ledge in the middle of a canyon a thousand feet long with lava flowing along the bottom. The walls are obsidian slick. A narrow ledge, which you might reach if you jump, runs horizontally above you —"* Her hazel eyes widened. "He said *imagine*."

Konrad lifted his brows then laughed. "Demuth, you saw past the distractions, when we were caught in the details. You should answer."

She turned to the owl. "The one sure escape is to stop imagining."

"Correct," said the owl.

Konrad stepped toward the owl. "We've answered your three riddles. We thank you for the pleasant game."

The owl rose in the air. "Fools." His voice reverberated. "The riddles are not yet finished." He hovered over us, blocking the sun. His wings stretched wider than the length of a horse.

The owl would never let us go. He'd give us riddle after riddle until we answered wrong, and then he'd consume us.

Demuth grasped my hand.

Konrad bowed. "We are fools, and we will answer the next riddle."

The owl settled back on the ground about ten feet from us. He was taller than Konrad. "What is my weight?"

"How are we supposed to know?" I whispered.

"We aren't. It isn't wisdom that will get us past the owl." Konrad bent his legs slightly and leaned forward. "I suppose you are *waiting* for an answer." He launched into the air, drawing his sword as he rotated.

The owl spread his wings as Konrad descended.

Konrad slashed, catching the owl across the shoulder. The force of the slash and Konrad's rotation combined. The blade bit. Red stained the white feathers.

The owl lurched backward, one wing hanging.

Konrad landed in a crouch. Feathers clung to his sword. "It will soon be half the weight that it was before." Konrad tossed a dagger.

The owl knocked it aside with his beak, then puffed his feathers. "I am not so easy to kill." The red faded. He pulled his wing back against him, as if uninjured. He dove forward as Konrad raised his sword, knocking Konrad to the ground and pinning him under his talons.

It was only a matter of seconds from Konrad's initial leap to his being pinned to the ground under an owl twice as tall as a man.

Could I get to Konrad's bow? Even if I could, it was unstrung and wrapped in an oil cloth. Konrad depended on his knives and sword to protect us, and only got the bow out for hunting. Could I get one of the knives he threw? I inched sideways.

A kerplop sounded. Peter, in human form, launched himself onto the owl's back, wrapping his arms around the owl's neck. He clung even as the owl flapped, ducked, and jerked.

Konrad groaned as the owl swiveled, and talons bit into him.

I dove for a knife. Where would be the best place to strike? His neck, an eye? I couldn't reach either. The stomach?

I rose and leaped on the owl. The blade deflected. I slid downward, pulling out feathers as I fell. He smelled like pine sap and cut hay. He should have smelled like a bog, like death.

His beak snatched the back of my dress, halting me before my feet reached the ground, then shook me, like a cat shaking a mouse.

My head snapped, and I tried to curl against the motion.

"Let them go!" Peter yelled from the owl's back.

The beak released, and I fell next to Konrad, my legs sprawled across his arm.

The owl stared down at me with large, yellow eyes. "I have one more question. And if you answer well, then the rest may go."

"Let me answer," Konrad gasped.

"No, the woman will." He lifted one foot from Konrad and

pinned me. "Tell me a truth, and I will bite off your head. Tell me a lie, and I will peck out your liver. Which will it be?"

I closed my eyes. He was giving me a choice in my death.

"It's—" Konrad began and cried out in sharp pain. "It's—"

The owl shifted and placed one taloned foot over Konrad's face.

Peter dropped to the ground beside us and grabbed the knife. He slashed as the owl knocked him sideways with his wing. Peter flew across the clearing, struck a tree trunk and slumped in a limp heap.

Demuth, in toad form, hopped toward us.

I had to answer before he killed them all. What would my final truth be? Or my final lie? The truth was I'd soon be dead. Which way did I want to go—decapitation or disembowelment? Decapitation would be quicker. My final truth.

I opened my mouth, and paused. Oh. "Owl, you will peck out my liver."

He laughed, a deep rumbling that shook the trees. He lifted his foot from me and then from Konrad.

Konrad leaped to his feet and placed himself between the owl and me.

The owl laughed louder and shrank in size. He spread his wings and flew into the branches. "She has answered well. You are all free to go. Fare thee well on your journey."

The owl flew away. As he flew, he called back, "Beware the growing madness that would shadow the armored man."

Konrad reached out to me and took my hand. He trembled. "My lady, are you hurt?"

My body ached, but I wasn't cut, nor was anything broken. "No. We should see to Peter."

Peter slumped at the base of the tree. A lump rose from the back of his shorn head. He had changed more. His breath came slow and shallow through actual lips instead of a stretched out mouth. His shoulders were broad, his arms and legs muscular through his rags. His head slumped sideways upon a thick neck. He looked like a blacksmith. A man strong enough to cling to that owl.

Demuth hopped up to us. "What are your injuries?"

"Peter isn't bleeding, but he has a knot on the back of his head," I said. "And I'm uninjured."

"Good," she said. "Then I need you to do exactly what I say until Peter wakes and can change me back."

Konrad stood from where he'd knelt next to Peter, and wavered.

"Konrad, lie down," Demuth commanded. "Now, before you faint. Hette, get the bandages from the saddle bag."

Konrad held his side and blood seeped from between his fingers. How had I missed that? "Konrad," I hissed. "Lie down like she said."

The rest of the day was a blur of cleansing and dressing Konrad's punctured chest wounds—the ones left by the owl's talons—applying a compress to Peter's head, doing whatever else Demuth instructed, and hoping I was doing it right.

Peter awoke near evening. He opened his black-lashed eyes and stared. "Where's the owl?"

"Hette answered the riddle," said Konrad as he lay next to a fire that I'd built. It had taken me more than an hour before it finally took to flame, even with their instruction.

Demuth sat near my side. "What was the answer? I didn't understand."

I glanced down at my hands, scratched from building the fire and raw from cleaning wounds with medicinal alcohol. "The owl said he'd kill me one way for a truth and another way for a lie. I told him he'd kill me the way that was the consequence for a lie. But if he killed me that way, it would make it a truth and invalidate his argument. It was the final riddle."

"No," Konrad said. "Not the final riddle. There was one more. But I don't know what it means."

"Then it is a good thing he didn't ask us to solve it," muttered Peter. "I've had enough riddles to last me every boring winter holed up in the mud." He picked up Demuth. "Thank you for kissing me."

Her toad mouth stretched wider. "I wasn't being any help. Thank you for protecting us."

He shook his head. "I tried. But it seems Princess Hette was the one who saved us."

I scowled. "We each had a part. Now kiss Demuth, and let her take over before I kill someone with my unskilled medical ministrations."

Konrad laughed and winced.

I bit my lip. *If the owl was the first part of the path, the part not even the wisest could find a way through, then heaven help us with what we'll meet next. A place that not even the bravest dare go.*

COURAGE

NOR THE BRAVEST DARE GO

"Hette." Demuth woke me with a gentle shake, her voice tight.

The chill dampness of dawn lay on my face. My head and body ached. I groaned and turned, pulling the blanket over my head.

Demuth shook my shoulder. "Hette. I need your help. Konrad has a fever."

Fever? I threw off the blanket and sat up blearily. "What can I do?"

She handed me a pot. "Get water."

I grabbed the pot and ran, my feet tripping through the undergrowth. We'd camped in the clearing where we'd met the owl. A shallow stream burbled not far from the camp. I dug down in the stream's gravel bottom until the pot had room to sit half submerged on its side. The birds twittered their morning songs. A deer wandered downstream and glanced at me before drinking. The water flowed into the pot unhurriedly. The birds, the deer, the water. None of them cared that we needed to make haste. Konrad had a fever. He'd never been ill, not even after the naiad captured him. Had I not cleaned his wounds well enough? Had the owl's talons introduced infection, or worse, a poison?

The pot finally filled. It sloshed against me as I ran back.

Demuth knelt and blew on the coals from last night's fire, urging them to catch on the new wood.

Konrad lay in a tangle of blankets, moaning. "I'm sorry. I'm sorry. I tried. Please."

I set the pot by Demuth, then knelt at Konrad's side. "It's all right, Konrad." I smoothed his tangled locks away from his face. His brow burned like a brick from the oven and was as dry.

His amber eyes flew open. He looked right past me, his gaze intense and frightened. "Please! Stop!"

"Demuth," I called. "What do I do? How do I help him?"

She looked up from measuring herbs into a cup. The pot sat on a rock in the middle of the fire. "Bathe his brow with a damp cloth. Sing to him."

I dampened a cloth with water from a water skin. I could have used that water to fill the pot, but I hadn't been thinking. I needed to think. I needed to be calm and reasonable, or I couldn't help him. I laid the cloth on his forehead.

Konrad's eyes closed again, and his words dissolved into meaningless moans.

Sing? I never sang.

Konrad jerked, tossing aside his blanket. I tried to tuck it back around him, but he struggled.

Sing?

I reached for memories of half-listened-to songs at long banquets. A simple song whispered—one a servant woman sang to her baby at the edge of the banquet hall. Each night she served us, then while we dined, she hushed her baby with the same lullaby.

I began to sing. My voice came hesitant and faint.

Hush, little prince, go to sleep;
Still are the birds and the sheep.
Garden and meadow are still;

Honeybee ceases her trill.

The notes broke on my dry throat. But I sang.

Moonlight with silvery beam
Pours on the window her gleam.
Sleep bathed in silvery light;
Hush, little prince, now sleep tight.
Sleep tight. Sleep tight.

Konrad stilled, only his head flinching back and forth. I repeated the verses as I tucked the blankets back around him and bathed his brow.

Demuth knelt next to me, holding a bowl with a white paste. "Bring the hot water."

Flames leapt around the pot. It steamed, and small bubbles rose to the surface. I poked at the wood with a stick, tumbling it to one side, then wrapped my hands in my skirt and leaned over to grab the pot. A stray flame caught the skirt fabric. I beat it out and tried again.

By the time I'd managed to remove the pot from the fire without catching flame or searing myself with boiling water, Demuth had unwrapped Konrad's torso. The deep puncture wounds were swollen and crusted in a yellowish pus. Red lines streaked outward over pale skin.

The water sloshed against me as my hands trembled. The heat seeped through the fabric and burned my legs. I ignored the pain.

I hadn't sanitized Konrad's wounds well enough.

"The water, please." Demuth's voice was calm, but the words came quickly.

I set the pot in the grass. It sizzled.

Demuth dipped the point of a small knife in the boiling water, then poured alcohol over it. "I'll need to lance the wounds and drain the infection." She held the knife over a pus-swollen puncture under his left arm. After a long breath, she sliced into it.

Konrad exploded. He flung his arms, knocking Demuth to the side, and leaped to his feet. He stumbled two steps, tripped over a rock, and fell face forward.

Demuth and I rushed to his sides, catching him before he hit the ground. He was heavier than he looked. We lowered him to the ground and rolled him on his back.

Demuth's jaw hardened. "Hette, can you hold him while I lance the infections?"

Konrad wasn't muscular like our guards. He was lean-muscled and lanky. All height. Surely I could hold him down. I sat sideways on his legs and placed my hands on his shoulders. His fever pressed like fire against my hands.

He flinched and moaned, but the outburst seemed to have drained him.

Demuth cleaned the knife again and sliced into the same wound.

Konrad leaped to his feet, and I tumbled to the grass. I could no more hold him down than a cat sitting in my lap could keep me from standing. He wavered on his feet, his eyes wide and unseeing.

"Konrad, please. We are trying to help you." I laid a hand on his shoulder.

He flinched.

"Please lie down," said Demuth.

He stood, panting and trembling, his face flushed.

Peter's voice came from a nearby tree. "I could hold him."

I bit my lip. Peter, as a man, was strong. He could hold Konrad still. But if Demuth kissed him then she couldn't tend to Konrad's wounds. I couldn't lance them. I didn't know how deep to cut, or what to cut, or how to drain them. Konrad needed both Demuth and Peter.

Blood tasted salty in my mouth. I'd bitten too hard on my lip.

But the salty sting would be better than what I had to do. "Peter." I closed my eyes. I had to do this. "Peter, I will kiss you so you can help Demuth."

Demuth opened her mouth, and words seemed perched in her silence. She closed it and nodded.

Peter looked between her and me and swallowed, his neck swelling with the movement. "Just this once."

"Just this once," I said. "I don't want to do this any more than you."

He laughed, and shuffled back half a hop as I knelt next to him. He was as afraid as I was. Was I so hideous? Or had he developed a loyalty to Demuth?

I lifted him so he was inches from my face. His bulbous yellow eyes stared at me, surrounded by warty skin. His wide line of a mouth pinched shut. He was bulgy, ugly, and poisonous. All I needed to do was give a quick, simple kiss. I leaned forward and touched my lips to his warty skin.

The world imploded. It wasn't like fainting where everything narrowed and turned black. More like riding at a gallop through fog. Air rushed in, in a grey dampness, folding over every part of me and sinking inward. As quickly as the fog came, it dispersed. My body was contorted into a strange shape, my legs and arms tucked against my body. Sounds came louder, the gurgle of the stream, the pop of the fire. Peter and Demuth towered over me. Their skin was a strange color, but the concern on their faces was clear.

"I'm fine," I said, ignoring the wrongness of my toad body. "Help Konrad."

Peter stood in front of Konrad and took him by the arms. Whereas Konrad was taller than Peter by a full head, Peter was wider and built like a small ox. "Lie down." Peter firmly pushed Konrad to kneel and then lie on his back.

Konrad bellowed and struggled as Demuth lanced and washed

out each chest wound, but Peter held him tightly, anchoring each arm and leg to the ground. Through the morning, Demuth cleaned each puncture, applied salve, and, as the pus gathered, drained, cleaned, and applied salve again. Even after she gave Konrad a settling tea, he still struggled against each cleaning. And each time Peter held him.

I watched. There wasn't anything else I could do. I'd cleaned his wounds wrong the previous day. Konrad's life lay in the balance because of my incompetence. A croaking cry ripped from my throat.

Konrad flinched as he lay flushed and panting after yet another cleaning.

"Hette." Demuth knelt next to me. "Will you sing again for him?"

"I wasn't good, even with my human voice," I croaked, my throat ballooning. "I'll cause him more harm than good with a toad voice."

She stroked the top of my head. "Will you try?"

"I will try. But if he becomes worse at all, I'll climb down a hole and hide my tears there." I began the lullaby.

Hush, little prince, go to sleep;
Still are the birds and the sheep.

Konrad turned his head toward me, and though his eyes were closed, his jaw relaxed.

When I'd sung the whole song three times, I tried another, one that Konrad had sung as we'd entered the thorn maze.

Led by sextant and book.
Timed by tortoise and hare.
Through darkness and mist,
we travel valiant and fair.

O'er bog and the fen.
Past naiad's still lake.
Price paid to the witch.
Lady's gift for Fool's sake.

My voice caught in my throat. I swallowed, and my toad eyes pulled inward with the motion. The witch's price had been high, but not too high for Konrad's life. Demuth would save him this time. I blinked away the tightness in my throat and continued to sing.

Onward, onward, we go,
our journey together is knit.
Bearing armor of courage
and daggers of wit.

The corners of Konrad's mouth twitched. He whispered, "daggers of wit." After that, he slept, even through the next cleaning of his wounds.

The day heated to the drowsiness of afternoon. Flies droned. My stomach rumbled. And before I knew it, I'd snapped one of them. I blinked and almost spat it out, but the fly strangely satisfied me. Almost as though it were a hearty slice of bread with butter.

The change to toad had changed my taste as well as my shape. An unexpected benefit. Perhaps the toad curse was kinder than the heart curse, or at least less emotionally wrenching. I'd survive a day as a toad, even if it wasn't comfortable.

I caught more flies while keeping an eye on Konrad. For the moment, he slept quietly.

Peter and Demuth knelt by the fire preparing other food. Demuth guided Peter as he chopped meat and mushrooms, then showed him how to sauté them in fat.

Peter leaned over the pan. "The witch liked to cook with toadstools. They never smelled this good. Toadstools are only good for sitting on."

Demuth chuckled. "Not that you could sit on one now."

"I could," he said. "I could sit on ten at once and have no trouble."

"Don't sit on the ones in the frying pan. That would be trouble."

He grinned. "What would you do if I did?"

I tried to tilt my head to the side. The conversation should have been awkward, but it somehow seemed to flow.

"I wouldn't have to do anything," said Demuth. "The fire would have punished you enough."

"And then I'd be—you'd have—" he scrunched up his face. "You'd have toad and toadstool fry." He grimaced. "That wasn't very funny, was it?"

I snorted, which came out as a sneezish croak.

Demuth laughed. "I liked it."

"It would have worked better if I was a toad when I said it."

She laid her hand on his. "I'm glad you're not."

Peter swallowed, his thick neck expanding with the motion. "We need more water. I'll get it." He leaped away with a pot.

Demuth moved the frying pan to the side of the fire, checked on Konrad, and came to sit next to me. "Hette, do you think—" she left the question unfinished.

Did she want me to kiss Peter more often so they could be human together? Was that why she was hesitating? Better to avoid that conversation. I hopped onto her knee. "Are you asking about his sense of humor? Because he's not funny."

She barked a short laugh. "Hette, you're one to talk. You don't even find Konrad funny." She let out a huff of air. "Do you think the sorcerer will break Peter's curse? I mean, after he breaks the curse on Konrad and restores your heart. After that?"

"I don't know."

"Me neither." She brushed her finger over my back. "And I don't know if I should even let myself hope for it."

"Hope for what?"

"That maybe he and I—" She lifted me from her knee and placed me back on the tree root. "It's nothing." She went back to the mushrooms and stirred them with a vigorous scrape of spoon on pan.

A fly buzzed around me as my thoughts buzzed within. *She likes him? Huh. Peter is good and kind, but a romantic interest? He's childish, awkward, ill formed, and a toad most of the time. He's—*

Peter bounded into the clearing with a pot of water and a large bundle of purple lupine. He set the pot down in the grass and held out the bouquet.

She blushed as she took the flowers. "They're beautiful, thank you."

He grinned and leaned forward, his lips slightly puckered.

She ducked her head. "Dinner's ready. We should eat before we have to change Konrad's bandages again."

They knelt side by side as they ate, a small space between them, which grew smaller as Peter scooted closer.

Demuth's face flushed, and a smile crept across it. She set her left hand on the ground between them.

Peter swapped his fork to his left hand and set his right hand on hers. His grin grew almost as wide as when he was a toad.

And then he fumbled his fork, dropping it on his plate, and scattered his food. "Ack!" He dove for the fork and tumbled the plate from his lap. He burst into laughter. "Maybe I shouldn't try to hold your hand while we eat." He raised his brows. "Afterward?"

She laughed, even as her blush reached her ears. "Yes. I'd like that."

They do like each other, I thought. *Is this what Konrad meant when he spoke of love? Sacrifice, caring, and kindness?* I swallowed a lump in my throat. *Why didn't the witch turn the sorcerer to a toad instead of Peter? I could turn the sorcerer if he tried to kiss me. If he kissed me, he'd become a toad. A sorcerer toad.* I chuckled, and it came out in a low croaking laugh.

"Hette?" Demuth came to my side. "I'm sorry. Are you hungry?"

Peter knelt next to her. "I'll change you back now. If you need me again, then—" he trailed off.

If this was their only time together, I'd not shorten it. "I won't kiss you again, unless I absolutely have to."

"You mean?" asked Demuth.

"I mean, I'm not kissing him again until Konrad is better and there's no possibility that you need Peter's strength to help you tend to Konrad."

"That may be days. What will you eat?"

"I know," I said. "And I won't kiss Peter each day for days. I can —eat—flies." I stumbled on the words. "They really aren't that bad."

Peter laid a finger on my head. "Thank you," he whispered.

He grinned at Demuth then turned back to me. "Earthworms are especially filling, if you'd like me to find you some."

He did, and they were better than flies.

The day passed into the evening. Konrad woke for a short time, and though he was not coherent, he drank a little broth.

"How is he doing?" I asked as Demuth checked each of his wounds.

"They are less inflamed, and the red streaks radiating out from them have almost disappeared. I think we've pulled the infections back to the puncture sites. Now we have to kill it there."

I hopped closer. "How long?"

"Another day, maybe two. Even then, he'll be very weak. We'll have to be careful that they don't reinfect."

"But he will get better?"

Demuth paused bandaging Konrad. "He'll get better. He's survived much worse. He's not allowed to die before his thirty-fifth birthday."

I shuddered. For a time I'd forgotten the cursed limit on his life. "He'll live much longer than thirty-five."

Demuth nodded. "If we have anything to do about it, he will." She finished bandaging him and left to lay out her bedroll.

I hopped over next to him. "Konrad, I remember the first time I saw you. You juggled a fork, a knife, and a pot of ink. You dropped the ink and scooped it up just before it hit the floor. No matter how difficult your acrobatics, or how impossible the save, you always did it."

I settled near his ear. "I was jealous of you. You always said what you wanted. I wanted that freedom, but royalty can never be unguarded. We have to wall our hearts behind dictates and commands. We have to think thrice over our words before we speak. I wanted what you had, and because I couldn't have it, I despised you."

I swallowed back a cry. "I'm sorry. I was wrong. You paid for your honesty in daily mocking. The truth that you told was rarely listened to. I could command what I wanted. Your only power was in suggestion, helping people see, if they would but look. I refused for years to look. And now I see. I want to be the queen you think I can be. I want to be a good ruler, both just and—kind. And I need you there beside me. I can't do this alone."

The next day was better. Konrad tossed and moaned less. Peter had little trouble holding him when Demuth dabbed an infection-killing ointment in the wounds. I sang for Konrad, the same two songs. Peter and Demuth took turns, but it seemed my untrained voice was more calming than either Peter's deep, vibrating tones or Demuth's clear, bell-like ones. Demuth taught me new songs. I sang and I talked and I sat in silence.

As evening drew into night again and the air grew colder, my body grew slower, as did my thoughts. The previous evening I'd rambled. I would not do so again. I'd been too unguarded. Instead I would watch Konrad until the cold forced me to sleep.

Firelight flickered across Konrad's pale face, over a scraggly beard, and danced off beads of sweat. *Sweat? Didn't Demuth say something about sweat?* "Demuth," I croaked. "Come here."

She knelt at his side and placed a hand to his forehead. "The fever is broken. He will begin to improve now."

Peter wrapped his arm around Demuth's shoulders. "I'll keep watch over him tonight. Sleep."

She nodded and wrapped up in a blanket. Soon her deep breathing sounded beside Konrad's rapid breath. Peter sat by the fire, his brow furrowed, his hand resting on Demuth's blanketed shoulder.

Konrad stirred and opened his eyes.

"Konrad," I whispered. "We are here. Rest."

He turned his head toward me, and his sleepy eyes widened. "Did you?"

"I kissed Peter so he could help you."

His face blanched. "I'm sorry."

"Don't be. It was the only reasonable choice."

"Thank you. I'll—"

"You'll rest so you can heal."

He smiled. "Thrice you've paid for my life."

"Once."

"Thrice. Hair, memories, and now toad form."

"It's what friends do."

"It is." His eyes closed, and his breathing evened into the deep rhythm of sleep.

The next morning, Peter offered to turn me back into a human.

"Peter," I said. "Do you know how to use any weapons?"

His brows rose.

I continued, voicing the thoughts that had rambled through my dreams. "Konrad is injured. I am the smallest one of our party and have never been trained in weapons. We need to protect Demuth so she can tend to any injuries we sustain. That leaves you as our most likely warrior. You are strong and fast. I will remain a toad while you practice."

He squared his shoulders. "I will give my best to defend each of you."

We rested two more days in the clearing where we'd met the owl. Peter filled the time with sword practice. When Konrad was awake, he gave instructions, but mostly he slept.

On the morning of the fifth day after the attack, Konrad's indistinct voice woke me. The early morning sun hadn't yet reached my spot on a tree root and my body was sluggish, but Konrad was speaking and no one else was answering. Had he fallen back into his fever?

I hopped toward the sound, past Demuth sleeping on the ground, then past Peter slumped over and snoring by the cold fire. They'd taken turns keeping watch at night, but sleep had claimed them both. I'd wake them if need be. I hoped Konrad was still healthy, or as healthy as a man could be five days after surviving an attack and infected wounds.

As I hopped closer, his voice clarified into words. "Can't you just be happy with what you have?" He knelt by the stream, shaving off the bristly start of a beard. "Yes, it's painful and a bit pathetic. But would you have it any other way?"

He tilted his head as if listening.

"True. There are many, many things you'd change if you could. But if you'd had your way, you'd never have had this chance to know her." He sighed. "You always knew she was clever, with a bladed courage, and beautiful. But what you knew pales compared to what you know now."

I stopped hopping. Who was he talking about?

He scraped the shaving blade along his bristly chin. "She's grown so much. I can't wait to see her as queen."

Oh. I swallowed. *That's who.* I hopped backwards. This wasn't a place for me to listen.

He continued. "Not that I have much chance to see that. It's always been my curse to die."

I froze. *He's not going to die!*

His face contorted from grimace to grin. "Heh, it's not as though I want to die. I don't. But what's important is that we get Hette's heart back, so she can be free. You understand, don't you? We'll not do anything to jeopardize that. No matter how much it hurts. Agreed?"

It was not agreed. We'd not continue our journey until he was healed.

He nodded at his reflection in the water. "Good. Besides, a month ago, who would have thought a princess would be calling a fool a friend? Maybe someday she'll find someone even closer than a friend. Maybe—"

A fly buzzed by. Instinctively I snapped it and made a chirping trill.

Konrad jerked and stared at me. His shaving blade slipped. A red line of blood beaded along his neck.

"Konrad!" I hopped to him. "Be careful!"

His face brightened to beet red. "How long were you listening?" The blood ran down his neck in a thin rivulet.

"Demuth!" I shouted. "Konrad's hurt."

As Demuth tended to a protesting Konrad, who insisted it was just a scratch, I settled in the sunlight on the far side of the clearing. I was a bit annoyed by Konrad's words at the stream and more than a bit embarrassed that I had been caught listening.

When the sun reached noon heat, he came and crouched by where I sat on a tree root. He coughed a few times, and his face tinged red.

Hopefully he wasn't going to bring up what he'd been saying that morning. It was awkward enough to hear it once. He thought me clever, with a bladed courage, and *beautiful*?

"Hette," he said. "We should continue on the sorcerer's path today."

It would have been better if he'd brought up the other topic. I stood on my four legs and puffed, the way Peter had once done to me. "No. You are not yet healed."

He shook his head. "I doubt the sorcerer gave us extra food. We've used up five days of it. We need to go."

"You've hunted for us before," I retorted. "You can replenish our supplies, if need be, once you are healed."

"Hette." His face pinched. "I already spoke with Demuth. It is time."

Demuth knelt by the fire, packing her healer's pouch. She was also preparing to go. She'd been preparing all day and I hadn't noticed.

"Demuth," I said. "He's not ready yet. I heard him this morning, talking about going no matter how much it hurt. He's not ready."

She paused wrapping washed bandages. "He's healed enough to travel, and he is right, we need to continue."

"And if I order you not to?"

"We'll continue anyway," said Konrad.

"Peter could hold you down."

"He could, but my struggles against him would be worse on my wounds than traveling."

Demuth knelt by me. "He's well enough. Will you trust me?"

I swallowed a croaking cry. Why did they want to continue when he wasn't ready?

I glared at Konrad. "You'll be careful?"

"Have I ever not been?"

"Often."

He laughed. "True. But I haven't died yet." He looked around. "What was it the owl said, the last riddle?"

Demuth stroked my head as she answered Konrad. "Beware the growing madness that would shadow the armored man."

"That still doesn't make sense," Konrad said. "Perhaps it will when we face it. For now we must go where not even the bravest dare go. But where is the start of that path?"

"If we had the book," I said.

"The book would lead us in a path that even the bravest would shudder to follow."

Peter lowered the sword from a practice swing. "A gravel path starts behind an oak tree that way." He pointed north.

"How did you know?" I asked.

He shrugged. "I thought it would be good to look for a path while Konrad recovered."

"Then," said Konrad, "that is the way we will start. But first, Peter, please turn Hette back to human."

We followed the path all afternoon. The way was fairly level, the trees spaced enough to allow plenty of sun, and the small animals of the forest were abundant and unafraid.

Konrad rode. Demuth and I walked beside the other horse. Its whole back was covered with bags and pouches, food for us, grain for the horses, ropes, fur blankets that would be too warm for summer nights, and more. The sorcerer had given us enough supplies that neither horse should have been rideable, but Demuth and I rearranged everything until there was space for Konrad to ride.

"It's your turn," Konrad said, swinging his leg over the saddle so that he sat sideways and half off.

"We enjoy walking." I said.

"Let me join you. I grow weary of riding."

"Then we can stop to rest."

He swung his leg back astride the saddle. "You win this time." He looked ahead. "The Black Forest is beautiful, when—"

"When it isn't trying to kill us," I finished.

"True." He laughed. "Though I was thinking, when we aren't following a book-bound kobold set on making our lives miserable."

"Peter is a much better path finder." I smiled as Peter puffed out his chest in Demuth's pocket.

Toward evening, Peter croaked a warning. "Something dangerous is ahead."

Konrad slipped a readied bow from its sling and pulled an arrow from the quiver on his back. I grasped the throwing knife he'd given me. I couldn't throw it, but I could stab. Demuth swapped places with Peter. And after I'd put Demuth in my pocket, Peter took the sword from Konrad. *We'd be ready this time.*

The trees ended in a ragged, bouldered cliff. Two paths wound down its face. The one that led south was wide and paved with flagstones. The clear path ended in a meadow at the base of the cliff. The second path led north. It crabbed its way between boulders, over a log spanning a section of nothingness, and ended in a cave several hundred paces from us.

"Well," said Konrad. "If the brave dare not take the second path, then it says little for the bravery of man. We've traversed worse."

"Have you?" a voice boomed. A man in silver-plated armor rode from the cave. His steed was the same silver color, and sunlight glinted off them like a mirror. "Have you defeated the silver knight in single combat? Have you faced the nightmares of the cave, nightmares that send the strongest of men into panic?"

He must be the armored man from the owl's warning. I gripped my knife. *We are not ready. We won't be ready until Konrad has fully healed and Peter has learned more swordsmanship. Maybe not even then. We should return to someplace safe and build our strength and—*

"Sounds about right." Konrad held his bow with an arrow nocked but not drawn. "Massive physical and mental battles. You'd think the person who made the path would be more creative."

"You discount my power?" the silver knight roared.

"No. I believe it takes great skill and resolve to face you and the cave."

The knight laughed. "Skill and resolve? It takes bravery to face me. Bravery that none of you have."

"And who would be brave enough?"

"A man who faces death and laughs."

"Done that. Daily."

The knight kicked his steed and rode between two boulders, closer to us. "You have not the bravery to face me."

"Do you have the courage to face me?"

"How dare you! I'll strike you down!" He urged his horse onto a narrow bridge made from a log.

Konrad lifted his bow. "If you had so much courage then you would face me on equal ground. Both of us unarmored."

The knight had reached the other side of the bridge and was halfway to us. "This is not my test, but yours."

"So, you get to kill all who pass this way in unequal combat. Where is your bravery?"

He drew closer, blinding us with his mirror-bright light. "I fought once in such combat and won. I've proven my worth to the master."

"And what was your reward?"

The knight paused and threw his gantlet to the ground, revealing a leather-gloved hand. "To be champion until another defeats me. And none have."

Konrad drew the bow. "Perhaps we will take the other path. You seem more a prisoner than a victor."

The knight raised a mace. "And you are a babbling coward. Only cowards would consider the other path."

"And you are not a coward?"

"I'll show you my worth!" He swung his mace and charged.

Konrad let the arrow fly. It struck the gap in armor below the knight's raised arm. "Quickly," he urged. "Down the other path."

The knight plucked the arrow out. Red stained its tip.

I stepped next to Konrad's horse. "You can't face him alone."

"Peter, grab her and go!" Konrad released another arrow. It glanced off the helmet.

Peter grabbed me and leaped onto the paved path. He leaped again. The air rushed, tearing Konrad's name from my open mouth. Again and again Peter leaped, taking us further down the paved path. Halfway down the cliff, he stopped and set me on the ground. Ragged breaths tore from him as he bent double.

I pushed around him and headed up the path. If Konrad still lived, I'd face the knight with him.

Horse hooves pounded.

I raised my knife.

Konrad rounded the corner of the path with our other horse galloping behind him. He pulled on the reins, and his horse slowed. His face was pale.

"Are you hurt? Where is the knight?" I asked.

A cruel laugh sounded from above. "Cowards. Fools. You'll live with your disgrace until your grave."

Konrad glanced up. "He won't follow us. We've taken the *coward's* path. And we will live beyond today because of it."

I sat hard on the ground. "I thought you would die. Don't do that again."

He dismounted. "And next time I say *go*, go."

"I didn't want to leave you."

He sat on the path and leaned against me, trembling. "Do you trust me?"

"I trust you to protect me, but not yourself."

He sighed. "I needed to guard your escape, but I stayed no longer. I knew he wouldn't follow when he said only a coward would take this path. We've taken the path that the bravest dare not go."

"You mean, this is the correct path?"

He laughed. "A riddle to trick us into death. A riddle based in pride and glory, and the unrefusable gauntlet. It seems the silver knight once took that challenge and won his imprisonment to face all others who came after. That would be my fate if I beat him. His path was only a dead end."

Demuth crawled from my pocket. "Figuratively and literally."

Peter panted beside us. Konrad clapped him on the back. "Thank you, my friend."

"So," I asked, still trying to understand. "The easier path is the right one?"

"This time, yes."

I sagged backward and leaned on my elbows. "Thank goodness for that. Let's get to the bottom of this cliff and find a place to camp. There Demuth will check your wounds."

"I'm unhurt," he protested.

"You were hurt before you fought."

We made camp under a rowan tree at the base of the cliff. The scabbing on two of Konrad's punctures had pulled loose.

Demuth sighed in relief and opened her medical bag. "It's not as bad as I thought it might be. Hette, please get the extra bandages. They're in Konrad's bag now."

I bit my lip as I rummaged through Konrad's bag. The last time I'd looked through his things, I'd opened the book and set us on a dangerous path. What would have been different if I'd trusted Konrad?

My hands closed over a roll of bandages. *Finally.* I pulled them out. They were wrapped around a small book. I shivered. *Another book.*

"Hette," Demuth said. "Did you find them?"

I ran to where she dabbed salve on Konrad's opened punctures. "Here," I said, holding out the bandages. "I'm sorry, Konrad. I'll put the book back. I didn't mean to pull it out."

He glanced at Demuth with a raised brow. "Did you wrap the bandages around it on purpose?"

Her mouth quirked. "You've told her the stories. I thought you'd want to show her the drawings."

"Why would she want that?" he asked.

I looked at the little book in my hands. "It's not magical, is it?"

"No." He laughed tightly. "Not at all. It's just sketches that Erasmus made. You can look."

"It won't change our path?"

"It's safe," said Demuth. "I think you'll like them."

"I want to see, even if you don't," croaked Peter from the ground.

I sat on the ground next to Peter, and with a held breath opened to the first page.

A young face stared at us with wide-eyed delight, as if he was as surprised to see me as I was him. Ink formed the lines, and watercolors filled in the shades of fair skin, raven hair and grey eyes rimmed with black. On the next page, he was older and more serious. One brow rose as if in question.

The same face hung amongst the family portraits. He *was* my great uncle. I'd accepted it, but it stung to see him. How did he become the sorcerer? Their faces were so different: one hard and proud, the other kind and curious.

I flipped the pages.

Other faces joined him: a woman with a gentle smile, babies, children; and then, toward the back after a long absence, my great uncle once more. This time his hair was almost white and his face cold with a hint of sorrow. It was the sorcerer's face. Beneath the drawing, shaky words declared, "Johannes, my friend, I promise I will find you."

My eyes stung. *Johannes is my enemy. But, maybe, the sorcerer still has good in him. We have to find his heart to truly see. And to do so, we have to finish the path.* I glanced back up the cliff we'd descended. We'd taken the path the bravest dared not go, and until we reached a stone horse we were safe—I hoped.

TEETH

SACRIFICE TEETH THAT A STONE HORSE
MIGHT EAT

MORNING CAME QUICKLY and the paved path continued through the forest. Konrad insisted on walking. I countered with a slow pace. He laughed and matched my pace.

Hours passed to the clopping rhythm of the two horses and the lighter tread of our boots. The easy path, sunshine, and birdsong lulled me. It seemed to lull all of us. Peter dozed in Demuth's pocket. Demuth had a far-off look. Even Konrad walked in silence, though he'd long since replaced my slow pace with a mile-eating long stride.

"Konrad," I said. "I'm worried about this path. It seems too safe. What do you think?"

"Mostly nonsense."

I stopped and turned. "What?"

"You asked what I think? Mostly nonsense, with a bit of hopeful wishing mixed in."

"Wishful thinking won't keep us safe. We need to be aware."

He flicked a knife from his belt. It skewered a falling leaf against an oak trunk. "I am aware." He retrieved the quivering blade from the trunk. "But I also won't spend my energy on worrying when I should be spending it on healing."

"Do you need to rest?" I asked. "You shouldn't have been walking this long."

Konrad held up his hand and laughed. "This pleasant walk is good for healing, and not nearly as jostling on my wounds. But do you know what is one of the best balms for healing?"

I shook my head.

"Laughter."

"Is that your answer to everything?"

He pulled out three knives and began to juggle them. "Laughter is like the rhythm that keeps these blades in a smooth cycle. Without that rhythm I'd slice my hand, or worse."

"So you laugh, instead of worry?"

"Not instead, but beside it. And beside despair, anger, and any number of soul-slicing emotions. I still have to juggle those emotions, but laughter keeps me from being injured by them."

"You feel all those other emotions?"

He added a fourth knife to the spinning circle. "Daily."

"And what happens when those emotions become too much or too many?"

He added his last two knives, tossing and catching them as he walked along. "Then I get cut, and I try to be more careful the next time." He caught each knife and slipped them back into his belt.

"How did you get to be so wise?"

He lightly tugged the belled cap that I still wore over the short bristles of my growing hair. It jangled. "By being a fool."

"And I suppose you were born with this skill?"

"No. I'll teach you now; the only cost is a laugh a day."

I raised an eyebrow. "Even if I wanted to, I do not laugh on command."

"I'll accept late payment. You already used one of the secrets of the fool when we faced the owl's riddles. You asked, 'If you ate a friend, would it kill you?'"

I grimaced.

The back of Konrad's hand brushed against mine. "It was a good question. A fool must never ignore a possibility, no matter how ridiculous it seems."

I glanced at Demuth, and whispered, "So the possibility that Demuth is falling in love with a toad?"

"That is not as ridiculous as you'd think," he whispered back. "Peter is a good man."

"I know. I wish—"

"We'll find a way for them, too."

Demuth glanced at us, as if realizing we spoke of them.

I coughed and pushed one of the cap's bells from my face. "Lesson two?"

"Watch for distracting information and use it to your advantage. The owl distracted us with many details about the lava trap and the tools we had. But Demuth noticed the wording that showed the sure escape. Semantics, and the multiple meanings of a word, are oft-used tools in foolery. For example, 'What loses its head in the morning and gets it back at night?'"

I scratched my scalp beneath the belled cap. I'd picked up one of Konrad's mannerisms. "A wraith or other undead?"

"Think semantics. Is there another way to look at it?"

"Dandelion? It loses its seed head to the wind and then grows a new one."

He nodded. "You are expanding your thinking."

"But it's not right?"

"Where is your head at night?"

"On my shoulders."

"Thankfully, yes. And where else?"

"In dreams."

"And?"

I grimaced again. "On the hard ground."

"And when you were in the palace?"

My thoughts drifted to soft mattresses, down comforters, and pillows—clean sheets smooth against my skin and a plump pillow cradling my head. Head, pillow, night. I snorted. "When I lie down, my pillow gains a head, and when I rise, it loses it."

"Well noticed."

We walked again in silence. The path turned onto a low stone bridge spanning a burbling stream. Beyond it, the forest turned into an orchard. Cherries hung in bright clusters from each branch.

Demuth glanced upward. "We should stop to eat, and fresh fruit will be good to add to our meal." She reached for a cluster.

"Wait, Demuth!" Konrad caught her hand.

"They're not poisonous. These are common cherries."

"But they may be magical," Konrad said. "Peter, are they safe?"

Peter poked his head from Demuth's pocket. After a moment he gave a short croak. "They aren't magical, but he is."

"Who?" I looked along the path and around at the trees, but couldn't see anyone.

"He's up in the tree," said Peter. "Over on the right. See his red leggings."

At the far end of the orchard, bright red leggings showed along the lower branches of a tree. Singing carried faintly back to us.

"Is he safe?" I asked.

"He feels harmless."

"Good, because the path takes us past him."

Demuth and Peter swapped places, and the two men walked down the path, while I trailed behind, guiding the horses and carrying Demuth in my pocket.

The singing became clearer. Bits of leaves and twigs fell from the tree.

A cherry a gold piece,
a bushel a copper.
An orchard for a song.

I am the keeper,
The mud and branch leaper.
No bird will stay too long.

"He sounds insane," I murmured.

"Crazy as a loon," Peter said.

The red leggings leaped down. A small man dressed all in red and with a cowled cap landed in front of us. He held large shears. "Crazy, you said? You be right. I'm crazy about cherries. But it be a difficult job to be evening their shadows."

"Why do you want to even their shadows?" asked Peter.

"Why, to watch out for thieving crows and robber robins. My master don't like his fruit being stolen." He blanched. "He's fae cold about theft. If the trees' shadows be all even, then I'll see the birds."

I shuddered. He was another of the sorcerer's servants. What test would we have to pass with him?

"But won't the shadows change as the sun moves?" asked Peter.

He stomped his foot. "So that's how they are doing it. Just waiting for the shadows to move. But I'll catch them. I'll trim the trees so I can see their shadow no matter what way the sun shines."

Would we have to help him solve his insane problem? Trimming the trees so he could see the bird's shadows was as challenging a riddle as any the owl gave. Maybe we could give a different solution. "Could you get a dog to bark at them?" I asked.

"No, no." He shook his head. "I must be evening the shadows. That is the only way. I'm crazy about cherries, you know."

"Can we help you?" Demuth said from my pocket.

He peered at us and smiled. "A talking toad. Toads don't eat cherries. Welcome, welcome. I thank you for your offer, but you have no hands, and I only have one shears. Thank you. Now I must be back to evening the shadows." He climbed back into the tree and began to sing as the shears snipped.

"We'll leave him and his cherries alone," Konrad said.

"Don't we have to help him?" I asked.

"Sometimes the best help is to accept someone's refusal for help."

"I don't understand."

He shrugged. "Will you trust me on this?"

I nodded, and we followed the path out the other side of the orchard. Maybe that test was to leave him to his insanity. Maybe.

Five days we traveled the paved path from early morning until the last of the evening died to darkness. We met no one else. Each night, by the flickering fire, Demuth checked Konrad's wounds until she proclaimed them healed, with no chance of reinfection.

Each day, Konrad taught me more about being a fool, from unraveling riddles, to looking beyond the expected, to finding the connecting points in contradictions.

"Life is a paradox," Konrad said, as we walked side by side along the tree-shaded path. "The scientists try to order each thing into categories, and thus to define all with sweeping generalizations. *All cats have long tails, soft fur, and distrust water.* Except when they don't. Some cats have no tails, others have no fur, and still others love swimming. The very categories meant to help us understand, limit us from seeing what doesn't fit."

"But without taxonomy, everything would be a confusion," I retorted. "It gives a framework."

He tilted his head. "True, and much good has come of that framework. But much blindness as well."

"How do you organize life?" I asked.

"By seeing individual creatures, things, and most of all, people, as uniquely themselves. That a man or woman can be many things at once. Even conflicting things. A gentle-natured man can be a butcher. A scholar can have a violent temper."

"Or the fool can be wise."

He laughed. "Seeing paradoxes and allowing that something may be many things at once is one key to wisdom."

"Are there others?"

"Many. When we faced the owl, you found safety in creating an incompatible statement. You gave an answer to his death riddle that invalidated both possibilities. As court fool, I've created incompatible statements to guide the king into seeing a better path than the one he pursued."

"When is one time you did this?" I asked.

He grimaced. "Do you remember when the king was angered by a cousin who plotted against him? He proclaimed that cousins could not be trusted, and all the cousins in the kingdom would be stripped of their titles and ranks.

"I stood beside the scribe who wrote down the edict and as he drew to the end, I said, 'Be sure to add that King Ludewig is stripped of his title and rank.'

"The king bellowed at me, but I explained, 'All cousins, as you have proclaimed, and if your cousin is cousin to you, then you are cousin to him.'

"The king laughed, and ordered the edict to be torn up, and instead punished only the one man who'd committed treason."

I did remember. Though I hadn't realized what he was doing at the time. I'd thought him the silly fool who'd made my father laugh and unknowingly had distracted him from a foolish edict. But Konrad had much more thought behind it.

"I see," I said. We walked in thoughtful silence. "Will you give me another riddle? I'm getting better at unraveling them."

He rested his chin on his fingers, then his amber eyes lit. "I'll give you three. Demuth, you know these, so no hints."

"I'll not tell." Her voice filled with delight.

"What grows larger the more you take away?" Konrad asked.

It sounded like an impossibility. But so did adding something to a barrel to make it lighter. I needed to look at it differently. What grew larger the more you took away? I walked musing as Konrad, Demuth, and Peter talked about other things. If you took away food, hunger would grow. Took away money in taxes, a serf's debt could get bigger. That fit the riddle. "Debt grows larger the more you take a person's money in taxes."

Konrad raised his brows. "An excellent and unexpected answer."

"It's not right?"

"It is very right. And fitting to come from one who will determine those taxes."

"What was your answer?"

"A hole."

I laughed. It was such a simple answer.

"Second riddle," said Konrad.

"Oh, don't say it that way," muttered Peter. "It brings back bad memories of an owl."

"Fair enough. Mary's mother had four children: April, May, and June were the first three. What's the name of the fourth?"

I laughed again. This time I knew. "You are using distracting information and categories. By the month names I should say July. But it isn't. It's Mary."

"You are learning. Are you ready for the last?"

I smiled. I was learning, and perhaps I'd get this last one as quickly.

Konrad's face turned serious. "You are in a stone room with no windows or doors. The only openings are three one-by-six-inch slits in the ceiling to let in air. The only thing you have is a mirror and piece of wood. How do you get out?"

Mirror and a piece of wood. I needed more information. There had to be hidden hints. "How thick are the stone walls? Is the floor also stone?

"A foot thick. The floor is stone."

"What shape is the wood?"

"A hand span by a hand span by two hand spans."

"Any sharp points?"

He shook his head.

A blunt piece of wood and a mirror. Even if I broke the mirror, would the glass be sharp enough to dig away at the mortar between the stones? "Is the wall mortared or stone set smooth on stone?"

"Squared stones set flush to each other without mortar."

"I could hammer at the stones with wood. If I could remove at least one stone, then I could remove others much more easily."

He inclined his head. "Each stone is a one-foot cube, weighing one hundred seventy-five pounds."

"I wouldn't be able to hammer it with a piece of wood. The glass won't help." I bit my lip and puzzled as we walked along. When we stopped for lunch I shrugged. "Konrad, I can't see any way to get out with the specifications you gave."

"See is part of the answer."

"I can't think in riddles anymore. Just tell me the answer."

He nodded. "You look in the mirror and see what you *saw*, take the *saw* and cut the piece of wood in half. Put the two halves together to make a *whole,* then just crawl out through the *hole*."

"That's not a fair riddle!" I cried. "The answer is impossible."

"The impossible is sometimes an answer."

I snorted. "I like your other riddles better."

"To be wise as a fool, you must be flexible to think even in the impossible and the ridiculous."

"I'll leave the fooling to you."

"For today at least." He handed me a piece of dried meat. "We'll have another lesson tomorrow."

"If tomorrow we don't reach the stone horse."

We reached the stone horse three days later, in the early morning. It stood beside a moss-covered cottage, and was about as big and mossy as the cottage. The horse stood on three legs and raised the fourth, as if ready to step from its rocky confines.

An old woman rocked in a chair by the front door. Wrinkles folded over wrinkles, so her whole face was like a shriveled apple. "Welcome. Have you come to feed my horse?" Her voice crackled like dry leaves.

"We are journeying to find the sorcerer's heart," Konrad said.

She rose from her chair. She was tiny, only coming up to my shoulder. Her face creased into a frown. "Most often they come for magic and power, and pay with their hearts. But you come to retrieve a heart?"

I shuddered. Who would ever sell their heart, even for magic and power? But that must have been what Johannes did.

"Yes, to retrieve a heart," Konrad said. "And we will not sell our own."

Her frown deepened. "If you are determined to go, then you must feed my horse to cross the flames and ice."

"How do we feed it?" I asked.

She turned to me. "One of you must knock out your front two teeth and place them in his mouth. You may take your time to decide."

We huddled together.

"Do you think it is another riddle?" I asked. "One where teeth represent something other than our teeth? Perhaps it means two ideas? Two biting riddles? Two—"

The old woman cut in. "It means teeth. No riddle."

We let out a collective sigh.

"It would be easier if it was hair. That grows back," said Demuth. "I haven't given anything up yet on this journey. I'll give my teeth."

"No," I said. "Maybe we could knock out the front teeth of one of the horses."

"Human teeth," said the woman.

"It was a good idea," Konrad said. "This part of the path requires sacrifice. I'll—"

"I'll give my front teeth," Peter said from Demuth's pocket. "I don't use them as a toad."

We looked at him.

"He has a good point," I said.

Demuth rubbed her finger along the top of his head. "I don't like it."

"You wouldn't like it for any of us to give up our teeth," I said.

Demuth's jaw trembled as she pulled Peter from her pocket. "Do you really want to do this?"

"No, but I will."

"I'll do it instead," she insisted.

"Demuth." Konrad laid a hand on her shoulder. "Let him sacrifice for you."

After a long moment she nodded and tenderly kissed Peter.

I turned my back as Konrad knocked out Peter's front two teeth. His cry carried through my covered ears.

"It's done," Konrad said.

Peter stood holding a handkerchief to his mouth. Blood stained the white fabric. He blinked back tears.

The old woman nodded. "Very good. Now place them in the stone horse's mouth."

Konrad stood on the tips of his toes to reach the horse's mouth. He placed the two teeth in it. The stones rippled, and the moss fell away. The horse lowered its leg and bent down its head. It tore up the grass.

"Peter," Demuth said, her voice barely above a whisper. "Will it be easier if you are a toad again?"

He nodded and kissed her. His mouth still bled in toad form.

Demuth dabbed his thin lips with a damp cloth. "Thank you."

"Quickly," said the woman. "Mount the stone horse."

"How can we mount it?" I asked. "The horse is taller than any of us."

"Kneel," said the woman.

The horse knelt, folding its stone legs beneath it. Konrad, Demuth, and I climbed on. The horse's back was broad, but not too much to sit across. And it was plenty long for the three of us.

"But what about our supplies? Our food, our water, our blankets." I asked.

"They'd burn. If you survive, you'll reach your path's end by nightfall."

"Burn?" I said. "How are we to survive?"

"Though you will feel the pain of the fire, if you don't make a sound through the flames, the fire will not injure you," she said. "However, if you utter a word, or even cry out while in the flames, your protection will end, and you will burn to ash." She took the reins of one of our horses. "I'll keep your horses fed until you return."

"What about the icy slope?" asked Konrad.

"Same rules. You will ride through a cold that will cause your bones to ache, but you must not speak or you will freeze solid." She patted the stone horse on the rump.

The horse lurched to its feet, and the world swayed.

As we galloped away, the old woman called. Her voice carried like the echo of a distant storm.

Hearken.
Fruits of insanity.
Death twined.

KOBOLD

RIDE THROUGH FLAMES AND UP ICY SLOPE

THE WIND WHIPPED against us as the horse galloped over rocky ground. Beyond the cottage, the land turned to huge boulders and steaming pools. The trees became scraggly. The air heated uncomfortably. How soon would we reach the flames, and could we remain silent?

"Konrad, do you think the horse will stop if we ask it to?"

"It doesn't have reins," he said, his voice whipped away by the wind almost as quickly as it reached me.

"Please try."

He grabbed hold of the thread-thin rock mane and tugged on it.

The stone horse slowed and stopped. Steaming pools surrounded us and sulfur filled the air. In the distance, flames licked across the surface of a river, sometimes bursting up in squinting brightness, covering every inch of water.

Konrad nudged the horse with his knees, and it walked toward the inferno, then stopped at its edge.

How were we to cross it? The river was wide. Even if the horse swam as quickly as it galloped, we'd be in the flames for many minutes. If the horse swam as slowly as a normal horse, we could be in the flames for half an hour. The old woman had promised that we'd be uninjured as long as we remained silent, but could we keep our silence under the pain of burning?

"The kobold never led us into this much danger," I said. "I wish we had Nyx back."

The sulfurous air stirred, and a gust of wind tore the scraggly leaves from the trees. It swirled in front of us and resolved into the kobold. She stood, a creature no taller than a child with pointed ears and red-and-black splotched skin. Wispy white hair sprouted under a red cap and hung in knotted locks over her grey dress. She grimaced as she stared up at us with dark brown eyes. "It took you long enough. I've been following you for days. But you didn't think of me until now? You are like all humans: selfish, forgetful, never remembering to thank."

"Nyx," I said. "Why were you following us?"

"Get down here where we can talk, or make space for me up on that stone beast," she said.

We each scooted backwards on the horse.

"More," she said.

We scooted until I, who sat between Konrad and Demuth, sat over the horse's back hips. Demuth must have been close to sliding off.

I wrapped my arms around Konrad's waist and leaned sideways to see around him as Nyx flew up and settled on the horse's neck.

"Why were you following us?" Konrad repeated my question.

She tugged at her wispy hair. "The cottage is gone. I have no hearth."

"And that means?" I asked.

"You humans know nothing." Her voice took on a quiver. "I'm a hearth spirit. And while I was trapped in that book, my hearth decayed."

"Can't you find a new hearth?"

"Germania changed. The people don't believe in us anymore. They just believe in science, and things seen, and…" She spat. "Books! I have to be invited to watch over a hearth. No one, not one single human, is looking for a kobold. I'm an outcast, a forgotten, a nothing."

"You want one of us to invite you to our hearth?" Konrad asked.

Her dark brown eyes brightened. "Some humans have more sense than others."

"We have none."

Her eyes darkened again. "None of you have homes?"

"Not until we finish our journey."

A sly smile wisped across her face and was gone. "And if you complete it, you'll invite me?"

Konrad shrugged. "I would if I had a home, but I live in the palace and sleep with the dogs."

"I've never had a home," croaked Peter.

"I can ask my parents if you can live in their hearth," said Demuth.

If the Kobold was planning to take over one of our hearths, we needed to make a deal, something that would benefit both sides.

"Nyx," I said. "I am a princess and soon will be a queen. My palace isn't large, but it has a hearth in each of its fifty rooms, plus a kitchen and a bakery with several ovens each. The grand hall has a central hearth with four openings facing north, south, east and west. It is the size of a small room and is lined with marble."

Nyx's eyes grew large, and her mouth fell open.

"You will have your choice of hearths if you help us complete our journey."

She licked her thin lips. "You will invite me to any of my choosing? Even the marbled room hearth?"

"If you help us, with no tricks," I said.

"You swear?"

"I, Hette, Crown Princess of Wurttemberg, swear that Nyx the Kobold may have her choice of any hearth in the Wurttemberg palace if she will help us complete our journey and all five of us survive, meaning Konrad, Demuth, Peter, Hette, and Nyx. And if she plays no mischief on us, though she may do so on our enemies."

Nyx laughed and danced on the front shoulders of the horse. "You will each survive, and I will be a palace hearth spirit. Oh, what the other kobolds will think when they hear. They mocked me for being out of home, but they will swallow their words. What fun I'll have. A whole palace!"

Misgiving churned in my stomach. "You won't be making mischief on the palace and its people, will you?"

Nyx sniffed. "Only on those who deserve it."

I shuddered. "Konrad? There are many who deserve it in the palace. Not the least the king."

"You've sworn, no going back now," he said. "Besides, a kobold's justice could be a good thing."

I shuddered again. "I think I just made my future reign more difficult."

Nyx settled astride the horse's neck, while the rest of us scooted forward till we each were secure across the stone horse's back. We started to explain the rules for the fire and ice.

"Yes, yes. I heard it all. I was there," Nyx said in a bland voice.

"Can you help us?" I asked.

"I'm a hearth spirit."

We waited in silence.

She huffed. "You humans truly know nothing. Hearth spirits have power over fire. I can make it hotter or protect you from the flames."

"All of us?"

After another long silence, the air around me cooled for a moment. Demuth let out a sigh behind me. Then the coolness fled.

Nyx panted. "All is too much. I can do the man or the two women. But not all three."

"And Peter?" asked Demuth.

"The toad is nothing. I can protect him with anyone."

Konrad's back tightened. "I'll go unprotected. I can hold my tongue."

"When have you ever held your tongue?" I said, and rushed on as Konrad's shoulders shook with a silent laugh. "You won't injure yourself again. We can go in several smaller groups."

Konrad nodded, and Demuth's grip loosened around my waist.

"We first must see who can guide the horse," Konrad said.

Over the next hour we found that we could command the horse to stop, go, turn, and to lie down to allow us on and off, without using words. We also found that the horse would obey Peter in human form, Konrad, and me, but not Demuth or Nyx.

"Perhaps Demuth is too gentle natured," Peter said.

I raised a brow. "And I am not?"

Peter swallowed and retreated into Demuth's pocket.

I snorted. "I've never been accused of being too gentle."

"I'll be more forceful." Demuth kicked the horse, but it continued to stand, ignoring her.

"No matter," Konrad said. "It will listen to three of us. We'll work with that." He stared out at the flames flickering across the water. The stone horse cropped at the scant grass. "Here lies the puzzle," Konrad said, scratching his curly locks. "How to get each of us across? Nyx can only protect me, or Demuth and Hette. But someone will always have to guide the horse back across the river, which negates part of the crossing."

"I can go any of the times," said Peter.

"But you can't guide the horse back in toad form," I said.

Demuth's hazel eyes brightened. "But he and I can trade places. The two of us can go first, then I kiss him, and he comes back in human form. And—" her face fell. "And then we are stuck."

"Nyx?" I asked. "Can you protect Peter in human form with another of us?"

"Make him human, and I'll see."

Demuth and Peter dismounted and kissed, then Nyx squinted her eyes shut. A cooling breeze passed over me and disappeared. Nyx shook her head. "He has as much mass as the tall man. I can only do the two women at the same time. Or..." she grinned. "I could only protect part of a person. Do you mind if your leg gets charred, or your arm? Maybe your face?"

"There has to be a way to get us all across, *safely*. We just have to find it." I broke a branch from one of the spindly trees and traced in the dirt, making a letter to represent each of us and a symbol for who was a toad when. Between the four of us—Nyx just watched—we scratched plan after plan into the dirt, and brushed them away.

"How about this?" Peter scratched out another option into the dirt. "Hette and Demuth go first. Hette returns with the horse. Konrad goes next. Demuth returns with the horse. Then Hette, Demuth and I go across together."

"It would work, except," Demuth said in a small voice, "the stone horse won't obey me."

How would we do it? There had to be a way.

Konrad laid his hand on my shoulder. "The woman said we'd be safe when we crossed. I will endure the pain of crossing without Nyx's protection."

"Pain doesn't have to leave a mark to injure," I retorted. "I know there's a way. It's at the edge of the other solutions, something that combines several parts."

I traced in the dirt and it finally came together. "Nyx. Can you protect us on this many trips?"

Nyx bent over to inspect the plan I'd etched in the ground. "Why not? It isn't the times but the mass that is the problem."

After everyone understood the plan, I mounted the stone horse. Even with it lying with its legs folded beneath it, I almost had to jump to get astride its back. Demuth climbed up behind me with Peter tucked into her pocket.

I nudged the sides of the horse with my boots, and it rose to its feet.

Konrad grasped my hand. "Be careful." Then he turned to Nyx. "You swore an oath to protect. Let not even an eyelash singe."

She flew up and settled on the horse's neck. "Of course. Kobolds keep promises."

A cool breeze cocooned me, lying over every inch of my skin, from my boot-enclosed feet to my capped head.

I reached around Nyx and grasped the stiff stony mane. It was time. I nudged the horse again, and we stepped into the river. The flaming water splashed, hissing against the horse's legs.

The horse stepped again and plunged. Water and flame enveloped us.

I swallowed a gasp.

Water covered the horse to its neck, and around my ribs. I clung tighter to its mane even as Demuth tightened her grip around my waist. The flames hissed and spit against my sides and shoulders, even as the cocoon of cool washed each away before it could burn.

The horse plunged again. Water and flames splashed into my face. I squeezed my eyes shut and bit my tongue. I couldn't feel the heat, but the scent and sounds of flames licking against me were real, as was the flickering light that showed through my eyelids.

The river's current increased, and flames swirled past. I tightened my legs to keep from being swept away. Demuth's grip tightened. And the horse swam, pushing its way across the river. The distant edge seemed to grow no closer. My eyes watered with the smoke. My fingers stiffened in the stone mane, and my shoulders ached.

The horse's movement changed. It was stepping again. Its neck rose higher from the flames, and then its shoulders. Water and flames dripped from my sodden and heavy skirt, dripping into the flames that licked around the knees of the horse.

Finally we stood on solid ground.

As soon as the horse lay down, I stumbled off its back and knelt, shuddering in the damp dirt.

Demuth wrapped her arms around me and wept, her face buried in my shoulder.

"I'm fine," said Peter from between us.

I laughed through my own tears. "Good, because you have to go back now."

Demuth kissed him, and he charged into the river astride the stone horse. The flames enveloped his form, as though he were being burned in effigy, and only a thin shield kept them from consuming him. He leaned forward, and the horse increased in speed.

Demuth shuddered, her whole toad body trembling, as she sat in my sodden lap.

The sun added its noon heat to the fiery river. Without a sextant, I could only roughly judge the passage of time, but the sun had moved about half an hour's time from when we'd started on the other side. Half an hour that had felt like half a day. "He'll be fine," I said.

Demuth stared at the river. "The woman said we'd be safe to cross as long as we were silent." Her voice trembled.

"And we were safe."

"Only because of Nyx," said Demuth. "Without her—" She shuddered again.

"Even with her it was terrifying. I don't even want to think about doing it twice more."

"But we will."

"We will because there isn't another way."

Konrad stood on the other side of the river, his hand raised to shadow his eyes. He stared in our direction.

I stood and waved to let him know we were well.

He cupped his hands around his mouth, but the words were swallowed up by the distance.

I placed my hand behind my ear.

He spoke again, but it was no use. He'd have to cross to tell me whatever it was.

The sun slowed in its movements as the stone horse struggled to cross the current, and Peter clung to its back. Finally he reached the other side.

Konrad clapped him on the back and mounted the stone horse, leaving Peter there, as was the plan. Konrad backed the horse away from the river and leaned forward. The horse galloped into the water. Nyx flew at his side in a smoky cloud, instead of astride the horse's neck. Konrad's face showed a pale blur through the hazy air. Flames flickered over him. His sleeve smoked.

Something was wrong. Though fire had surrounded us, none of the flames had taken hold. Why were they on Konrad? Was Nyx unable to protect him fully?

I cupped my hands around my mouth. "Nyx, protect him!"

Konrad dipped his hand in the water and splashed over the smoking sleeve. With the water came flames. One landed in his hair, the bright yellow turning his russet-blond curls black. He doused himself again, but the tossed water spread more flames. His left shoulder burned, as did his right forearm. He slipped from the back of the stone horse on the upriver side, keeping his hands gripped in the horse's mane.

If he lost his grip, the river could rip him around the horse and downstream.

I twisted my skirt in my hands. If only it was a rope that I could throw and pull Konrad safely to our side.

He dunked his head into the river and only his hands showed, grasping the mane. A moment later he came up. Water and flames streamed down his face. Again and again he dunked under.

I stood as close as I could to the flaming water, without stepping in. "Nyx! Help him!" The shout ripped from my chest.

Nyx flapped a hand at me, as if I was distracting her. Maybe she was giving her all to protect him. Maybe we'd worn her thin with the first two trips. Maybe we should have waited longer between crossings for her to recover. Would Konrad make it?

He drew close enough that I could see his expression. It was pained and determined.

I clasped my hands together. "Please," I whispered.

He glanced up at Nyx and waved one arm. The flames snuffed out in his hair and clothes. They still licked around him, splashing over him, but no more of him caught fire. He pulled himself back astride the stone horse.

Why had she waited to protect him? She'd promised to shield him. Why hadn't she?

As the horse splashed up onto the bank, I stood with my arms folded. "Nyx, how could you?"

"It was his request," she said with a pout as she settled on the ground.

I spun around and glared at Konrad. "Is that true? You requested that she not protect you?"

He shook his head, and bits of damp and burnt curls fell to his shoulders. "I wanted to know if I could endure it. Nyx promised to provide protection as soon as I signaled to her."

"But why? Did you think you needed to prove your bravery? You've never been more of a fool!"

"If I could endure it, that would mean on the return trip we could cross all together. Then you wouldn't have to cross multiple times."

"Do you think I care more about that than for your safety?" My voice rose in volume.

He dismounted from the horse and crumpled to his knees.

I dropped beside him. "Are you hurt? Demuth can tell me what to do. Or we'll get across the river and back quickly so she can tend to you herself."

"No." He shook his head and more seared hair fell. "I'm not injured, not a single burn."

He was pale and bits of ash clung to his cheeks and forehead, but his skin was unmarred by blisters or burns. The old woman had been right. The fiery passage was possible. But even though it was, Konrad hadn't needed to prove it.

I squeezed my hands into fists in my lap. "Demuth and I have faced as much danger as you on this journey. You've respected us enough to allow us to brave what we needed to without coddling us. You saw us cross safely. So it doesn't make sense that you'd put yourself in danger just to make it so we had fewer crossings."

His mouth quirked in an apologetic half-smile. "I'm a fool. I don't have to make sense."

"Konrad," Demuth said from my pocket, her voice forceful. "You need to tell her."

"Tell me what? What aren't you telling me?"

He frowned at Demuth. "It isn't her truth to bear. She has enough burdens."

"You promised to tell me the truth," I said.

"I promised I'd speak the truth, not that I'd tell you everything I know—that would take a lifetime."

"She needs to know," Demuth said, her voice bristling. "If you don't tell her, I will."

He scratched his head, and more seared locks fell to his shoulder. "I don't know how much longer the journey is to reach the sorcerer's heart, and I turn thirty-five in sixteen days."

"Sixteen days!" I said. "But you said you had six months!"

"I said I had less than half a year."

"You implied six months!"

"I didn't want you to worry."

We'd been traveling sixteen days from the tower. Five of those days were Konrad healing, so it was possible to return along the same path in eleven days, if we were truly near the place of the sorcerer's heart. We needed to hurry. I swallowed my heated words. "Is that why you wanted to journey so soon after you were injured by the owl?"

"Yes."

"I see."

He rubbed his skin through a hole burnt in his sleeve and spoke quietly. "You were right. Nyx's protection was worth us taking separate trips. If we have the time on the return journey, I will gladly take longer, multiple journeys and not feel that again."

"What did it feel like?" asked Demuth.

He blanched, but said with a shaky chuckle, "Each spark burned like a hot iron pressed to my skin."

My stomach constricted. Why hadn't he told me of his birthdate sooner? We could have traveled faster. We could have emptied the horses of some of their luggage and all ridden. We could have found a faster way to get safely across the river—somehow. I clenched my jaw from speaking.

He hesitantly met my glare. "I'm sorry to have worried you."

"Is that all you're sorry for?" I said quietly.

He dropped his gaze and stared at the ground.

I stood, my legs trembling more than they had when I'd crossed. "You're here now. Rest. We'll return with Peter soon." I turned my back to him as I spoke. Ice edged my voice even as tears pricked my eyes. I blinked. I wouldn't cry. He didn't deserve my tears. He'd not trusted me enough to tell me the truth. He would die in sixteen days, unless we hurried.

I mounted the stone horse. Both fear from the first crossing and fear for Konrad tightened my chest like a vice. After taking a deep breath against the pressure, I kicked the stone horse and he plunged in.

The crossing took just as long and the fear built even quicker. Once on the other side, Peter kissed Demuth so we were back within the mass limit for Nyx's protection, and all three of us crossed to join Konrad on the far side.

It should have been easier. I'd crossed twice before and knew it would not hurt, but if anything the third time was the worst. My logical mind froze. Only my will-locked jaw kept me from screaming as the flames licked against my skin, but did not burn. I squeezed my eyes shut and tightened my legs to make the stone horse go faster. An eternity in flames, and then hands closed around my waist and lifted me from the horse.

Konrad held me as I shuddered through the visceral fear.

My shaking in his arms turned to laughter—witless, unthinking laughter.

He held me still, until even my laughter died into weary gasps.

"I'm not hurt," I said, standing, pulling away a little. "And we only have sixteen days left. We should go."

"If you are ready, my lady."

"Not, *my lady*. I am Hette, your friend. Someone who trusts, and whom you *trust in*. If you will endure the actual pain of the flames to shorten our journey, then I can endure just the fear of them." I glanced into his face. "Konrad, you've changed. Back at the stream, you were still ready to die on your thirty-fifth birthday as long as you helped me. But now you are fighting to live. Why?"

He looked across the flaming river. The back of his hand brushed against the back of mine. "I've found more reasons to live."

I trembled, but it wasn't in fear. It was something else, just as powerful. "Good. Because you're not going to die. We won't let you. Right, Demuth?"

"Right," she said.

"I won't let him die, either!" croaked Peter.

I slipped my fingers into Konrad's large hand. "Let's go."

The horse galloped as quickly as it had when we first set off from the woman's cottage, taking us far from the fiery river and into woods filled with pale lacy maples and deep green oaks. In the distance, a mountain rose above the trees. It was pure white and glistened in the afternoon sun. Less than an hour later, the trees thinned and we faced a smooth slope of translucent crystal, pyramid shaped and perfectly balanced.

"So this is the icy slope?" Konrad dismounted and laid a hand on the crystal. The crystal pulsed like a star and Konrad leaped back, tucking his hand under his arm. Cold hit, biting through my still sodden clothes. And then the cold was gone, and the summer forest breeze brushed by.

"We should build a fire and dry our clothes before we go," Demuth said from behind me.

"We don't have time," I said. "Konrad only has sixteen days."

"But we'll freeze solid if we don't."

"Won't hurt me," said Peter. "I'm used to being frozen. But Demuth's right, the rest of you can't."

"It will take all night to dry the clothes," I argued. "We don't have time."

Konrad laughed tightly and pulled the horse to turn away from the crystal. "I shouldn't have told you my birthday. All our deaths won't keep me alive longer. We will dry our clothes."

Nyx hunched on the horse's neck, quietly swearing.

"Nyx," I said. "Can you dry our clothes?"

"Of course," she said, and cursed again. "But I will not go up that crystal."

"You promised."

She spun around and faced me, standing on the horse's shoulders. "I am a kobold, a hearth spirit. That extreme cold will snuff my flame. You might as well ask a bird to fly underwater."

"Then we will not ask you to come," said Konrad. "The rest of us will make the journey together—no back and forth this time. The old woman said we'd survive as long as we didn't make a sound."

Nyx flew up in the air. "You had better survive, because I want that palace hearth." She snapped her thin fingers and a warm glow, like standing in the summer sun, spread over every inch of me. My clothes dried and radiated like a fire-warmed blanket.

"Thank you, Nyx." I pulled the warm cap lower around my ears, jingling it.

Konrad, Demuth, and even Peter added their profound thanks. Much more flowery than mine.

If Nyx could dry our clothes and make them glow with warmth, could she also—?

"Nyx?" I asked. "Could you—"

"I can't go with you."

"Not that. Could you send some of your warmth with us?"

She tilted her head, then grinned. "Each of you stuff stones in your boots and pockets, and wherever else you want to be warm. The larger the stone, the better."

We hurried around, stuffing stones into our boots, tucking them into stockings and sleeves. Binding them to our heads under caps or with strips of fabric. I folded my shawl in half and filled it with stones along my back.

Then we mounted the stone horse again.

Nyx snapped her fingers, and each stone glowed. Lastly, she

laid her hand on the stone horse, and he glowed a rosy red, giving us an uncomfortably hot seat. "Go," she said. "The stone horse will keep its heat the longest because it's so large, but your other stones will only last a short time."

Konrad leaned forward and the horse galloped onto the crystal face. Cold hit us as soon as the hooves clacked onto the surface.

Nyx called, "Don't be fools and get yourselves killed."

We didn't answer. We could not say anything until we'd passed this part of the journey.

The heated stone horse radiated against my legs, even as the cold slid like a knife over my exposed face. I leaned into Konrad's back, burying my face in the scorched and holed fabric of his wool jacket. The cold slipped down my neck and through the cap. The three heated stones nestled in the cap did little to offset the icy fingers that pressed like a vice on my temples.

Demuth's arms tightened around my waist, and her whole body shivered against my back.

The sharp clack of the horse's gallop rang like anvil strikes on the crystal. Wind rushed by us, but Konrad blocked most of it. Only my arms, wrapped around his waist, and my clasped hands bore the brunt of it. I had the best spot between Konrad and Demuth. They were both exposed on at least one side.

My legs ached as the cold seeped deeper. It was worst between the tops of my boots and the bottoms of my skirts, where only my wool stockings provided a layer of protection. The warmth from the stone horse fought against the creeping cold. The cold pushed harder. One by one the rocks in my boots, sleeves, cap, and in my clasped hands, dulled and then froze into icy stone.

My jaw ached as I clenched my teeth. I would not speak. My bones throbbed with each anvil strike of the stone horse's hooves against the crystal slope.

Cold. Achy, jarring cold.

The world slowed. The anvil strikes of the horse's hooves

dampened. The wind stopped knifing my arms and hands. My feet disappeared at the end of my aching legs, which prickled in the in-between state of warring temperatures. The vice on my head turned to a muffling pressure. Sleep.

I rubbed my face on Konrad's rough wool jacket. I couldn't sleep. If I did, I'd fall from the horse and freeze.

Demuth's arms loosened around my waist.

I kicked her leg with my boot. The impact shot up my aching leg.

Her grip tightened again.

How much longer?

Cold. Enfolding, comforting cold.

The world came to an abrupt halt.

"So, three have come," a proud, pinched voice said. "And without any magical abilities. Impressive. Though they look half dead. What think you? Shall I invite them in?"

A growl answered.

"Ah, yes. You're right, there is a fourth, and he has a little magic. But the woman without a heart intrigues me most. We'll see what she has to say."

I fell and didn't stop.

ALONE

Cold stone lay under my cheek and hands. Not the shattering cold of the crystal slope, but cold that seeped through my wool dress and woke the aching memory of that ride.

"Konrad? Demuth? Peter?" My voice came out hoarse and muffled. No one answered.

I pushed to kneel and wavered on my knees. "Konrad?" My voice echoed, as if I were in a large room or cave. It was as black as a cave, though near scentless. Only a light tang of stone, but not of moisture or animal. And there was no sound but my own rapid breathing.

Where's Konrad, and the others? Are they safe? Are they—I shook my head to cut off the thought. They were alive, they had to be. And I needed to find them. To do so, I first needed to figure out where I was.

I crawled in the dense darkness until stone met my forehead. *Oof. One wall.* After rubbing my head, I stood and inched along the wall until my boot hit another. The corner was a square angle. *A room, then, not a cave.* Another slow inching along that wall brought me to another corner, and then a third and a fourth.

Maybe the corners weren't square. Was there a fifth wall

making this a pentagonal room? I inched along the wall, until I'd found four more corners. No seam or crack caught my rough fingers as I brushed them along the walls. *No door, no bars, a solid stone room.* Just like the riddle. But I had no mirror, nor piece of wood. And the riddle had not taken into account that an enclosed room would have no light to see in the mirror. And even if it had, no word play would help me escape.

I swallowed to ease my rapid breathing. My heart thumped wildly, clicking and ticking, as the gears slipped past each other. I needed to be calm. I couldn't help anyone if I passed out from fear. *Focus on something I can do.* What could I do? Learn more about the room.

How large of a room? I increased my stride and walked blindly along the walls, counting corners and paces between them. *Thirty paces, corner, forty paces, corner, thirty paces, corner, forty paces, corner.* Again I circled. Same paces, same corners. It was a rectangular room thirty paces by forty paces.

Is there anything else in the room? Or anyone? I huddled in a corner, listening. Nothing but my own breathing. *What if*—I bit my cheek. *They are alive. Maybe here, maybe somewhere else, but they are alive. The room is large, and breathing can be light. Maybe they are still unconscious, and I don't hear them over my own movement.* I had to know what was in the center of the room: my friends, a pit, or nothing. But how to mark my way and where I'd been? I unwrapped the wool knitted shawl from my back, scattering stones. I bit off the knot at one end, unraveled it, and rolled the yarn into a ball. It would be my skein of yarn to guide my path across the one-hundred-twenty-pace square room.

If Konrad, or Demuth, or even Peter were here, I'd find them. I anchored the yarn with one of my boots and crawled along a forty-pace-long wall, letting out the yarn on my non-wall side. Stone hit my head. I'd reached the far side. I pulled Konrad's cap lower over my forehead to buffer against the next time. I anchored the yarn with my other boot and crawled back across the room, that time following the line of yarn I'd left, letting out more on my other side. Again and again I crossed the room, each time I anchored the yarn with the boot that I'd used along that wall from the previous time—until the yarn ran out. I only found a smooth stone floor and one empty bucket.

I rerolled the yarn and crawled to the other forty-pace-long wall, then restarted the process. Maybe the yarn wouldn't cover all the way to the middle, but it would help me know if anything lay on that half. If I still didn't find anything, *or anyone*, I'd cut across diagonally and work my way from the middle.

Nothing, nothing, nothing. The thoughts echoed as I huddled along a wall. I'd covered the room from each wall and cut across diagonally. Nothing. No one. Alone.

A stone room with no escape. Worse, an empty room. Alone.

"Konrad!" I cried, and his name echoed back: *Konrad, Konrad.* "Demuth, Peter!" I stood and shouted. "Konrad! If you can hear me, please answer! Konrad!"

Nothing but echoes.

"She is ingenious," said a proud, nasal voice. "Plotting quadrants and using yarn from her shawl to mark the way in the dark. A formidable mind."

I froze in the corner where I'd huddled, dozing in and out of fear. Someone was in the room with me. But no slide of a door or rasp of a lock had announced him.

A yip echoed.

"Yes, she'll need water eventually. But she's not submissive enough yet. She'll survive another day without it."

A low growl reverberated.

"You forget yourself, wolf. Perhaps I'll wait two days before giving her water. I can bring her back from the edge of death if I desire. Just as I can keep others on the edge of it."

Others. What had he done to my friends? Anger burned in my chest. "If you hurt Konrad, or Demuth, or Peter, I'll—"

"See," said the nasal voice. "Still too much fight."

I lunged to my feet and pushed through the dark toward the voice.

Laughter surrounded me and then was gone.

"Come back! Tell me what you've done to them!"

Echoing silence answered.

I stumbled around the room, tripping and rising, until I could no longer push back to my feet. I lay on the cold stone and shivered.

"Please," I whispered. "If you are listening, whoever you are, please have mercy on us."

Time passed, measured by my intensifying thirst. It parched my throat and stuck my tongue to the roof of my mouth. I hadn't drunk anything since we first mounted the stone horse, before the fiery river and the icy slope. None of us had. How many days had it been?

My thoughts drifted, forming into half-awake dreams, vibrant in the darkness.

Konrad kneels next to a street urchin and gives him a copper. "A full belly and a forged friendship is worth a little metal."

Demuth holds my hand and counts with me as I fight cursed emotions.

Konrad rips the snake from my leg, and holds me safe until I push him away.

Peter rebukes me when I call Demuth maid. "It isn't who she is, only what she does."

Konrad covers my fears with stories. "There once was a shepherd, famous throughout the whole land for his wise answers to questions…"

Demuth cries with me as we leave my dead horse in the bog.

Peter leans forward, and the witch places her hand on his warty cheek. He gives up memories to save Konrad.

I touch the fool's cap on my head. Konrad smiles, a gentle sad smile. "I would give you a bear-skin cap if I could. But I only have a fool's offering. I can't even return your sacrifice of hair."

We sit between thorn walls, and Konrad teaches me the meaning of love.

My eyes pricked but no tears came. I lacked the moisture. My throat tightened around the unsheddable tears. I'd told Konrad I'd never seen the kind of love he described, but he'd shown it daily. He'd given me kindness, patience, and trust. He'd spoken the truth, even when I didn't like it. He'd brightened my days and comforted my nights. So had Demuth and Peter. I was wrong. I knew what love was. They'd surrounded me with it. My chest tightened into a painful knot.

Water dripped into my mouth. I licked it with a thick tongue.

A hand supported my head.

I struggled to sit. "Konrad?"

"Hush," a voice rumbled beside me. "I am not him. But he lives, as do the others."

A rush, like the fluttering of a thousand birds, passed over my skin, leaving me limp. They were alive.

The rumbling-voiced man came again.

"Are you helping my friends too?" I asked as he lifted my head.

"As much as my master will allow." He spooned a savory broth into my mouth.

"Who is your master?"

"The Sorcerer."

"He can't be. We already faced the sorcerer in the thorn-walled tower."

"That man is but a servant of the Sorcerer, a heart-bound slave like the rest of us."

I choked on the broth. Heart-bound slave? Had the Sorcerer stolen Johannes' heart just as Johannes had stolen mine?

The rumbling voice continued in the dark. "He hasn't decided yet what to do with you. You have no heart for the Sorcerer to bind. And because you are human and not fae, you have no true name for him to enslave you with."

"True name?"

"If you find—" His voice cut off in a pained howl. The bowl clattered to the floor, splashing broth on me. He panted, and his voice drew away. "Forgive me, I cannot say more."

"Please, don't go," I cried out, rolling to my knees.

"I've said too much. You will speak with my master soon."

"At least tell me how many days we've been here."

"Three."

Three days. Konrad only had sixteen days left before the crystal mountain. Now he only has thirteen.

"Please," I pleaded. "Konrad has less than two weeks to live. Don't make him spend it alone in darkness. Please let us all be in the same cell."

"I'm sorry," he said, and was gone.

The water and broth brought back my ability to think.

Johannes sent us on an impossible journey to get back his

heart. If this sorcerer was so much more powerful than Johannes, then what hope had we? We hadn't even been able to defeat Johannes when Konrad said his true name.

True name? The rumbly-voiced man had said only fae had true names. Johannes wasn't fae. Did that mean saying his name only partly diminished his powers. Was this sorcerer fae? Did he have a true name?

If you find—the man had started to say. If I found the sorcerer's true name?

He said his master could enslave others by a fae's true name. Would it hold true for the master, too? If I knew the sorcerer's name, could I command the sorcerer and free us, and even get Johannes' heart?

It seemed the only way. But how to find his name?

Would the man tell us his master's name? Could he? He'd started to say something and couldn't finish. But he had at least started. He had some free will. If he knew more of our story, would he tell more, even against his master's command?

The man brought water, broth, and a little bread each day. But he never spoke again, despite my questions and pleading. I told him our plight, Konrad's family curse, Peter's transformation, and my stolen heart. I shared about Demuth's quiet kindness, Peter's sacrifices, and Konrad's foolish wisdom and bravery. I begged him not to end our long journey this way, to let us at least be together. His only response was quiet whimpers.

The time passed in dark slowness. Each time the man brought food meant another day less for Konrad to live. Eleven days, eight days. I couldn't wait longer. I grabbed the servant's hand. "Take me to your master. I will bear the consequences."

He gently withdrew his hand and was gone.

The next day I leaped on his back. It was broad and he wore a furred cloak. I clung as he walked. A wall struck my head and forced me from his back, as if he could walk through stone, but I could not. The same happened the next day, and the next. My head ached from the repeated impacts. Five days, then three days, before Konrad's thirty-fifth birthday. Would the sorcerer wait until Konrad was dead?

Even if I could force my way to speak with the sorcerer, what would I say? The servant had pity for me, but the master had withheld water until I was near death. I'd find no pity from him. Instead I had to find his name. But how?

My thoughts circled into the rut of despair.

No, I can't give up. I must be ready to face the sorcerer. If I am allowed to see him, I can at least guess at his name. His true name. But I know nothing of the sorcerer. I rubbed my aching head. *Or do I?*

He must have been the one the witch spoke of. Johannes could be no more than a hundred and thirty, yet the witch said I was the first bride the sorcerer had sought in over three hundred years. She must have been thinking of this sorcerer, not Johannes. Why hadn't I caught the discrepancy before?

What else did I know? The path to the sorcerer was riddled with dangers. I paused and wrapped my arms tightly around me. *Riddled.* The path was *riddled.* Each step required us to think and solve. Even the first words he spoke in my cell were about my formidable mind. Were we his entertainment in the dullness of an immortal, solitary life?

Would he give us some riddle to his name? I had to try. If only he'd let me speak with him.

"Please," I whispered into the dark. "Please just let me speak with the sorcerer. Don't let Konrad die alone."

NAME

WHAT NAME WILL YOU GIVE WHEN FACED WITH TRUTH?

"Come." The rumbling voice surprised me. He hadn't spoken in so long. It was two days before Konrad's birthday, if the servant fed me once a day.

A large, calloused hand took mine and led me through the dark. The dense blackness lightened into grey.

I glanced at the man who led me. He was a hulking shadow, shaggy around the edges. The grey brightened and I gasped. A wolf-headed man, taller than Konrad and broader than Peter, strode beside me. Thick black fur covered him, yet he had arms and legs like a human, and his hands and feet were furless.

He led me down a stone passage. Soft, glowing spheres floated along the edges. The passage ended in a cavernous room walled with white crystal, bright as a full moon. I squinted.

"So you've come at last." It was the nasal voice.

I blinked. A figure in white came into focus. He stood in the center of the room, beside a column of crystal. He not only wore white robes, but was white, as if bleached of color. White hair, white skin.

The wolf-man led me closer, then left my side and exited the room.

His master smiled with lips the color of bluish ice. His eyes looked cataracted, white in the center of pale blue. But they followed me.

Cold rushed over me as it had on the crystal slope. Was his name Ice?

"Please." I knelt before him.

"Please? Please grant my boon?" he mocked. "Please use your magic to save my friends?"

"Please give me another riddle."

His bushy white brows rose. "An interesting petition. Very well, what kind of riddle do you seek?"

"Your name."

He laughed, and the room snapped with the cold sound. "You are an intriguing and dangerous foe. Well met and well said. You may have three guesses to my name."

Three guesses. It was more than I could have hoped.

He smiled. "But you must pay for those guesses. If you guess correctly, I lose everything. So, you must also lose everything if you guess wrongly. I will take your heart from my slave, and I will take you to wife."

I trembled. Being wife to the corrupted Johannes would have been hellish. But to this man? This fae of ice?

"And if I don't guess at all?"

"You've proven interesting. If you don't guess, then I will give you a choice. It's more than I give others. You can choose death, or become my wife."

"And my friends?"

"They will die or they will serve me, whichever I desire." A chiseled sneer formed. "Will you give me a name?"

I shuddered again. It was the next line from Johannes' riddle, *What name will you give when faced with truth?* If I gave a name and guessed wrong, I faced worse than death. If I guessed right, we could all be free. If I didn't guess at all, I could die, but there was no assurance of that escape for my friends. These were the truths I faced.

"I will guess." I stared into his eyes. "But you promised me a riddle, and you have not given it yet. What is a riddle to your name?"

He turned his back on me. "My servants told you my name. I will give you no more hints."

His servants told us his name? So there were riddles? I rushed over what each had said along the path. They hadn't said much, except for the crazy man in the cherry orchard. He'd said the same thing many times. Crazy about cherries. What else? Something about shadows. He kept trimming the trees to even their shadows. No that wasn't it. He spoke oddly. He was *evening their shadows.*

Was his name to do with the shadows falling in the evening? Was his name Nightfall? But what had that to do with cherries? The sorcerer said his servants told us, not just one. What had the others said?

"Hette!" Demuth's voice rang across the room. The wolf-man released her at the entrance before disappearing again. She ran to me, wrapping me in her arms. "Oh, Hette, you're alive!"

"No speaking." The sorcerer's voice chilled the air.

Demuth stumbled back from me, her mouth pressed shut. Her hazel eyes widened, and she made sounds in her throat. I grabbed her and pulled her close again. The sorcerer wouldn't allow us to speak together, but I would hold her as long as possible.

Demuth buried her face in my shoulder, and her tears soaked into my sleeve.

Focus. What was the old woman's riddle? She had given one. *Hearken. Fruits of insanity. Death twined.* Fruit and cherry. Insanity and crazy. But nothing about shadows. Death twined, maybe.

The wolf-man entered, carrying Peter in his large hands. Peter lay shriveled and still, his eyes closed.

"Peter," I gasped.

Demuth spun around, grabbed him from the wolf-man, and clutched him to her heart.

Peter's eyes slowly opened. His wide mouth spread into a grin. "I knew I'd see you again."

The sorcerer silenced him too.

I wrapped an arm around Demuth's shoulders and laid a hand on Peter. *The sorcerer's name. I have to figure out the riddle. They will not die because I lack focus.*

The sorcerer's name had to do with fruit and craziness. What else? What had the silver knight said? Mostly boasting and challenges. Had he spoken of fruit or even any riddles?

How I wished I could speak with Demuth. She remembered words exactly.

Remember. The owl. His parting riddle. We'd spoken of it often enough that I knew it word for word. *Beware the growing madness that would shadow the armored man.* I thought it referred to the silver knight, but what if it was also the sorcerer's name?

Madness, like crazy and insanity. *Growing* madness, fruit and cherry. Another connection. Shadow. The crazy man had also said shadow.

Heavy, stumbling steps echoed across the room. The wolf-man entered half dragging Konrad, holding Konrad's arm over his own shaggy shoulder. Konrad's head hung down, and his curly, half-burnt locks concealed his face.

I let go of Demuth and rushed to his side. "Konrad, I'm here."

He lifted his head. Dark circles shadowed his sunken eyes. "That is good, because I don't feel quite here myself."

"Konrad, descendant of Erasmus," intoned the sorcerer. "I've studied the spell on you. It is a curious one, made by foolish fingers and untested magic. A knotted mess of man's invention and witch's spells. And it ends with your death. I will make it right—for a proper price."

Konrad straightened his legs and back. "You say it ends with my death. Will none other carry the curse?"

The sorcerer laughed. "You spent a lonely life to ensure that. And you will die a lonely death unless you pay."

A smile twitched at the corner of Konrad's mouth. "You'd like me to ask the price, or are you expecting me to just agree?"

"You have two days left to live. You are not in a place to bargain."

I slipped my arm around Konrad's waist. Demuth came to Konrad's other side, and the wolf-man stepped back as she pulled Konrad's arm over her shoulder.

Konrad trembled, but his smile grew. "I like to bargain, but I'm not afraid to walk away from a bad offer."

The sorcerer stepped closer. An icy air settled over us. He sneered. "I will give you all the life that has been drawn from generations of your family. You will live centuries instead of days. All I ask is your heart in exchange. It is a small thing."

Konrad laughed. The rich sound bounced off the crystal walls, and the sorcerer winced. Konrad said, "And I thought I was the fool here."

"You reject?"

"I'd sooner eat nightshade."

Nightshade. It is a fruit. It causes a person to act crazy. Evening the shadows. Nightshade.

I moved between Konrad and the sorcerer. "Your name is Nightshade."

The sorcerer froze, as though he'd become the ice he appeared to be. Then he laughed. "That is not my name, and you have used one of your guesses."

"Hette?" Konrad's voice trembled, lacking the bravado he'd shown to the sorcerer.

"Silence," said the sorcerer. "You've rejected my offer, and you will await my sentencing. I may still take your heart, but I will not give you the long life of health I first offered."

Konrad's lips clamped together, as had Demuth's.

I pressed closer to Konrad's side and stared at the sorcerer. Nightshade. It fit everything. Even the death twined. As it had twined through the thorns. The sorcerer had reacted. It had to be close to his true name.

Demuth had called it crazy cherry nightshade. The man in the orchard said *crazy about cherries*. Again, it fit. Was it his full name?

I swallowed, "Your name is crazy cherry nightshade."

The man snorted. "No sorcerer would bear such a ridiculous name. You have one more guess and then you are mine."

I closed my eyes. If I didn't guess, would he let me choose death? But I couldn't leave Konrad, Demuth, and Peter behind to slavery. What was his name? What?

Konrad took my hand in his and caressed a finger over my palm.

Shivers ran up my arms. It was similar to, yet nothing like the cursed emotions. Something sweet and comforting.

I winced as Konrad's caress grew more forceful, a trace across the pad of my hand and then a downward swipe. He wasn't caressing. He was trying to tell me something. I grimaced. Emotions, cursed or not, were distracting.

He paused and traced again. *T—O—L—L—K—I—R—S—C—H—E.*

Tollkirsche. That was what Demuth had called it. The nightshade that twined in the thorns. Tollkirsche, an elegant name for a deadly vine. An elegant name for a sorcerer of death. A true name for a poison-hearted fae.

T—O... He traced, but it was different... *U—C—H.*

Touch. I shuddered. I'd forgotten the other requirement for conquering the sorcerer.

Konrad squeezed my hand and then let go. It was time. I had one chance to touch the sorcerer and say his true name.

I bowed my head, as if dejected.

"Have you given up?" the sorcerer sneered.

I lifted my head just enough to see him through my lashes, and let my lip tremble. "If I don't make a third guess, will you still give me a choice between death and marriage?"

"If you don't make a third guess, I will allow you the choice." His sneer tilted into something akin to relief.

I had him—hopefully.

I bit my lip. "You appear to be ice. How would I survive a marriage to you?"

He laughed. "I am like ice. But I will make you immune to my cold, even if it isn't comfortable."

My stomach tightened to a knot. "I can't. I can't promise to marry you, unless I know I won't be frozen solid by you. Death would be preferable."

"I'll give you a small taste of what I feel like, in exchange for your answer."

I bowed my head again, hiding the hope in my eyes. "I will tell you whether I choose death or marriage afterward."

He strode to me, dropping the temperature with each step. His sneer widened as I shivered.

I kept my head down as he reached out and touched the back of my hand. Needles of ice shot through my nerves and then deadened to a dull ache.

"See," he said, "I can even make it enjoyable. I can—"

I grabbed his wrist with my free hand, and gasped. It was like grabbing an icicle at midnight. "Your name is—"

"Silence!" he roared. Wind ripped through the room, billowing his robes.

I clung to his wrist as the winds buffeted me, and icy air filled my lungs and froze my teeth.

"Tollkirsche." I winced as the word scraped over my iced throat.

The winds died, as if a door had slammed shut on a storm. The sorcerer's wrist grew warm and sticky. He crumpled to his knees. Black, purple, and pale green bled along his robes. The green formed into leafy vines, the purple into flowers, followed by black berries. His eyes turned purple and his lips black over pale green skin. Black hair flowed over his shoulders. A sickly scent filled the room.

"Tollkirsche." I released his wrist. "You will free Konrad of the curse."

He blinked his purple eyes and sneered. "My name both gave you power over me, and also took away my magic."

"You have to break the curse," I cried. "He'll die if you don't."

"I'll die before him." Tollkirsche turned grey and his skin shriveled. The sickly scent turned dusty. He collapsed inward, and a pile of dried twisted vines lay where he'd been.

I dropped to my knees by Konrad, where he lay sprawled by the wind. We'd been so close.

Konrad laid a hand on my arm. "I still have two days."

I swallowed a sob. "It took us sixteen days to get here. Not even the stone horse could make it back in time."

"I know," he said. "But the fae, who could not lie, assured me that none other will bear this burden. It ends with me. It is more than I'd hoped for."

I tried to smile. "These will be the two best days of my life."

"They had better not be. You will still have Demuth and Peter, and you will find other friends. Maybe you'll even love someone enough that you'll be willing to put up with their quirks for a lifetime."

I buried my face in his shoulder, unable to say the rest. There was only one I would be willing to do that for.

BLITZ

MY HEART LIES IN STONE HANDS

"My mistress." The wolf-man's voice rumbled.

"What?" My voice came out harsh, as I clung to Konrad.

"You have freed me," he said. "And thus I am at your service. If you command, I will strive to save his life."

My chest spasmed. I looked up. "Can you save him?"

"If you command me, I will."

"Hette," Konrad said, warning strong in his faint voice. "Don't rush into an agreement."

"I order you to save Konrad," I said.

The wolf-headed man touched Konrad's shoulder, and Konrad went limp. He laid a second hand on my shoulder as I rose in anger. His icy blue gaze met mine. "He is close to death already. My old master, Tollkirsche, tried to break him. If he is to survive the run, he will need to sleep."

Demuth placed a hand on Konrad's chest, then let out a breath. "He's alive."

I held the wolf-man's gaze. "What run?"

"It will take the one who cast the spell to remove it. But I can lead you to his heart and carry Konrad to his side."

"Can you do it in two days?"

"I am Blitz." He grinned a wolfish smile. "I run like lightning."

Demuth and I ran on either side of Blitz down crystal halls lit by a floating, flickering light. His wolf head atop his human body towered over me, while thick black fur covered him, except for his hands and feet. He carried Konrad's limp body in his arms like a child.

"I could carry all of you," he said. "But I cannot speak in my wolf form, and there is much you must know. When you spoke Tollkirsche's true name, you broke the web of spells he created and shattered his power. The crystal mountain is no longer cold nor the river flaming. It will make the return safer. But we must return each heart along the way."

"Each heart?" I asked.

"I promised, if our old master's power was broken, I'd return the hearts to my fellow bound-servants."

"Do it after you take Konrad."

"A fae cannot break a promise." He turned the corner, and we circled downstairs into a black pit. "Just as Tollkirsche could not freeze your mouth shut before your third guess, because he'd promised you three guesses."

"How many servants?"

"Five, the last being Johannes. He is the youngest of us, the only human, and the most troublesome to my old master."

"Troublesome?"

"He is human and has no true name to control his actions. He paid for magical knowledge with his heart. Tollkirsche agreed to it, calling Johannes the first person worthy of being his apprentice, despite his weak humanness. That was the start of Tollkirsche's fall."

"How so?" I held my side. The stairs were unending, and I was still weak from my imprisonment. Blitz paused, and I leaned against his furry side.

"Johannes discovered the darkness of the sorcerer's magic and tried to kill him. Tollkirsche punished Johannes through his heart, freezing out goodness. But Johannes was resourceful. He escaped, and it took me six months to find and imprison him in the thorn tower."

Blitz started down the stairs again, and I ran beside him.

"Tollkirsche was a patient man. He had chosen Johannes as an apprentice and waited for the time that his heart no longer resisted the touch of dark magic. For years, Johannes stayed trapped in the tower, inventing precise, geared tools and weaving them with magic. Some of his tools grew plants on the stone walls. Others pulled water from the air. First Johannes sustained his magic and himself with the life pulled from the tangled vines that imprisoned him. Tollkirsche laughed as Johannes drained the land of all plant and animal life. Only the imprisoning vines survived. When there was nothing left to sustain him, Johannes wove a spell and connected his life to that of another man, and that man's descendants, freezing Johannes' life into a single un-aging day."

"Konrad's family curse," I whispered.

Blitz nodded. "Tollkirsche called for him then, ready to teach him, but Johannes resisted each call. His heart had grown cold as stone and barely beat, frozen into a hard wall against the sorcerer. After a hundred years, Tollkirsche released him from his thorny prison, just for the enjoyment of seeing what havoc Johannes would wreak on the world."

We finally reached the bottom of the stairs. The flickering light revealed a room with six crystal statues: a wolf, a young woman with rose-braided hair, an elf dancing, a knight, an owl, and Johannes. The only color in the translucent white room were six red hearts; some held in maw or beak, others in hands. Glittering shards were piled along the wall.

"Why are you telling me this?" I asked.

"To warn you." Blitz set Konrad on the floor. "I've watched Johannes over the years. Tollkirsche was heartless and cruel, but I knew what to expect of him. I cannot predict what Johannes will do. He is broken and twisted. Sometimes he seems to be noble, and other times more hateful than my old master."

I bowed my head. "Like what he did for his best friend, and then against him and his family."

Blitz nodded. "Or against you. He is human and thus doesn't have to keep his promises. Even if you give him his heart, he may go back on his word."

"But he's the only way to save Konrad."

"True. You may want to keep his heart hostage until he's undone the spell."

"But won't his heart restore him to his goodness?"

"I don't know. It may. I wanted to warn you. Do what you will with the knowledge." Blitz took the beating heart from the crystal wolf's maw. The wolf statue shattered, splitting the air with the sharpness of broken glass. Blitz pressed the heart to his chest, and it sank into his black fur. He fell to his hands and knees and transformed into a huge black wolf, taller and longer than a horse. Even larger than the stone horse which had carried us all. His howl rang and bounced along the crystal walls. He panted, then stretched onto his hind legs and turned back into a wolf-headed man. "Quickly," he said. "Gather all the hearts."

I ran to Johannes' statue and touched the heart. It was cool, stiff, and pulsed slowly. Could Johannes still be good? Would his heart warm when back in his chest? Would he lift the curse for Konrad? He would. He had to. I lifted the heart from the cold crystal hands, and the statue crumbled at my feet.

I held the heart out to Blitz. "What do I do with it?"

"Wrap it in fabric," he called over his shoulder as he ran from the room.

I tore fabric from my dirty petticoat, wrapped the stiff heart, and placed it in a deep pocket of my apron. Demuth did the same with another, and the owl statue lay in rubble. Soon, each statue lay broken. Three hearts thumped against me through the thick layers of apron and skirt. The ones from the woman and the elf were warm and beat stronger than Johannes'.

Blitz returned with two water sacks, a sheathed sword on a belt, and something like a saddle, but larger, with many leather straps along the edges. "When I turn back into a wolf, mount this on my back and bind Konrad's legs and arms to the saddle. You must also bind your legs, or you will not be able to keep on me. But first drink. It will help with the journey." He held out one of the water sacks.

I tilted it into my mouth. A sharp vinegar liquid burned my throat. I coughed, sputtered, and swallowed. Some went up the back of my throat and stung my nose.

Demuth handled it a little better. Peter coughed the most and crawled deeper into Demuth's pocket. "I'll wait for water next time," he grumbled.

Blitz turned into a wolf, and in a longer time than it should have taken, we buckled the saddle to the huge wolf and secured each of us to it. The sword that Blitz had given us hung heavy against my left leg. Demuth could have kissed Peter so he could carry it, but I wanted her available to help Konrad. Besides, we were riding a wolf. No one would dare attack us, and the sword provided a comfort, even if only an illusion that I could protect Konrad. Time was our only enemy now.

Blitz lifted his head and howled a bone-rattling cry, and a hole opened in the crystal wall. A vast forest stretched below us. The sun shone over the horizon, either sunrise or sunset.

The slope of the mountain blurred as we descended. Wind tore the belled cap from my head and flattened my skin against my bones. The forest flashed by. I buried my face deeper against Konrad.

Blitz was appropriately named. He was fast like lightning.

We splashed through a river, and something caught the shoulder of my dress.

Words ripped by my ears. "What—!" and the rest was unintelligible.

As quickly as we began, we stopped outside the stone horse's cottage, and the winds ceased. The first sound after the sudden silence was Nyx cursing. "Green logs and soot-stopped chimneys, what did you do!" She clutched my shoulder with bony fingers.

"Hette defeated the sorcerer," said Demuth breathlessly. "And we are trying to save Konrad's life."

"Good." Nyx let go of my shoulder and resettled her red cap over her wispy white hair. "Because if he dies, I can't have my palace hearth."

"You defeated him?" The old woman hobbled out of her hut, her eyes bright in her shriveled face.

Blitz gave a short growl. He couldn't speak while in wolf form. I would be his emissary. It would be quicker that way.

I reached into my pocket and withdrew the heart that had been with the young woman's statue. It must have been the heart of the old crone. "This is yours."

She darted forward with more speed than seemed possible and unwrapped the warm beating heart. She clutched it to her bony chest and sighed as it sank in. "Finally, after three hundred years." She bowed to me. "You have my undying gratitude, my lady." Her gaze swept over us. "It is cold riding lightning; you'll need blankets." She snapped her fingers, and three blankets settled over us, tucking in around, covering from head to boots.

Nyx coughed from where she floated in the air.

The woman laughed like leaves crushed underfoot. "The hearth spirit wants a blanket too? Well, get on and hold tight." She snapped her fingers as Nyx settled on the wolf's neck. A blanket wrapped around Nyx, covering her from red cap to grey dress. The woman waved a hand. "Watch for—"

The world blurred before she finished. Wind rushed and roared, but the blankets stayed firmly tucked, and the hours sped by. I jerked awake as the blurred world resolved into a cherry orchard, or what had once been a cherry orchard.

Fallen trees littered the ground, trunks crisscrossed and crimson cherries scattered like marbles. The afternoon-warmed air smelled sweet and woodsy. The small, red-clad man sat on a stump, his cowled cap pulled back from his head, revealing his pointed ears and elfin features. His chin rested on a fist, and his elbow on a wood chip-covered knee. An ax lay at his side.

He didn't look up, even when Blitz nudged his shoulder with his nose.

I reached into my pocket and withdrew his heart. It was smaller than the woman's, but hotter and fluttery. The sooner I gave it, the sooner we could leave. "Here. Your heart."

He blinked. "Did you say heart? Not cherries or shadows?"

"Heart. Take it quickly. We must go."

He stood and extended a trembling hand. "First, the compulsion to trim the shadows is gone. And now my heart is back." He unwrapped the dirty fabric and brushed his fingers over the beating muscle.

"Blitz, let's go."

A low growl rumbled from the wolf.

"Elf," I said. "Put it back in your chest."

He took a deep breath and pressed it to his red doublet. As it disappeared, his eyes cleared. "Insanity of repetition is too high a cost for unending peace. You've broken my chains and my insanity.

I must repay." He held up a flask. "This will cure weariness, fill bellies, and speed your journey." He poured a little into Blitz's mouth then handed it to me.

It was thick, honey-sweet, and scented with cherry blossoms. Fiery warmth tickled my throat and spread outward. It tingled along my skin and lifted the weary ache of days of imprisonment. If anything could help Konrad survive the next part of the journey, it was this.

"Blitz, we are giving this to Konrad. Please wake him."

The wolf shivered and growled. His body began to change shape. He darted forward, slipping from the saddle. We thumped to the ground, our legs still bound to the saddle. Thankfully, the rigid leather extended further than our feet.

Nyx floated, scowling in the air. "Why'd you make that foolish order? Now you'll have to undo all the straps, and re-saddle, and redo the straps. A lot of wasted time."

I hadn't expected Blitz to need to change shape to break the sleep spell on Konrad. Nyx was right, it was wasted time. But Blitz had already changed and laid his hand on Konrad's shoulder, waking him as I had ordered.

Konrad struggled against the bonds that held him face-down against the leather saddle. "Hette, Demuth, Peter?"

"We're here." I worked to unbuckle straps that held his arms. "We are taking you back to Johannes with his heart. He'll break the curse."

"How long was I asleep?"

"Half a day, maybe."

"Half a day." Blitz nodded. "You have until noon tomorrow before the curse takes effect. I will get you there by morning."

Konrad jerked his arm free as I undid the buckle, then slumped forward as if that movement had been too much. "Don't force me asleep again." His voice came muffled against the leather.

As soon as Demuth and I were free from the saddle, she supported Konrad while I lifted the flask to his lips. He swallowed, and his pale face took on a warmer hue. He struggled to sit. "If I wasn't going to die tomorrow, this would make me live for years."

"I won't let you die tomorrow," I said, making him take another swallow from the flask.

"So said my mother to my father. It didn't change the curse," Konrad said morosely. "This is why I never married. Couldn't do that to another family. Hurt enough to see my father go and then my mother waste away in grief. You have to promise not to do that. Of course you won't. You are too practical. Besides, we are only friends, which is more than a fool like me could ever hope for. I only wish I could be there to see all the good you will do as queen. At least you'll get your heart back. And I'll have fulfilled my duty."

"Konrad, stop it! You are not going to die."

Blitz laid his hand on Konrad's shoulder, and Konrad slumped. "I'm sorry, my lady," Blitz said. "Tollkirsche tried to break him so he'd agree to give his heart—a freely given heart is more powerful to a sorcerer's magic. Konrad wouldn't bend. Instead, parts of him shattered. I don't think he believes he can live beyond his thirty-fifth birthday."

"Does the curse truly take effect tomorrow at noon?"

Blitz nodded. "I can see spells, and that is when his comes to a knotted end."

"Then we'll have to just unknot it before that point. Let's go."

The magical blankets and the potent cherry potion kept me warm and awake as we sped through the night. They must have had the same effect on Peter, for he sang, his voice strong enough to carry over the roar of the wind. A silver full moon crossed the sky and sat near the center when Blitz slowed and ascended a cliff.

It was the cliff where we'd faced the silver knight. Peter silenced as we reached the top and Blitz turned and descended the other path. The night was soft around his quiet padding over a log bridge and toward the cave, our shadows preceding us.

Demuth shifted behind me. "I've got the silver knight's heart ready." She paused. "I wonder what he will give us in thanks?"

"If he takes it and sends us on our way, that will be the best thanks he could give," I said.

Demuth rested her hand on my leg. "Konrad is strong. He'll heal from Tollkirsche's abuse once the curse is broken."

I swallowed. "I've never seen him so melancholy. It frightens me."

"Do you remember his lesson on juggling knives—"

"—and emotions?" I finished. "Yes. He said laughter gave him the balance to handle the other intense emotions. Has he always lived with those fears about death and not having family?"

"Always."

"How did he do it?"

"As he said, laughter, and a stubborn will."

I laughed tightly. "He is stubborn."

"He is." Demuth squeezed my hand. "Stubborn enough not to want any of us to sacrifice for him. But, we are as stubborn as he."

I let her comfort carry away the worst of my fear for Konrad. We'd save him, whether or not he agreed.

Peter croaked a warning. "He's coming."

The silver knight burst from the cave. "You seek to sneak past me in the night! That is a coward's path!" He raised his sword.

"Sir Knight," Demuth cried even as Blitz stepped back. "I have your heart."

"Heart! I have no need of a heart!" He charged, swinging his sword in an arcing path at Demuth.

Blitz leaped backward at the same time that Peter hopped from Demuth's pocket, bellowing a night-shaking shout. "Never!"

The arcing sword and Peter entered the same space—and the blade sliced into him. Peter flopped to the path.

"You dare smite him," Nyx hissed as she grabbed the heart from Demuth's hand. Flames licked around the muscle. The knight fell from his horse and clattered to the ground.

"You destroy my chance at a palace hearth," she said. The flames leaped higher. The silver knight writhed on the ground, his armor clanking.

"Stop it!" Demuth cried as she fumbled to unbuckle her legs. "Just stop it." She slipped from Blitz's back and picked Peter up. Moonlight glistened off slick liquid spreading across his chest.

"Peter." She held him to her heart. "Peter."

My throat tightened.

The clanking of the knight stilled, and Demuth's quiet weeping filled the air.

"Demuth." Peter's word was gasped more than spoken.

Her face hardened in the moonlight. She lifted Peter.

"Don't," I commanded, trying to undo the saddle buckles. "It won't save him. His injuries will carry over to his human form. He'll die, and you'll be stuck as a toad."

Her shoulders squared, and she kissed him.

White fire burst from Peter's small form, enveloping him and Demuth in a column of flames.

I jerked against the leather buckles that held me to the saddle.

"Nyx," I cried. "Stop the flames!"

"I can't."

"Blitz!" I commanded.

He whined and shook his huge shaggy head.

The blinding white flames concealed Demuth and Peter. No screams came from the inferno.

I hid my face against Konrad's back. "Demuth," I whispered. "My friend."

The crackling of the flames filled the air.

Why did she kiss him? Why did he burst into flames? Why does magic have to be so awful? Why? Why! I sobbed, shaking against the slow rise and fall of Konrad's sleeping breath. *We need to go or Konrad will also die.* I swallowed, preparing to command Blitz to leave, but the words wouldn't come.

"Demuth." It was Peter's voice. "My lovely, wonderful Demuth."

I lifted my head and blinked away tears.

The white flames flickered in a low circle around two figures facing each other. Demuth looked up into Peter's face. His ragged shirt was torn from neck to navel, but his skin was whole beneath. He was fully human, with no toad characteristics. A bull-necked, broad-shouldered man with a wide smile that showed his two missing teeth—the ones he'd sacrificed to the stone horse.

In Demuth's hands lay a toad's shriveled skin.

Peter traced a finger across her cheek, then cupped his hand behind her neck and leaned down. As their lips met, the toad skin slipped from Demuth's hands and fell into the white flames.

"How?" I started, then shook my head. "Don't tell me how. I'll ask later. Let's go."

The saddle was only built for three, but Demuth and Peter used the same buckles to bind both of them to Blitz's back. Peter shifted the sword belt so the sheathed blade didn't dig into Demuth's leg. We were wonderfully crowded as Blitz sped off again. Konrad breathed steadily in front of me, and pressed close behind were Demuth and Peter. We were all alive; somehow, unbelievably alive.

Blitz had hardly started when he stopped again. A large, white owl settled on the ground in front of us. "You've returned."

A tremor ran down my back at his soft words that were punctuated by beak-clacked consonants.

"We have your heart." Demuth's voice shook.

"And no more riddles," added Peter, as he held out the heart with one hand and grasped the sword with the other.

"A heart and no riddles?" The owl hopped and spread his wings, fluttering a short distance, and settled on Blitz's head.

Sparks flew off Nyx's red cap. "You will not touch or test them this time, owl. Take your heart and go."

The owl tilted his head toward me. "You've grown in strength, both in companions and courage. But not courtesy."

Blitz growled.

"Ah, Todesfall," said the owl. "You know I cannot understand your wolf speech. Change form so we can speak as friend to friend."

Todesfall? Blitz's name is lightning, *not* death. My chest tightened. *He's proven honorable. We have nothing to fear—from him. But will the owl delay us further by wanting to speak with him?*

"Blitz," I said. "You can speak with him after you deliver us to Johannes."

The owl clacked his beak. "Blitz, is it? You've gained new masters. What happened to our old one?"

The night sky paled, and the first of the morning birds twittered. We had until noon before Konrad's curse came to a knotted end, but even Blitz's speed would be slowed by the maze.

I gritted my teeth. "Honored owl, your old master is dead. We bring you your heart as Blitz promised. Take it and let us go."

"He is dead? That is good." The owl spread his wings and silently brushed by us, snatched the heart from Peter's hand, and swallowed it. He landed on the ground and hooted triumphantly. "Ah, it is good to be my own master again. Master of riddles and no man's servant."

"Let's go," I said.

The owl grew to a man's height. "You may not pass."

"You promised," I cried.

"I made no promise. And I must know how Tollkirsche died before you go. Ah," he sighed. "It is good to say his name out loud. No more compelled silence."

We would get nowhere until his curiosity was satisfied. "Blitz," I said. "Reason with him."

The wolf trembled beneath us and shrank into the wolf-headed man. He crawled out from under the saddle. "Rätsel," he growled. "My mistress solved the riddle of Tollkirsche's name and destroyed him. You should bow to her in thanks and aid her in her journey."

"Intriguing." The owl fluffed his feathers as he settled on a stone facing Blitz. "This woman solved our master's riddle? How did she even know to ask it? The larger question is, why have you taken a new master, when you fought so hard against your servitude to our old master? What spell of compulsion has she placed on you?"

"None. I help her freely."

"That is truly a riddle. Todesfall, the werewolf who would be king of the black forest, is freely letting himself be saddled and carrying these mortals according to their bidding."

"You let them pass."

"They answered the riddles," said Rätsel.

"They didn't," said Blitz. "In her imprisonment, she told me all you asked. They did not answer your weight. It was an answer that not even the wisest could find unless they had magic. You were the gatekeeper, charged to only allow those with magical ability, as well as wit, to pass. Yet you gave them another riddle and allowed them through."

"I allowed the man's witty statement that my wait was for his answer. These magic-less mortals intrigued me. However, I'm not giving myself into their service."

"I don't ask for your service," I said, as I finished unbuckling the saddle straps from my legs. "We've given you your heart and your freedom. You will let us pass."

The owl closed his eyes and grew larger. "As I said, you lack courtesy. If you've solved the riddle that destroyed my hated master, then you can spare the time to solve another."

Nyx flamed, floating by my shoulder. Peter crouched beside Demuth with his sword protectively drawn as she unbuckled the saddle straps from Konrad's arms and legs.

I stepped from the saddle. "Blitz?"

He shook his head. "I cannot defeat him in combat, and I doubt I could stop him from injuring you. The riddle is the only way. I did not expect this of him."

"You didn't." The owl laughed. "You've grown soft in your servitude, while I've stayed true to my name."

Rätsel—riddle—the old owl was rooted in riddles. And we had not time for more of his games. Could we force our way through with magic?

I turned to the flaming Kobold. "Nyx?"

She grinned and darted forward in a flurry of flames. Balls of fire flew from her hands and struck him, searing the white feathers black. A sickly scent wafted up with smoke.

He ruffled and the black fell to the ground, leaving unstained feathers. "Your pitiful magic is less dangerous to me than the tall one's knives."

Peter sprang to his feet.

I laid a hand on Peter's arm and faced the owl that was taller than I. "I will answer your riddle, if you let my companions go on without me first."

Rätsel snapped his beak and grew so large that he dwarfed what Blitz would be in his wolf form. "No."

"You promise to let all of us go without injury or delay, if I answer?"

"I promise you and your companions swift and safe passage to the thorn tower if you answer correctly. No consulting with your companions. I want to hear it from the mind that destroyed Tollkirsche. The first words from your mouth are your answer. If you answer wrong, I will ask another, more difficult riddle, and another until you answer one correctly. We can take as long as we want. Eventually, you'll get where you want." He chuckled. "Oh, the joy of being rid of the compulsion to eat those who answer wrong. Human flesh is nasty, and it is a waste to kill clever minds."

Konrad lay limp on the saddle. He had only hours left of life. Between us and an end to his curse stood a near-invincible, riddle-crazed owl. He wouldn't hurt us, but he had effectively trapped us. I rubbed my forehead. I needed to think like a fool, and to do it quickly. "What is your riddle?"

"Which is stronger—the heart or the head?"

Which is stronger—heart or head? It is by my head I reason. By my head, I've kept going when cursed emotions threatened to overpower me. By my head, I've figured riddles and even destroyed a mighty sorcerer. Logic and reason have saved us many times.

Yet, the heart motivates to action. The heart is behind Demuth's compassion and Peter's sacrifices. The heart is behind Konrad's courage and kindness. The heart allows friendships and joy. The heart allows to see beyond what the head thinks is possible.

But the heart can be corrupted, just as the head can be cold and calculating. Either, without the other, is dangerous.

I looked up into the owl's golden eyes. "The strongest person balances his head and his heart. If one is more powerful than the other, the person is weak. Which are you? Strong or weak?"

The owl tilted his head. "According to your definition, I am weak. And happy to be so." He chuckled. "I would that I could keep you for your conversation, but I have promised passage for a correct answer. Sometimes I wish I were not fae and could break promises as easily as you weak humans do." He prostrated himself on the ground. "I can carry two of you at a time to the tower. Who will go first?"

I looked at Blitz. "Do you trust him?"

"He will not betray his promise," said Blitz.

"Then wake Konrad, and I will go with him to face Johannes."

LAUGH

KONRAD RODE in front of me in silence after I finished telling him all that had happened since facing Tollkirsche. The wind ruffled his curly hair as he clung to the back of the owl. The forest spread beneath us, and in the distance, the gaping scar of the thorn maze and sharp tower broke the green.

"Hette," he finally said.

"I don't want to argue."

"I don't either. What good would it do? What is done is done. We must plan for what's coming."

"What is there to plan?" I said. "We give him his heart, and he breaks the curse on you."

"And he restores your heart."

I snorted. "Yes, that too."

"Don't tell me you forgot the whole reason we came on this adventure."

"Perhaps, for a moment."

"If you forgot that, then do not forget that Blitz cautioned you against trusting Johannes. We need to be prepared with our own tricks."

"What sort of tricks?"

"Distraction and sleight of hand."

"So you are ready to fight to preserve your life?"

He chuckled. "An interesting question, coming from you. For a practical woman, you have a tendency to throw yourself into peril —making deals with evil sorcerers, befriending werewolves, and challenging invincible owls to duels of wits."

"I'm only following my friend's example."

"That friend had best turn his life around and be a better example," he said.

"That friend will have a lifetime to change his ways."

Silence fell between us. Konrad's back warmed me even as the chill wind whipped around us.

"Hette, promise me—"

"Promise you what?"

"Promise me that no matter what happens today, you will live life fully. Keep friends, create joyful memories, and rule the kingdom with both wisdom and compassion."

"Not without you."

"Even without me. Please promise me."

"I'm human, not fae. Even if I promised, the only way you can make sure I'll keep it is to be there beside me."

His shoulders rose and fell as if with a silent sigh. "We should plan. Rätsel, could I interest you in a game of wits against our esteemed apprentice sorcerer?"

The owl gave a hard laugh. "An intriguing offer. What do you have in mind?"

Johannes stood outside his tower as the owl landed. A gentle breeze rippled his blue and cream robes and his pale hair. "So you've returned, and you've even convinced the riddle master to lend you a ride. Interesting. Have you brought my heart?"

"We have." I slid from the owl's back, and Konrad followed. He staggered as he landed, but steadied when I lay a hand on his arm.

"Was it worth the cost?" Johannes smirked. "It seems you've lost several companions, and Erasmus' grandchild is not well. Wouldn't it have been easier to just promise your heart to me and rule beside me?"

"Whether it was worth the cost or not," I said, striding toward him, "it is paid, and now you must fulfill your agreement. Restore my heart, and I will restore yours."

"Must I?" He kissed his fingertips and blew across them to me.

Hette, beautiful wise Hette. My queen. His voice twined inside my soul. *Come to me. Bring me my heart, and we shall know true happiness.*

"No."

He blew a second kiss.

A deity stood before me with broad shoulders, narrow hips, and a catlike grace. Chiseled brows arched above soul-searching grey-black eyes. Perfect satirical lips parted, inviting me to meet them with my own.

I took a shuddering breath. It shouldn't have been this difficult. I'd fought against his cursed emotions many times, but I'd grown weak in my time free from them. I needed to focus, to keep to our plan. I needed not to feel. I closed my eyes against Johannes. "No." I forced the word between gritted teeth.

"Is that so, my queen?" A third kiss whispered on the breeze.

A rich, sandalwood scent twined, pulling me. Slender fingers brushed against my cheek, traced along my jaw, and played through the short hairs at the back of my neck. Lips caressed the corner of my mouth, my ear.

My limbs ached. My empty lips yearned to meet his. I needed him. I was nothing without him.

No! This isn't love. This is artificial, forced, and false. Real love makes a person more, not less. Real love is what Peter and Demuth *have, a connection so deep and a desire so great that they sacrifice and fight for each other, and that they find joy in each little moment together. Real love is full of trust and truth. Real love never forces or demeans. Real love is—*I opened my eyes. Konrad stood at my side and slightly in front of me, his face fierce and his hands on his knives. I laughed.

I laughed, even as the longing wrapped around me, drawing me, stretching me out between where I was and where Johannes stood. "I know what love is, and it isn't in the emotions you create. You may make my life miserable with longing, but you can never make me love you. It is a choice, and I've chosen another."

Johannes' brows rose. "Unexpected. Very well, let us proceed with the negotiations." The tangle of emotions faded.

I locked my knees against the sudden release. I needed to stay strong. We weren't done yet.

Konrad pulled out two knives and juggled them with one hand, the ease of his motion belying the intensity of his gaze fixed on the sorcerer.

"Johannes," I said. "We will exchange hearts at the same time. Bring mine out, and I will reveal yours."

He tilted his head. "How do I know you have it?"

I pulled a wrapped bundle from my pocket. It thumped slowly in my hand. I carefully unwrapped it and revealed a pale, pulsing muscle. "Can you feel what happens to your heart?" I drew a knife and pricked the muscle. A bead of blood formed.

Johannes clutched his chest. "You are ruthless. Are you certain the love you've chosen isn't to yourself?"

"Perhaps," I said grimly. "Shall we proceed? Restore my heart to my chest, and I will give you yours."

"Not so, my queen." A mocking smile spread across his face. "How do I know you won't kill me, through my heart, once you have what you want? I will give you your heart, but until I hold mine, I will not replace it in you."

"And if I return your heart, how will I know you will fulfill your promise to me?"

"You don't. Neither of us trusts the other. But you will, at least, have your heart back."

"True. I accept your conditions. Rätsel will carry yours and give it to you after you've handed me mine. My fool will guard our every move and can pierce you or your heart if you make a false motion."

"Agreed." He withdrew a blue-wrapped bundle from a pouch at his waist and raised a knife. "Would you like equal assurance of it being yours?"

The ticking clockwork quickened in my chest. "Yes."

"Then tell your fool not to kill me for it."

"Fool," I said coldly, "kill him only if he draws more than a drop of blood."

Konrad smiled and added a third knife to his one-handed juggling. The blades winked in the mid-morning sun. Three more hung in his belt.

Johannes pulled back the blue wrapping and revealed a bright red muscle. With a swift motion, he pricked the heart with the tip of a knife.

I stumbled forward as pain shot through my chest, as if someone had thrust a dagger through my left breast and ribs all the way to my heart. And then it was gone.

Konrad caught my arm with one hand, even as he juggled knives with the other.

"I'm unhurt. Johannes truly has my heart." The sun slanted down on us. I squinted in the mid-morning glare. It was taking too long. We had to hurry, but not act as though we were in a hurry. I pulled away from Konrad and offered the heart in my hands to Rätsel. "Let us make the exchange."

The owl plucked it with his beak and walked beside me to Johannes with a quick shuffling gait. A drop of blood beaded on the heart in his hands. I reached out and wrapped my hands around it.

Johannes placed a hand on top of mine. "You could still marry me, and I'll restore your heart to you. Your *yes* is binding enough for us to let go of the rest of this charade."

His words were simple and calm, without the layering of cursed emotions, and also more powerful.

I gritted my teeth against the unexpected spell. "No." I took my heart and pulled my hands from his.

He sneered. "You may come to regret that choice."

I ran back to Konrad's side. My heart pulsed strong and steady in my hands.

Rätsel dropped the heart into Johannes' hands.

He exploded into a fury of winds. "This is not my heart! Where is it?!"

With a laugh, Rätsel spread his wings and sprang into the air. The winds hit us a second later, throwing both Konrad and me to the ground. Konrad's juggled knives scattered. I tightened my grip on my heart and cried as pain squeezed my chest.

"Where is my heart?" Johannes strode forward, the winds buffeting us, and then he stumbled and the winds stilled.

"It is here." Konrad held a heart with a knife pressed against it. "And it will stay here until you agree to our terms."

"How?" Johannes trembled. "You have no magic."

"But my friend does." Konrad stood. "Rätsel created the illusion, Hette created the distraction, and I pricked your heart when she pricked the illusion. Now that she has her heart safely back, we can truly negotiate. You will restore her heart, fully and uncursed."

"No." I slipped my heart into my pocket and stood. "Johannes, you must first take the curse from the Fool."

Johannes' brows rose. "Why would you care? He's not royalty, or powerful, or anyone of importance."

"Then why should it matter to you? He's served me well. That is enough, and it is a small thing in exchange for your heart."

He made a dismissive motion. "I'll take the curse from him, not that it's shortening his life much. Only a month or so at most."

"A month?" Konrad's face flushed and the knife trembled in his hand. "Do I only have thirty-five years and a month to live—that you take only a month?"

Johannes clutched his chest and hissed. "Be careful. If you kill me now, I cannot remove the curse or restore the princess' heart."

"Konrad, please," I whispered.

Konrad blew out a breath and steadied his hand.

Johannes straightened. "The spell doesn't work that way. It pulls a little life from each of Erasmus' children and grandchildren, dividing out and pulling less from each as the family grows larger. Your family must be in the hundreds now. So it should only be a month. You'll live much longer than Erasmus."

"Then you made the curse wrong," said Konrad. "The oldest child carries the full burden, and they've each died on their thirty-fifth birthday. I am the fifth from Erasmus, and I am in my thirty-fourth year. Will you take my life also?"

Johannes laughed coldly. "So I created the spell slightly wrong. It did what I needed it to."

I shivered. Johannes was no longer the man of Konrad's tales. That man had died long ago. I lifted my chin. "You will break the curse on him, or you will die."

"Very well." He closed his eyes, and his brows furrowed. Sweat beaded on his forehead as he muttered unintelligible words. He gasped and stumbled to his knees. "It is tangled and intertwined with my magic. If I break the link, I will lose my power." He stared at Konrad. "My life and work is worth more than yours. Without my power, I might as well die. But if I die, so will you."

"No. You have to remove the curse. I can't lose him. Please," I pleaded, no longer able to hold onto my cold act toward Konrad.

Johannes scoffed. "You love the fool?"

Love him? I pressed myself against Konrad's side. I would have grasped one of his hands, but one held a knife and the other held Johannes' heart. "No, I don't love the fool. I love Konrad."

Konrad jerked.

Johannes groaned as Konrad's knife pricked his heart again.

"Hette?" Konrad asked. "What do you mean by love? Friend love, correct? That's all I am to you."

I laughed as the words caught in my throat, "My foolish, wise Konrad. If I ever marry, it will be to you and none other."

"You can't," he stuttered. "I'm just a common fool, and I'm cursed."

"You said to not pigeonhole people into categories. Plus, you are not going to die." I lifted my chin. "Johannes, you will remove the curse on Konrad, now."

"You reject me in favor of the court fool. You—" Johannes stepped forward, then stumbled, clutching his chest.

Blood beaded on the pale surface of the heart around the point of Konrad's knife. "Take another step and it will be your last."

"Konrad, don't!" I cried.

Johannes sneered, even as his face paled. "Once, I gave your ancestor life, and now you will take mine. But my curse will follow your family. It will pass onto the oldest child of your oldest cousin. Is that what you want? If you let me live, then I will make the curse end with you."

"It already will," said Konrad. "A fae, who cannot lie, informed me that it ends with my death."

Johannes gnashed his teeth.

"Please," I pleaded. "End the curse on him. Let Konrad live. We'll give you your heart. I'll make you a king."

Konrad stiffened next to me.

"You are the rightful heir," I said. "I'll abdicate. You won't have your magical powers, but you'll have the power of a ruler and all your wisdom."

Johannes stroked his chin. "That is a possibility. A kingship in exchange for losing my magic and giving him his life."

"No." Konrad spoke firmly. "My life is not worth a whole kingdom being ruled by a madman. I'm sorry, Hette. I wish we could have restored your heart, but at least he won't be hurting you more." He slid the tip of the knife deeper in the heart.

"Stop," I cried.

"Wait!" Johannes tumbled forward. "Her curse won't end with my death."

Konrad froze. "What do you mean?"

Johannes panted. "I added a thread of spell to her heart when I pricked it, and it will perpetuate past my death. Little things will trigger the emotions, a picture of a man with black-rimmed eyes, a scent of sandalwood, a color of azure fabric, a name—Friedrich."

Cursed emotions flooded me, stinging me like a whip of longing and desire. A lifetime of this and Konrad dead. "No," I whimpered. "Please, no."

"He's bluffing," said Konrad. "Just as he was about the curse following my family. Your curse will end with his death."

"What if it doesn't?" Johannes' voice came silky smooth. "I can break that thread, for a price. A promise of a kingdom and your hand in marriage, then I'll break both his curse and yours."

My stomach heaved. He was corrupt and evil. Konrad was right. I couldn't give Johannes my kingdom. Hundreds of thousands would suffer under him. But if I didn't, Konrad would die.

How did the sorcerer become soulless? The Johannes of the stories had a heart full of honor, friendship, and sacrifice. His heart was—*his heart.*

"Give him his heart," I said.

Konrad's jaw tightened.

"Trust me. Give him his heart. Blitz can hunt him down later."

"I'll cut him down first." He handed the heart to Johannes. "Now, put it where it belongs."

"Fools." Johannes traced a finger over the heart wounds, sealing them as if they'd never been pierced, then pressed the heart to his chest. It sank through his cream-colored tunic and disappeared. His eyes widened, and he collapsed.

His form lay crooked on the ground, his breath came in little gasps, and his eyes stared unseeingly into the sky. The sun was near its apex.

"Do you have smelling salts?" I asked.

Konrad laughed. "You will make a good fool yet."

"And you will be there to teach me each trick." I knelt by Johannes and shook his shoulder. "Wake up."

Konrad knelt next to me and held a knife near the sorcerer's throat.

"Wake up," I shouted and slapped Johannes' cheeks.

His eyes fluttered open and he stared into Konrad's face. "Erasmus? Have you finally come?" His brow crinkled. "No, no. You have to leave, now. It is dangerous here. I am dangerous. Go quickly before I lose my mind again. Go, now." He pushed against Konrad.

"Be still," said Konrad gently. He slipped the knife back into his belt. "You have your heart, and Tollkirsche is dead."

"Nightmares," muttered Johannes. "Nightmares and terrors, and I was the beast."

"Johannes," I said.

He looked at me, and his eyes widened again. "Mother? No, she died long ago. Who are you?"

"Your grandniece, many generations later. You've been gone for a hundred years. But please, we need your help. Konrad will die this hour if you don't break the spell on him."

"Grandniece? Konrad?"

"There is a spell between you and him. Can you still see it? Do you remember your magic?"

He cried out in pain. "It wasn't just nightmares. Oh, how can you let me live?"

"Can you break the curse?"

"There are two." He looked between us. "One on this grand-child of my friend, and one on you, my grand niece. But my magic is in shards. It was built in the hole in my chest. And now that hole is filled. I don't know if I can pull enough power together to sever one curse, let alone two."

"What is the curse on Hette?" Konrad asked.

"It is a love spell. When triggered, she will feel strong emotions for me."

"Will it carry on after your death?"

He closed his eyes, and his face paled. "Yes."

"And Konrad's curse?" I asked.

"I am a monster. I only meant it to preserve my life through my imprisonment, until I could escape. Erasmus offered to help, and I thought the spell would spread out over his family. I thought I'd escape quickly and end the spell before it even took effect. I thought—" He clutched his head. "Oh, I am a monster."

I lifted my chin. "Break the curse on Konrad."

"No," said Konrad. "You'll be stuck with the cursed emotions."

"I'll laugh them off, but I cannot laugh you back."

Johannes groaned. "I am a monster."

"Then stop being one and help Konrad," I snapped.

He blinked. "Yes, my lady." He closed his eyes and perspiration formed on his brow. His lips moved in silent words, and his fingers flickered as if untangling a string.

Konrad stared into my eyes, "Are you certain? If I die, I will pass onto the next world, but you are taking on a life of trial."

"I am certain." I tried to laugh, though the thought of the curse tightened it to a squeak. "Besides, Johannes held the curse off from impacting me while we quested for his heart. He can do that again. We just have to keep him alive."

"I still don't understand how you can love me, a fool."

"It's no more foolish than that you could befriend a heartless princess."

He leaned closer, his amber eyes never leaving mine. "Not just befriend. I thought it was safe to love you. That when I died, I would leave behind no broken heart, because no princess could love a fool, especially not a princess who'd vowed never to marry."

He loved me! I'd thought he did, and now I knew. I grinned. "You were wrong."

His mouth quirked. "I often am." His hand brushed my cheek, soft and hesitant. "I promise you, sometime we will find a way to return your heart to you."

"If reasonably possible," I said. "I'm not going on another quest for that." I pressed my hand over his and held it to my face, "And you're not either."

Konrad stiffened and gasped.

"Konrad!"

He slumped to the ground. The sun shone directly overhead. Johannes still muttered spells.

"No." I pressed my ear to Konrad's chest. His heart was still.

"No!" He couldn't die. Not now. Not after everything. Not when he had given me hope, given me love. "You can't die!"

"Hette." It was Demuth.

Blitz stopped beside us. He'd finally made it through the maze. Demuth slid from his back, followed by Peter and Nyx.

"His heart isn't beating," I cried. "Johannes is trying to break the spell. He is so close. Konrad can't die yet."

She laid her head on his chest, then knelt and leaned her whole weight on his chest with her fists. "Hette, blow air into his lungs."

I pressed my mouth to his and blew. Air came out his nose. I pinched it and blew again. His chest rose.

Demuth pounded his chest.

Blow. Thump, thump.

Konrad, breathe.

Blow.

Konrad, you have to live.

Thump, thump.

You said to move on in life without you.

Blow. Thump, Thump.

But I don't know how a tree can blossom without the sun.

Blow.

Please.

Thump, thump.

Please.

My tears dripped as I pressed my lips against his and blew again and again, filling his lungs with my air. Willing his heart to beat again.

I'll try to be the queen and woman you believed I could be. I'll be kind and wisely foolish. I'll use my heart beside my mind.

Blow. Thump, thump.

Please don't leave me to do it alone.

Johannes gasped. "It is done."

Konrad shuddered and took a deep breath.

Demuth stepped back as I flung my arms around Konrad and kissed his cheeks, his forehead, his—

He met my lips.

PROMISE

A SHORT TIME LATER, though Demuth assured me it was more than a few seconds, and long enough for me to learn that all the cursed emotions were but shadows of something much richer and more nuanced, we sat together: my beloved, my friends, and my former enemy, to discuss what to do next.

Konrad leaned against Blitz, the wolf-man supporting him. Despite Konrad's weakness, he had enough strength to hold my hand. His fingers traced over mine, caressing away my fears.

Peter and Demuth knelt across from us on the hard dirt, their sides pressed together and hands intertwined.

Johannes lay on his side, his head resting on rolled-up blue robes, his face pale around his dark eyes.

Nyx sat close to him, studying his face with impish delight. What miseries would she play on him? I almost felt sorry for him.

Rätsel hadn't returned, and I wished to thank him, but perhaps it was best. He could have turned our plans into more riddles.

"Demuth," I said. "How did you know how to save Konrad's life? How did you know to—whatever that was?"

"It is a technique from Persia. I heard about it from a storyteller."

"Do you know his name? I must thank him."

"Her name was Kamilo. She was a young Greek woman. But she was a traveling storyteller. I doubt you will find her."

"I will honor you, and her, by naming the new class at the physician's academy after you both. The Demuth Kamilo heart technique."

"You are in an expansive mood." Konrad traced a finger along my forearm.

"And why shouldn't I be?" I laughed and kissed him. "But you are right. We must attend to more practical matters. How do we get out of this forest and back home?"

"I suppose you want me to guide you," grumbled Nyx.

"Preferably not," I said.

"I will carry you," said Blitz. "But five is more than will fit on my back. I could take you in two journeys."

"No. I'm done with riddles of who will go and who will not. We will travel together, and we'll trade off who is walking. Lightning will just have to travel at a mortal's pace for a time."

And so we did. When we arrived back in my kingdom we stopped by the mineral baths where I supposedly had been staying to restore my health. Gold, provided by Blitz, in addition to what I'd initially sent was enough to ensure our story, including the part that they'd needed to shave my head to allow the release of heat from a terrible fever, as well as the assurance that I was well and truly healed.

Little else had changed. The king was still stubbornly alive and on his sick bed. No countries had invaded. No barons had rebelled. And a list of noblemen awaited times to court me. That list accidentally fed Nyx in her new hearth. Mischief did happen more often in the palace, but it was *almost* always deserved.

Demuth and Peter married within a month and returned to her parents' town, where she resumed her healing practice while Peter apprenticed to a blacksmith. Letters frequented between us.

They were first read and written by Demuth's parents, and thus kept to safe topics, but Peter quickly learned to read, and soon letters arrived in his creative spelling, telling of more exciting news, such as a coming baby. Demuth sent drawings of her and Peter and their daily life. Even if she couldn't read or write, her thoughts came through clearly in pictures.

Blitz made his home in the deer park, and rumors of an enormous wolf spread, contradicting other rumors of a wolf-headed man. Combined, the rumors turned the park into my undisturbed haven.

Bestian took Johannes under his care. Johannes slowly regained his vitality, and, along with it, some of his magic, though he was hesitant to use any. Three months after we returned, he snapped the last of the spell between him and me. He'd only semi-successfully kept the cursed emotions away during that time, and it was good to have it fully severed.

Where Johannes had once been charismatic and cruel, he became reclusive, hiding away from all but a few people, and apologizing for everything, even if he had nothing to do with it. Not that Nyx would have let him get away with anything. She appointed herself as his guardian, to ensure he never fell back into evil, and did so through much mischief and teasing. Over time, they forged a friendship that brought a quickening to his steps. He even started inventing again.

My heart I kept locked in a silver box, waiting for the time Johannes was strong enough to restore it, if ever that time would come. The mechanical heart wasn't so bad. It was heavy, and the ticking was irksome to fall asleep to, but it pumped my blood.

As for Konrad and me—that was a riddle that took time to untangle. Laws and expectations didn't change for love. And as I wasn't yet queen, I couldn't order the changes.

～

I stood outside the king's bedchamber, wearing the full armor of royalty, from corseted red brocade and stiff collar to toe-pinching shoes. The wig, a tower of blond curls, itched over my short hair. The itch was a distraction from the question: *Will he listen?*

I set my jaw. I was almost thirty years old. I was no little girl to tremble at the glance of her father. I was a woman who had faced sorcerers and death riddles. I would someday be queen.

A page stood at the door with his eyes respectfully averted. He'd wait as long as I needed before announcing me. He'd even give a believable excuse if I turned and walked away from my appointed meeting with the king. But what then? Though I could refuse to marry any of my suitors, I could not choose to marry a commoner. A princess had to marry one of noble rank. But a princess could not bestow that noble rank. For six months, I'd tried everything I could to persuade the king to bestow some noble title on Konrad, not that he allowed me more than three audiences with him in that time.

I'd tried everything, except to tell my father the truth.

I composed my face into an emotionless mask and nodded to the page. "Please let His Majesty know I am here."

He entered and returned a short while later. "He will receive you now."

The vast room was thick with the tang of medicines. A fire warmed it to an oppressive heat. Low-burning lamps did little to offset the dimness of the closed curtains. In the center of a massive bed, buried in blankets and surrounded by pillows, lay an emaciated man. A crown sat upon his head. A woman in a low-cut dress and too much makeup sat on the covers next to him. Four guards stood at the edges of the room, while servants moved in quiet efficiency.

I bowed. "Your Majesty."

He scowled. "Daughter, have you come to pester me again about bestowing knighthood on the court fool? He's provided me with rich entertainment, yes. He's guarded you faithfully to and from the baths, yes. He's made you smile, which is a feat of magic. And yes, the largest point of your argument, he saved my life once. However, he's only done what is required of a servant and fool. The answer still is—and will always be—no."

"I have not come to pester, Your Majesty." I sat on a chair next to his bed. "I've come to tell you a story."

"A dry story." He laughed and coughed. The woman held a handkerchief to his mouth.

"A story to rival the court fool's tales, and a story for your ears only."

He raised his brows. "An intrigue then, a bit of gossip. I didn't think you cared for those. Very well, everyone leave. I will listen to this *story*. Though prepare a good wine to rehydrate me from its dryness."

The room cleared of servants, woman, and guards. As the door shut, I leaned forward. "Father."

"Father, is it?" He laughed again. "You haven't called me that since you were a bratty little thing, before you turned as rigid as a figure in a Swiss clock."

"Father, do you know the story of Prince Johannes, the one who disappeared from court more than a hundred years ago?"

"The one my ancestor supposedly killed to gain the throne? Yes. It's a lurid tale, depending on who tells it, but not a new one. If you don't have something of more interest to share than a dusty tale from a century ago, you may go."

"I know where Johannes disappeared to, and what happened to him. He wasn't killed by our ancestor, but he was almost killed by me."

The king settled further into his pillows and sighed contentedly. "I will hear your tale weaving. Tell on."

～

Silence settled after my last words. The king lay staring at the gold-trimmed canopy above him. He snorted. "Not the most expertly told tale. Not even moderately well told. But nothing contradicts. Which means it is probably true." He turned his head and stared into my face. "You want to marry the court fool?"

"I will marry Konrad."

A tired smile settled on his face. "You remind me of your mother. She had a fiery will, and what she wanted happened. I didn't think you had any of her in you."

"You never tried to know me."

He snorted again. "My mistake." He sat up. His body shook with the effort. I placed several pillows behind him.

"Hette," he said. "Being a ruler isn't easy. You have to keep those in power happy. They won't be happy if you marry the fool. Just marry a noble and take the fool as a lover."

"No."

"No? You are telling the king no?"

"I will marry Konrad and only him. Whether it is now, or when I become queen, I will marry him."

"You do understand that even if I make him a knight, or even a baron, he will always be remembered as the court fool."

"They will eventually come to see his wisdom."

"I doubt it. People don't change opinions quickly, and nobles are the slowest. Are you willing to take on the whispers and mocking of the court? Are you ready to reign beside a consort who will never be taken seriously?"

"My decision isn't based on what they think."

"Many of your decisions will depend on what they think, if you want to stay in power."

"I will take into consideration their viewpoints in matters of state, but not in matters of my heart."

"Clockwork though it be?" he said.

"The organ is clockwork, but my emotions are my own, as is my mind."

"Hette, my girl, if you are going to do this either way, before or after my death, then I might as well knight the fool." He chuckled. "I'm only doing it to preserve my life. Who knows if you'd try to shorten it to make yourself queen sooner."

"Your Majesty!"

"Don't tell me it hasn't crossed your mind. And I will remain silent about the tale you told. We don't need our kingdom to fall when you become queen because they learn they are being ruled by a part-clockwork atrocity."

"I'll abdicate before it comes to that. Johannes could always rule."

He hunched over in laughing coughs. When he caught his breath, he wheezed, "That old, broken sorcerer. Never. He had his chance and threw it away, twice. My daughter is too quick-witted for him." He settled back into his pillows. "No. The next ruler will be you. And despite the odds, I'm betting that you will accomplish things no other ruler has ever dared try." He grimaced. "And turn this whole kingdom on its head in the process. Send the fool to me when you leave. I know the exact knighthood to bestow."

My hands trembled. "Thank you, Your Majesty."

He closed his eyes. "Practice your storytelling before visiting me again. I expect to see you in a week. And no more calling me *Your Majesty*."

"Thank you, Father."

The grandfather clock ticked in the corner of the receiving room to a slower beat than the one in my chest. Soon, soon, soon.

I paced to one wall and back. A fire pushed the deep winter

chill from the room but did little to calm my nervous energy. An impish face flickered for a moment in the flames.

"Nyx," I said, "go back to your marble hearth. This is a private conference."

A laugh crackled with the flames, and the fire flared, then died down to a normal burn.

The clock struck three, each metallic bong a heartbeat of waiting.

I settled on the small sofa and watched the door. After a knock, a servant entered with a tray of coffee and pastries, followed by Herzog Heinrich, my father's chamberlain. He sniffed disdainfully and said, "Sir Konrad, Knight of das Paradox, Avenger of der Schmetterling, and Protector of das Gelächter."

I lifted my hand in a gentle gesture that only shook a little. "He may enter."

Konrad stepped into the room, and I caught at a laugh. He looked so different. Instead of his usual clashing diamond jerkin and striped leggings, he wore a tailored green and cream doublet and hose. His normally wild curls were trained into reddish-blond ringlets. He raised his brows above his amber eyes in a hesitant, unasked question.

"Please, Sir Konrad, have a seat," I said.

He settled next to me on the sofa, and our knees touched. The corner of his mouth twitched.

"The rest of you may leave," I said with an upward tilt of my chin.

The servant left with a curtsy. Heinrich lifted a brow, but when I held his gaze, he bowed and left.

As the door swung shut, Konrad clasped my hands. His mouth quirked. "Knight of the Paradox and Protector of Laughter are fitting titles. But Avenger of the Butterflies?"

I lifted my chin and stiffened my lips against a smile. "I find it fitting. You avenged the butterflies that I'd mercilessly pinned to a board when I was a youth."

"There is only one butterfly I'd avenge now." He slipped his hand behind my back and pulled me closer. His fingers traced along my jaw and cupped behind my neck. The first kiss was a gentle brush, then another, deeper and sweeter, and another.

When he'd described love in the thorn maze, he'd not explained that the fire the poets spoke of was a real part of it, and all the cursed emotions were but poisonous shadows of something rich and sweet. Or maybe he had, but I hadn't understood. I probably still didn't understand. I had a lifetime ahead to find out what real love was in all its many layers.

"You're thinking too much," Konrad murmured.

"What do you mean?" I pulled away enough to look into his rich amber eyes.

"I can tell when you are distracted."

"I was thinking about how you explained love and how much I still have to learn."

He laughed. "Only you would be thinking about the analytical side of love in the middle of a kiss."

"Do you still love me, despite it?"

"I love you *because of it,* and so many other reasons." He lifted me from the couch onto his lap. "How did you convince the king to knight me?"

"I remembered something a wise fool once told me."

"And what did this fool say?"

"Who but fools can tell the truth to the great ones? I decided I needed to tell him the truth about our journey and my heart."

Konrad's mouth opened in surprise. "He listened?"

"I think he finally respects me. At least, I interested him, and he wants me to be the next ruler, and not just a wife to the next ruler."

"I have much to learn from you, my lovely Hette."

"Not lovely. I'm too sharp, both in body and personality, to be called that. And when we are married, you'll have to see me without my wig, and my hair is still unseemly short. I won't go into our marriage with false flattery."

"I saw your hair when it was non-existent in sacrifice for me. Besides." He lifted the wig from my head and ruffled his hand through the fine, flyaway locks. "Your hair is beautiful at this length. It frames your face and adds a softness to your elegant, high cheekbones."

I smacked him on the shoulder. "I said, no false flattery. I got enough of that from Johannes and the cursed emotions."

"It's not false, but I'll rein myself in until you are ready to hear it. Johannes ruined some perfectly good truths."

My brows furrowed. "Why do you think he went through all that work to try to marry me? Some other princess would have married him even without his taking her heart, though I shudder to think what would have become of them."

"I asked him."

"And?"

"The part of him that was still him wanted to fulfill a promise to Erasmus to start a golden age in his kingdom. Marrying you and becoming consort to the queen seemed the best way to achieve that. It wasn't logical, but he clung to the idea and put all his energy into achieving it."

"He was a tangle."

"Still is, just a less dangerous one. Though I'll never truly trust him around you, my lady."

"You think he still wants me?"

"I can't see how he couldn't. You are the most brilliant, capable—

"False flattery," I warned.

"I didn't say anything about your looks."

"You can go back to your quips. I like them better." I scooted from his lap and stood, facing him. "But we are distracted. Emotions do that, both the real and the cursed. You are a knight now. I wish very much that we could do as Demuth and Peter and go to the priest and be married today, but we can't. There is much to plan. First—"

"First," said Konrad, as he knelt in front of me and took my hands in his, "you are the sunlight that brings light to each of my days and brightens the darkest corners of my soul. I know I am but a fool, but I promise to listen to you without judgment, and to walk beside you through the trials of life. I promise to trust you and tell you the truth, even when it's hard and you don't want to hear it. I promise to rejoice with you on the good days, and hold you when the burdens of ruling are too heavy. I promise to keep trying, even when I blunder or you frustrate me, or we are both at our wits' end. Most of all, I promise to bring laughter into your life. May I walk this life with you?"

Tears dripped onto our held hands. Mostly mine. I couldn't speak. If he'd promised me unending happiness or to protect me from all harm, it would have been hollow. But instead, he promised to be with me through whatever life threw at us. And he'd already proven that promise repeatedly.

I withdrew my hands and walked across the room. A small silver chest sat on a shelf in the corner. I handed it to Konrad.

He took the silver chest and looked into my face with hopeful longing.

I lay my hand over his. "Herzog Heinrich told me the safety of the people is in the heart of the ruler. He was right. But what he didn't realize was that the heart of the ruler needs a place of safety too. Konrad, the safety of my heart is in your hands."

THE BARD

THE BARD SLIPPED the gold watch out again. "The tale is told. The heart is not mended, but the queen is whole. And the fool has found his match."

John spoke before he realized the words were slipping through his lips. "A queen truly married a fool?" The honest curiosity in his voice surprised even him.

She raised her thick brows. "She did, and they brought about an age of wise foolishness and heart-led reason. Something that has sadly been lost in the hundred years since their reign. Memories are short when stories are lost." She opened the watch. "But I remember."

He shook his head as confused and uncomfortable thoughts fought within him. "I—" he faltered. "I don't know what to think of it."

"You're thinking. And that is enough for now." She smiled ruefully. "Come next rest-day, and I'll take you to the land of the Franks and a never-ending week."

~

Read *Gift: A Heartless Hette Novelette* to see more of Hette and Konrad.

· · ·

If you liked *Heartless Hette,* please leave a favorable review, even if it is just a sentence. And please, share with a friend. I created the book, but the story lives through readers like you.

Keep reading for *Food for Thought* and *Research Notes.*

BOOKS BY M.L. FARB

THE KING TRIALS
The King's Trial (also an audiobook)
The King's Shadow

HEARTH AND BARD TALES
Vasilisa
Fourth Sister
Heartless Hette

HEARTH AND BARD SHORT STORIES
Flight: A Vasilisa Novelette
Birth: A Fourth Sister Novelette
Gift: A Heartless Hette Novelette

FREE SHORT STORY
East of Apollo's Palace

FAMILY AND HUMOR
When I Was a Pie: and Other Slices of Family Life

FOOD FOR THOUGHT

"Memories are short when stories are lost." How do stories help us remember and really understand? Why do we need the stories in addition to facts?

"Many things are foolish to those who only see things in categories. But life doesn't sort so neatly." How does categorizing things help us bring order to life? And how can it blind us to what doesn't fit into categories?

Peter said, "It isn't who she is, only what she does." How are we more than our job or position in society? How can we see past position and title to individuals?

Demuth said she became a healer because she wanted to "help others, especially those who are ignored by society." Who do you know who is ignored? How can you reach out to them?

Konrad laughed to help balance out his other emotions. He said, "Not instead, but beside it (worry). And beside despair, anger, and any number of soul-slicing emotions. I still have to juggle those emotions, but laughter keeps me from being injured by them." How can humor help us deal with the intense emotions of life instead of being buried by or burying them?

Lust can be described as similar to "the lead sweetener. It feels good but it never satisfies. And eventually it poisons all the emotions." And love can be described as similar to "the sunlight that brings a seed to bloom, changing it from a hard pit into something beautiful and useful. Love nurtures life." Yet both involve intense emotions. What are the similarities and differences between the two?

Hette answered the owl with, "The strongest person balances his head and his heart. If one is more powerful than the other, the person is weak." How can we balance the two?

RESEARCH NOTES

Research for writing is a delightful journey of discovery. Below, I've included some of what I learned along the way.

The idea for this book came from my oldest son. He told me about a dream he'd had of a sorcerer who stole half a princess's heart. I used that idea seed with his permission and combined it with the fairy tale "The Princess Who Never Laughed". The result was *Heartless Hette*.

Can you find nods to these tales?

- Grimm Fairy Tale: "Shepherd Boy"
- Grimm Fairy Tale: "The Six Swans"
- Grimm Fairy Tale: "Hansel and Gretel"
- Grimm Fairy Tale: "Sleeping Beauty"
- Grimm Fairy Tale: "Red Riding Hood"
- Grimm Fairy Tale: "Rumpelstiltskin"
- "Käthchen and the Kobold"
- Birbal Tale: "Golden Gallows" (from India) *A Caravan from Hindustan by James Moseley*

- "The Magic Brocade" (from China), *Mightier Than the Sword by Jane Yolen*

Names and Their Meanings

When writing a story, I choose names first based on nationality (in this case, German) then on name meaning. (See also the pronunciation guide at the beginning)

- Hette: Home Leader
- Konrad: Bold Counsel
- Friedrich: Peaceful Ruler
- Johannes: God is Gracious
- Bestian (from Sebastian): Venerable
- Demuth: Modest
- Erasmus: Beloved
- Peter: Rock
- Georg: Earth Worker
- Nyx: Daughter of Chaos
- Rätsel: Riddle
- Blitz: Lightning
- Tollkirsche: Deadly Nightshade

German Inventions and Discoveries

https://en.wikipedia.org/wiki/
List_of_German_inventions_and_discoveries

Sextant:

"A common use of the sextant is to sight the sun at noon to find one's latitude. Held horizontally, the sextant can be used to measure the angle between any two objects, such as between two lighthouses, which will, similarly, allow for calculation of a line of position on a chart."

https://www.naturepl.com/stock-photo-bluegreen-nature-image08129221.html

Erasmus Habermehl helped invent the sextant. Thus another reason for Erasmus' name. https://en.wikipedia.org/wiki/Erasmus_Habermehl

Black Forest

"As deep, dark and delicious as its famous cherry gateau, the Black Forest gets its name from its canopy of evergreens. With deeply carved valleys, thick woodlands, luscious meadows, stout timber farmhouses and wispy waterfalls, it looks freshly minted for a kids' bedtime story."

https://www.lonelyplanet.com/a/nar/688bf7f3-0556-4787-affo-edfaea162660/1324973

Rowan tree: "The European rowan (Sorbus aucuparia) has a long tradition in European mythology and folklore. It was thought to be a magical tree and give protection against malevolent beings. The tree was also called 'wayfarer's tree' or 'traveler's tree' because it supposedly prevents those on a journey from getting lost."

https://en.wikipedia.org/wiki/Rowan#Folk_magic

For more about the Black Forest and some beautiful pictures:

- https://handluggageonly.co.uk/2015/01/27/7-magical-photos-will-make-want-visit-black-forest-germany/
- https://en.wikipedia.org/wiki/Black_Forest

A Court Fool

Germany kept the position of court fool long after he disappeared from other world courts. The court fool's position was a contradiction with the scientific advancements and logical thought process of Germany, yet the rulers saw the value of his contradictions and his ability to see things from a different angle.

"And who but fools ... was able to tell the truth to the great ones of the earth? Priests and pastors are too timid, and cameralists (German scientists) too bound up with the projects of the ruler." *Four Fools in the Age of Reason* by Dorinda Outram.

Sapa

For part of *Heartless Hette* I wanted to use the example of an ancient poison that was also sweet. In my search for such an item, I discovered the ancient Roman sweetener sapa. It was perfect, with characteristics which increased the depth and breadth of the story. If you want to learn more about the history and effects of sapa: https://www.smithsonianmag.com/arts-culture/sugar-of-lead-a-deadly-sweetener-89984487/

Kobolds

Kobolds are very much like the kitsune of Japan. They attach themselves to a house or family and sometimes help them, while other times they play tricks on them. A person has to be very careful not to offend the household kobold. (If you want to learn more about kitsune, read my novel *Fourth Sister).*

https://en.wikipedia.org/wiki/Kobold

German Lullaby

The lullaby Hette sings for Konrad when he is fevered is a traditional German Lullaby, "Sleep, My little Prince, Sleep", written by Friedrich Wilheml Gotter.

https://www.mamalisa.com/?t=es&p=4039

Cardiopulmonary Resuscitation (ancient CPR)

When writing the scene where Konrad's heart stopped, I

wondered if there was any ancient form of CPR. I was delightfully surprised to find that it's been around since the 15th century.

"Burhan-ud-din Kermani, a physician in 15th century Iran, was first to describe 'Cardiopulmonary Resuscitation' (CPR), in ancient Persia, as a combination of 'strong movements and massive chest expansion' (for induction and support of breathing), and 'compression of left side of the chest' (equivalent of cardiac compression)."

https://en.wikipedia.org/wiki/History_of_cardiopulmonary_resuscitation#

ACKNOWLEDGMENTS

First of all, thank you, James, for telling me your dream about a sorcerer who steals half of the princess's heart. Your dream inspired this story.

Writing is very much a family endeavor here. My husband and children brainstorm with me, two of my children always beg to read a draft, and they all listen and offer suggestions when I read a final draft to them before publication. I couldn't write without you. Thank you!

In particular, thank you to:

My husband, Jesse Farb, for brainstorming on Johannes' backstory, and suggesting witty remarks for Konrad to say. Many of them made it into the book. Also, thank you for putting together a German pronunciation guide. I needed it.

My sister-in-law, Sunni Smith, for reading drafts, then brainstorming over the phone. Those were delightful and productive hours. You are a brilliant writing buddy.

Jesse, and all our children, for helping develop the many riddles in the "Owl" and "Teeth" chapters. The geek is strong in our family.

I also want to thank my amazing alpha and beta readers: Tori Gollihugh, Sunni Smith, Joe Gilbert, Shelly Ruble, Jackie Wilson Cope, Justena White, Luna Salvatore, Rachel Deibler, Jacque Stevens, Divya Ramji, Marie Lewis, and Rachel Perez, for your insightful critiques and suggestions.

Thank you to my editor, Annie Douglass Lima. I truly appreciate your fine-tune edits and polishing.

Thank you, Lara Carter, for creating the beautiful cover. It is perfect.

Thank you, W. R. Gingell, for your brilliant reworking of my blurb.

And most of all, thank you to my Heavenly Father. Thank you for showing me how to create.

ABOUT THE AUTHOR

Ever since I climbed up to the rafters of our barn at age four, I've lived high adventure: scuba diving, mud football with my brothers, rappelling, and even riding a retired racehorse at full gallop—bareback. I love the thrill and joy.

Stories give me a similar thrill and joy. I love living through the eyes and heart of a hero who faces his internal demons and the heroine who fights her way free instead of waiting to be saved.

I create adventures, fantasy, fairy tale retellings, and poetry. I live a joyful adventure with my husband and six children. I am a Christian and I love my Savior.

You can contact me at:
    mlfarb.author@gmail.com
    mlfarbauthor.com
    instagram.com/mlfarb_author/
    twitter.com/farbml
    facebook.com/mlfarbauthor

www.ingramcontent.com/pod-product-compliance
Lightning Source LLC
Chambersburg PA
CBHW061057190726

48286CB00006B/1787